MYST

KILLING CUSTER

KILLING CUSTER

MARGARET COEL

BERKLEY PRIME CRIME, NEW YORK

THE BERKLEY PUBLISHING GROUP
Published by the Penguin Group
Penguin Group (USA)
375 Hudson Street, New York, New York 10014, USA

USA | Canada | UK | Ireland | Australia | New Zealand | India | South Africa | China

Penguin Books Ltd., Registered Offices: 80 Strand, London WC2R 0RL, England
For more information about the Penguin Group, visit penguin.com.

This book is an original publication of The Berkley Publishing Group.

Berkley Prime Crime Books are published by The Berkley Publishing Group.
BERKLEY® PRIME CRIME and the PRIME CRIME logo are trademarks of Penguin Group (USA).

Library of Congress Cataloging-in-Publication Data

Coel, Margaret, 1937–
Killing Custer / Margaret Coel.—First Edition.
pages cm.
ISBN 978-0-425-26463-8 (Berkley Prime Crime hardcover)
1. O'Malley, John (Fictitious character)—Fiction.   2. Clergy—Fiction.   3. Holden, Vicky (Fictitious
character—Fiction.   4. Women lawyers—Fiction.   5. Custer, George A. (George Armstrong),
1839–1876—Fiction.   6. Celebrity impersonators—Fiction.   7. Arapaho Indians—Fictions.
8. Murder—Investigation—Fiction.   9. Wind River Indian Reservation (Wyo.)—Fiction.
10. Wyoming—Fiction.   I. Title.
PS3553.0347K53   2013
813'.54—dc23   2013019110

FIRST EDITION: September 2013

PRINTED IN THE UNITED STATES OF AMERICA

10   9   8   7   6   5   4   3   2   1

Cover illustration by Tony Greco & Associates Inc.
Cover design by Lesley Worrell.

For my mother, Margaret Speas,
whose gentle voice guides me still.

ACKNOWLEDGMENTS

Many thanks to all those who took an interest in this novel and generously helped me navigate tricky areas of expertise, especially Mark Stratmoen, deputy coroner, Fremont County, and Detective Sergeant Fred Cox, Lander Police Department, both in Wyoming (with apologies to Detective Cox, who is nothing like Detective Madden in the story). And to my friend Veronica Reed in Albuquerque, and my family, especially my daughter, Kristin Henderson in New Mexico; my niece Denise Saxon in Colorado; and my nephew John Dix in Virginia.

And thanks to my group of astute readers who were willing to read some very rough drafts and make helpful suggestions: Karen Gilleland, Beverly Carrigan, Sheila Carrigan, Carl Schneider, all of Boulder; and Virginia Sutter, Ph.D. and Jim Sutter, of Wind River Reservation.

And a special thanks to the many 7th Cavalry, Civil War, and Old West reenactors in Colorado and Wyoming who generously spoke with me about their experiences impersonating historical people and reenacting historical events. My hat is off to them for their dedication to authenticity and for educating new generations about our common past.

It's a good day to die!
Brave up, brother! Hoka hey!

—Eagle Elk, Sioux, at the Battle of the Little Big Horn
from *Custer's Fall* by David Humphreys Miller

KILLING CUSTER

1

DRUMS POUNDED AND trumpets blasted. The noise floated ahead of the parade. Crowds lined the curbs on Main Street in Lander and clustered around aluminum chairs and ice chests. The sun blazed like a hot poker. A dry, scorching breeze ruffled the flowers in the pots hanging from the streetlamps and snapped at the brim of Father John O'Malley's cowboy hat. He fished two dollars out of his blue jeans pocket, purchased two tall glasses of lemonade from the Girl Scouts behind one of the booths, and handed a glass to Bishop Harry. They made their way through the crowd toward a vacant space as the parade came down the street. A giant, multi-legged monster. It was the second Sunday in June, the Moon When the Hot Weather Begins in the Arapaho Way of marking time, and the breathless days were already beginning, the heat gathering and settling in for the summer.

"Hey, Father John!" A man's voice cut through the undertones of conversation and noise, the blare of trumpets, and the harsh staccato of drums. Father John glanced around and lifted his lemonade glass toward Edna and Mike White Eagle, who were pushing a baby carriage along the sidewalk. Brown faces mingled with white, sunburned, freckled faces. Lander sprawled along the southern border of the Wind River Reservation in the middle of Wyoming, and Arapahos and Shoshones from the rez joined the town folks every year for the parade that preceded the big county rodeo. He hadn't missed the parade in ten years at St. Francis Mission on the rez, eight years as pastor. Long enough to watch kids grow up and have children of their own, to settle into the rhythms of the seasons. Summer meant parades and powwows, rodeos and tourists.

Bishop Harry waved to a group of Arapahos across the street, then leaned forward and said something to Ellen Redbird seated in an aluminum chair. Father John smiled. The Right Reverend Bishop Harry Coughlin was enjoying himself. He liked getting out with the Arapahos, being part of the life here. But he couldn't stop worrying over the mission. What if there were an emergency? Father John had assured him phone calls would be transferred to his mobile, so anyone needing help could reach them. The old man had arrived at St. Francis almost two years ago with orders from the provincial superior to take it easy, recuperate after two heart attacks and bypass surgeries. Bent forward, with a U-shaped fringe of thick, white hair and slitted blue eyes in a face that might have been blasted out of sand, the bishop worked harder than any assistant priest Father John had ever had. Technically he was a guest, not an assistant. Father John had given up trying to get the old man to take it easy. He'd take it easy later, he always said, which meant, Father John knew, when he was dead.

"Colin's riding with the warriors." Lou Morningside, an Arapaho elder, moved in close. A mixture of pride and worry creased his narrow, brown face. He was stoop-shouldered around a ropy, chest-sunken frame. He had long black hair cut through with gray and pulled into a wiry ponytail that hung below his tan cowboy hat. "He's gonna compete in the rodeo tonight. I got a bad feeling. I wish he'd skipped the parade."

Father John waited a moment. Lou had passed over the polite preliminaries, the how-are-yous and how-do-you-like-the-weathers. He'd launched into what was on his mind. "What's going on?" Father John said finally.

"Custer's back."

The parade passed the flower shop, the bakery, and the restaurant across the street and carried itself forward. Blue pickup in the lead, wrapped in red, white, and blue streamers. Hoisted over the cab, a white banner with large red print that said, "Welcome Fremont County Rodeo." The Wind River High School band followed, Arapaho and Shoshone kids with dark, serious faces, marching, playing flutes, trumpets, and trombones, eyes straight ahead shadowed by the peaks of blue uniform caps, the drummer in the lead, pounding the drum.

"The Seventh Cavalry?" Father John moved close to the old man to make himself heard. He felt the same unease that had come over him when he'd read the list of parade entries in the *Gazette*. Reenactors of General George Armstrong Custer's 7th Cavalry. Thirty troopers who had marched in parades across the country led by a Custer impersonator named Edward Garrett. County fairs, rodeos, civic celebrations, Pennsylvania, Florida, California, Illinois, and always a big hit, according to the newspaper, always marching to war. The 7th was passing through on the way to

Montana for the reenactment of the Battle of the Little Bighorn on its anniversary, June 25. What a coup for the parade to have the cavalry, a real incentive to bring out the crowds. Father John remembered dropping the newspaper on his desk as if it were on fire. Custer? In Indian country?

"Who decided that?" Bishop Harry leaned into the conversation.

"Nobody asked us," Lou said. "Colin went into town and told the organizers: 'If *he* marches, we march, too.'"

The band with Indian kids had moved past, the sound of brass instruments fading, drumbeats drifting behind. Then came the Lander Valley High School band, with drums, flutes, and trumpets blaring loud enough to drown out the Indian band ahead. Passing now, a long line of floats decorated in a rainbow of tissues and paper flowers with beautiful girls in flowing dresses and cowboy hats waving to the crowds, tossing red and white carnations. Banners with large colorful letters fluttered on the floats: Rotary Club, Mike's Auto Dealership, Lions Club, Gillespie's Good Food, Summer Reading Program for Kids, Kiwanis Club, Lander Kiddie Camp.

A space opened behind the floats, then a short, wide-shouldered man in a blue cavalry uniform with yellow cords running down the sides of his pant legs, black boots, and a blue cap rode down the middle of the street. He lifted a brass coronet and blew the tune of "Garry Owen," swinging from side to side, mischief and amusement in his eyes. Behind the bugler rode the 7th Cavalry. Some looked like cowboys, with light-colored canvas pants, slouch hats, and beards and goatees. A few in fringed leather jackets; others in canvas jackets. Most wore blue uniforms. "Authentic impersonators of Custer's men in dress and appearance," the newspaper had said. The horses pranced and balked and neighed so that, instead of rows, the columns advanced in waves behind a sergeant holding aloft a red-and-blue guidon with crossed swords in white. At the head of the column rode three men. Custer was in the center, riding a muscular, chestnut stallion with a blaze and three white fetlocks.

My God, Father John thought. It might have been the man himself, the resemblance to photos of Custer was so strong. The man rode tall and straight-shouldered, master of his stallion, which pranced along. He wore a fringed white buckskin shirt and trousers with a light gray, wide-brimmed hat pulled low over his forehead. A dark blond handlebar mustache obscured his mouth. He faced straight ahead, but Father John saw the way his eyes darted back and forth, taking in the crowds at the curbs.

The riders flanking him wore blue uniforms and peaked hats. Mounted on smaller horses, which made them seem shorter and less important than the man between them. Major Marcus Reno and Captain Frederick Benteen, Father John guessed, officers under Custer.

A low roar started up, like a gust of wind crashing about, and Father John looked around. Groups of Arapahos and Shoshones were shouting and waving their arms, faces dark and angry. "We remember the Washita," someone yelled. Other voices shouted: "We remember Wounded Knee." "Go back to hell." Father John watched a white couple pull two children close. Other whites started moving away from the Indians, stepping back onto the sidewalk. A few of the troops turned toward the crowd and waved, as if they were being cheered on, an air of invincibility about them.

"Why'd he come here?" Lou said, almost under his breath. "Killed the Cheyennes at Washita." He was shaking his head, remembering an old story he'd probably heard from his grandfather. "Peaceful people, Black Kettle's people. Went to the Washita to get away from all the troubles on the plains, and Custer followed them. Lot easier to kill peaceful folks than warriors." The old man gave a little laugh. "Oh yeah, Custer didn't want to go near the warriors. After Washita, the Cheyenne warriors put their pipes out on his heels."

The first time Father John had heard that expression from one of the elders, he had wanted to ask what it meant. It was impolite to ask for the gift of information, and he had remained quiet. Then the elder explained that Cheyennes had followed Custer's tracks across the plains for eight years after Washita, until 1876, waiting for the chance to kill him.

"Wounded Knee massacre in 1890," Lou was saying, pulling out the memory of another story. "Big Foot and his people trying to get away from the soldiers in a freezing blizzard. The 7th mowed them down—women, children, old people—all of them killed. Troopers bragged they did it for Custer. Called it revenge for the Little Bighorn."

The troopers rode in front of them now. The old man drew in a long breath and nodded toward the columns of Arapaho warriors riding up next. "I tried to tell Colin, no good was gonna come from Custer being here."

Father John watched the mounted Indians—about thirty, he guessed, the same number as the troopers—drawing closer. It was hard to recognize anyone. All the warriors had painted their faces. Some wore long, feathered headdresses, others cowboy hats, black braids hanging down their backs. A few in buckskin shirts and trousers, but most were shirtless, chests and arms streaked with red, black, white, and yellow paint.

"Do you see Colin?" Father John bent his head toward the elder.

"Looks like Crazy Horse," Lou said, nodding toward the warrior in the center of the first row. "Smeared his face with dirt, 'cause Crazy Horse's vision told him to cover his face with dirt and braid his hair with grass, then nobody could shoot him. They stabbed him when they killed him."

Father John kept his eyes on the warrior with a face the color of putty and what looked like stalks of green grass woven into his braids. He rode bare-chested, skin painted in geometric symbols that made it look as if he had on a shirt. His tan canvas trousers looked old and worn. He wore moccasins, beads flashing in the sun.

The crowd cheered and waved as the warriors passed, but Father John could hear the angry shouts and taunts farther up the street. There were fewer people about, vacant places where white families had congregated. Groups of people were heading down the sidewalk, as if the fun had wooshed out of the parade like air out of a balloon. He could feel the tension crackling through the cheers.

The bishop stepped over. "I think we've seen everything." He might have read Father John's mind.

Before Father John could reply, the warriors broke into a gallop, two abreast on both sides of the street, hugging the curbs. The crowd moved forward, craning to see, pressing against one another. Two women pushed themselves into a vacant spot in front of him. The warriors galloped along the sides of the cavalry, crossed in front and circled back. Around and around they rode, whooping, hollering shouting, making double circles that forced the cavalry to a standstill.

Father John hurried along the sidewalk, dodging past groups of people, his eyes on the circling Indians. The rest of the parade had moved on. Just as he reached the front of the cavalry, the warriors swirled about, shouting and shaking their fists overhead, and formed into neat columns, side by side, ahead of the cavalry. A smooth, expert maneuver that Father John had seen at rodeos and horse shows. A dare ride, an old tradition. Circling the enemy, showing contempt and superiority, daring the enemy to do anything. The warriors had circled the troops, as if they were counting coup. Now they rode ahead.

The cavalry had stopped moving, stranded in the middle of the street, the gulf between the troopers and the warriors widening. Something was going on. Three horses in the lead, riderless. Father John dodged through the little groups gathering at the curb. Troopers were dismounting, running to the front. They crowded around the buckskin-clad figure lying in the street. The parade had moved half a block away, the shouting and cheering a dull, muffled echo. One of the troopers straightened up and scanned the crowd. "Medics," he shouted. "Get the medics."

As if they had materialized out of air, two uniformed policemen ran down the middle of the street toward the stalled cavalry. Behind them was a man in khaki trousers and a white shirt carrying a blue kit with First Aid written across the sides and a woman in green scrubs with a folded stretcher under one arm. The troopers were standing up, backing away from the man in the street. Father John could see the bushy handlebar mustache, the prominent nose and sunken cheeks, the wide-brimmed hat lying next to his head.

The crowds started stepping off the curb, but the policemen flapped their arms and motioned them back. Across the street another policeman was trying to control the people surging forward.

"He's been shot," a man shouted. The words reverberated through the crowd: He's not moving. He's not moving.

"God help us." It was Lou Morningside's voice, and Father John realized the elder had come up beside him. "The warriors did it again," he said.

"Did what, Grandfather?" Father John said.

"Killed Custer."

2

THE AMBULANCE BLOCKED the double glass doors at the emergency entrance. Father John had followed the sounds of the siren up the winding hill and into the parking lot next to the sign that said Lander Regional Hospital. After Lou Morningside offered to give the bishop a ride back to the mission, Father John had jogged down the side street to the Toyota pickup and started after the ambulance. Now he pulled into a space set aside for clergy and hurried across the sun-seared pavement. The automatic doors parted. Cool air wafted over the lobby. Across the expanse of green linoleum, beyond the plastic bucket chairs hugging the walls, two troopers in blue uniforms, gripping their caps against their chests huddled near the metal door that Father John knew led to a warren of examining rooms.

"Doctors are with him now." The voice erupted through the small metal communicator in the center of the window on the right. A red-haired receptionist on the other side gave him a smile of recognition.

Father John thanked her. He didn't know Edward Garrett. Yet he'd had the sense he'd seen him before when he'd first ridden into view. Hundreds of photos in books on American history he had read over the years. George Armstrong Custer, elevated to brevet brigadier general after leading a brave assault on the Confederates at Gettysburg, the boy general, seated on a velvet stool. Later photos, posed outside a tent on the plains, reduced to lieutenant colonel fighting skirmishes with Plains Indians. Seated at a desk inside his tent, Libbie Custer reading in a nearby chair, a domestic scene suffused in contentedness.

Father John walked over to the troopers. The shorter man, black-haired and thick-necked. The other, taller, a sallow complexion and an experienced look about him, with white curly hair and light blue eyes fixed on some vacant space. They had ridden on either side of Edward Garrett. "Father John O'Malley," he said, extending his hand. "I'm sorry about your friend."

"Nicholas Veraggi." The black-haired man slid a moist, smooth palm into Father John's hand. He had a stubbly black mustache and dark, brooding eyes under bushy black eyebrows. "Also known as Major Marcus Reno, second in command to General Custer. I for one never called him friend."

"I say the same." The white-haired man took Father John's hand. "Philip Osborne or, if you like, Captain Frederick Benteen."

"Who is he?" Father John said.

"George Armstrong Custer? General. Colonel. Whatever you like," the black-haired trooper said. "Arrogant sonofabitch. Only a matter of time until somebody put a bullet in him. There was lots that wanted to."

"I meant Edward Garrett?"

The white-haired captain squared his shoulders and seemed to grow an inch taller. A hat line ran through his hair above his ears. The blue eyes were rimmed in red and watery, as if he had been staring into the bright sunlight. "Colonel Edward Garrett," he said. "Retired, U.S. Army. Fought in Iraq during Desert Storm. Another tour in Iraq and one in Afghanistan. Mean and crazy as Custer. Sure knows how to summon Custer's ghost." He shrugged. "It's a game of pretend," he said, what passed for laughter rumbling in his throat, "but it takes you back, gives you something else to think about than the world falling apart today. I was in Iraq, and I'm here to tell you, I'd rather have been fighting Indians on the plains."

"Maybe Benteen thought his world was falling apart," Father John said.

The trooper shook his head. "He had his place, and he knew what it was. Ground wasn't shifting all the time."

"You've known Colonel Garrett long?"

"Since Desert Storm. I heard from Veraggi here that the colonel had a Seventh Cavalry gig. Traveling the country in RVs, reenacting the Battle of the Little Bighorn." He tried for another laugh. "So I contacted the colonel. Turns out he was looking for a man that resembled Benteen. He took me on. Hell, I've been a Civil War buff since I was a kid. Loved reading about the old battles. Still do. I followed all those great commanders—Sheridan, Sherman, Crook—out to the plains where they was fighting Indians after the Civil War. Custer, too. One of my idols; that is, until I got to know him."

He drew quiet. His eyes had an inward, worried look, as if he were rereading a text of his own words and wondering how they portrayed him. He was like an actor always in costume, playing a part. "Maybe Custer was a great guy. I guess we don't know."

Veraggi was shaking his head. "You ask me, Garrett got Custer just right. Narcissist of the first order. I hated the man. I mean, Reno hated the man."

"His wife loved him," Father John said. A memory flickered at the edge of his mind: the contented scene inside the tent, a woman following her husband across the plains, sharing the hardships. American History, the Civil War years, for junior and senior students at the Jesuit prep school in Boston where he'd taught before his own world had come crashing down and his superiors had sent him into alcohol rehab for the third time. He had known it would be his last. He would either start to recover or spend the rest of his life in an alcoholic haze, sick, depressed, and lonely. A year later he was at St. Francis Mission with the pastor, Father Peter, the only Jesuit willing to take him on.

The metal door swung back and a young woman stepped past. She paused a moment, allowing the door to close behind her. Father John recognized her from previous visits to the ER with parishioners: heart attacks, diabetic comas, car accidents, and, more times than he wanted to think about, shooting incidents. The doctor was beautiful with an air of competence about her. Probably in her thirties but looking ten years younger, with shoulder-length brown hair and hazel eyes that peered out of round, frameless glasses. Her white coat flapped around dark slacks. Clipped to the coat was a white plastic tag that read Eleanor Henderson, MD.

"Hello, Father." She looked past the troopers. "You're here for Colonel Garrett, I assume."

"How is he?" Father John said.

"I'm sorry." She shook her head.

The lobby went quiet for a moment. Muffled sounds of the hospital—doors shutting, phones ringing—came from far away, another place and time. "Would you like to see him?"

Father John nodded.

The doctor glanced from Veraggi to Osborne. "You were friends?"

Father John waited for the reply, but the troopers nodded solemnly in unison, as if Garrett's death had erased the old animosities.

They followed the doctor past the metal door and down a corridor with light green walls and vinyl floor and white charts hanging on closed doors. Footsteps tapped out a syncopated noise that reverberated around them. The doctor pushed open a door and waved them inside.

The man who had impersonated Custer lay on a gurney, a bulky figure under a white sheet. The doctor stepped over and lowered the sheet from his face. Father John felt his breath stop. The resemblance between Colonel Edward Garrett and Custer was even closer than it had seemed at the parade. The man on the gurney had close-cropped blond hair, not the long curly locks that had brought the Cheyennes to nickname Custer "Long Hair." But wasn't there a reason? Father John tried to capture a dim memory: Custer had decided to have his head shaved before he'd left Fort Lincoln on the last campaign of his life. But he hadn't shaved the bushy handlebar mustache that—another memory surfacing—he'd worn to protect part of his face from the fierce sun of the plains. The man's eyes were closed. Something peaceful about him, an end of striving.

Dr. Henderson kept her place on the other side of the gurney, eyes fixed on Garrett's face, as if she was having trouble reconciling the two parts of her profession, life and death. Father John lifted his right hand over the body and made the sign of the cross. "May the all-loving God have mercy on your soul," he said, "and forgive any sins you may have committed. May Our Lord Jesus

Christ give you the peace and joy that he promised to those who
love him." He prayed the Our Father silently—for both men, he
realized: Colonel Edward Garrett and George Armstrong Custer.

When he turned around, the troopers had left the room. He'd
been lost in prayer and hadn't heard the door open or close.

"HELLO, FATHER." THE man in the entry a few feet from the troopers
was about six feet tall, muscular with close-cropped brown hair
and a rugged face, crisped by the sun. He wore blue jeans, a white
shirt under a leather vest, and a tan straw cowboy hat. Father John
had known Detective Al Madden for five or six years. Once in a
while he would come to St. Francis Mission to request the pastor's
help in locating some Arapaho suspected in a burglary in Lander
or a drunk and disorderly or a drug deal. Arapahos were tight-
lipped; no one wanted to snitch. And Father John had found himself adopting the same attitude. He didn't like being thrust between
the police and the people. He'd spread the word on the rez, he
would tell the detective, point out that by turning himself in, the
suspect might win sympathy from the prosecutor. He would say he
would accompany the person to police headquarters. He would
always encourage the suspect to call Vicky Holden, the Arapaho
attorney. Sometimes it worked. He and Vicky would show up at
Madden's office with a scared, trembling Arapaho.

"You connected to Garrett?" the detective said.

"I never met him."

The detective gave a brief nod. The priest had come to pray,
bless the body. He glanced from Father John to the two troopers.
"You were riding alongside him." He said. "See anything that
might be helpful?"

Osborne ran a hand through his white hair. A pained expression crossed his face. "We've already told the cops that nobody could've seen anything in the confusion. Damn Indians racing horses around us. Set my horse to bucking and neighing. All I could do to stay mounted. Same with the other troopers. Bugler was lucky he didn't get trampled."

"How about you?" The detective turned to Father John.

The cavalry had just passed when the Indians started the dare ride, Father John said. He'd hurried down the sidewalk to see what was going on. When the Indians had moved ahead, Garrett was on the ground.

Detective Madden took this in for a moment, then dug past the front of his vest and produced a small notepad and pen. He flipped open the pad and started scribbling. "Family, as far as you know?" He looked up at the troopers.

Veraggi had put on the cap and pulled it forward. "Heard he's got a daughter in these parts. Said he was buying a ranch outside of Dubois so he could be close to her. That's all I know. He wasn't much on jawing about his business. Pretty much kept to himself."

"Went visiting up in the hills west of town couple days ago. You ask me, that's where the daughter lives." Osborne slapped his cap against his thigh. "Came to drilling practice ten minutes late. Wasn't unusual for him to show up late. Took off whenever he wanted, showed up when he got around to it. Used to brag how Custer did that. He said commanders make their own rules."

"West of town is a big place," the detective spoke under his breath. "Any idea where I can find her?"

"I heard she was at the high school last evening to hear him speak," Veraggi said. "Auditorium was packed with folks wanted to see and hear Custer." He was shaking his head.

"Long line waiting to shake his hand. Folks pawing at his buckskin shirt," Osborne said, and Father John thought he detected the smallest undercurrent of envy in both the troopers' voices. "Heard him mention Dorothy once. That wasn't his wife's name."

"Wife?" The detective flipped to the next page.

The troopers looked at each other a long moment. "Can't say for sure," Osborne said, taking a step back. "Belinda Clark impersonates Libbie, the little missus. Garrett said he was expecting her any day. She was going to the Little Bighorn reenactment with us."

Detective Madden walked over to the door, pulled a cell out of the case on his belt, and, dipping his head, muttered something. In a moment he was back. "I should know in a few minutes if there's a Dorothy on any of the titles of houses up in the hills. Soon as I have a few words with Dr. Henderson, I'll drive up and give her the bad news. Anybody care to come along?"

"We weren't personal friends," Osborne said. He and Veraggi started moving toward the door.

"Hold on," the detective said. "I've got officers heading to the campground where the cavalry's been staying. We'll want to talk to everybody. No one fires up his RV and drives out of here until I say so. That clear?"

The troopers nodded, and for a moment, Father John half expected them to salute. Then they were through the sliding glass doors and hurrying toward the parking lot.

FATHER JOHN RODE in the passenger seat of the black, unmarked car with Detective Madden gripping the steering wheel and working his way west. Finally he settled back, steering with the crook of one finger. "Lone wolf is the impression I'm getting of Garrett. Living in the shoes of a man that died over a hundred years ago. What do you know about the fellow?"

"Only what I read in the *Gazette*. Travels around the country with impersonators of the Seventh Cavalry. They march in parades and rodeos and county fairs. They were a big hit in Philadelphia last month."

"I was thinking about Custer, the guy Garrett thought he was."

"He was killed at the Little Bighorn in 1876."

"Sioux, wasn't it?"

"Sioux, Cheyenne. Even Arapahos were there."

"Any Indians have a reason to shoot him again?"

"Hard to imagine," Father John said.

"You ask me, Indians don't forget. Maybe somebody wanted to make a statement. Shoot the guy impersonating Custer, almost as good as shooting Custer himself. I heard the shouts at the parade. How they remember Wounded Knee and other old battles. Maybe somebody didn't like Garrett making Custer a big hero again."

Father John felt an uneasiness gnawing at him. It hadn't gone away, he realized, since he'd read the article in the *Gazette*. What the detective said was true. Arapahos lived by symbols, invisible pictures of reality. He tried to shake off the possibility that someone from the rez was involved, but he could see where the investigation would go. As clear and obvious as the foothills ahead. He closed his eyes, and the craggy, worried face of Lou Morningside appeared on the inside of his eyelids. His grandson, Colin, had dressed like Crazy Horse, the Oglala chief who had led the attack on the 7th Cavalry at the Little Bighorn.

"Revenge for massacres over a century old?" he said. "Sounds like a weak motivation to kill a man." He didn't say what he was thinking: Colin should call Vicky right away.

"Never know what motivates a killer," Madden said.

"What about the troopers? I got the impression that Veraggi and Osborne didn't care much for the man."

"Nobody was armed. The city wouldn't give them a permit to carry. Don't need armed soldiers marching down our streets."

"Neither were the Indians," Father John said. "Most were half naked. How would they conceal a gun?"

"All the same. Indians hated Custer." The car slowed down, and Madden swung right. At the end of a long, dirt driveway, a two-story log house nestled against the peach and red outcroppings that jutted from the sagebrush-studded earth. Shadowing the out-croppings and the house were peaks of the Wind River range. A young woman in blue jeans and a blue blouse leaned against one of the pillars of the porch watching them drive up.

"Bought the place last year," Madden said, pulling in close to the porch steps. "Name is Dorothy Winslow. Only name on the title."

The woman didn't move as they got out. She looked a lot like her father, Father John thought.

3

"DOROTHY WINSLOW?" MADDEN stopped at the foot of the porch steps. Father John walked across the hard-packed driveway and stood next to him. "Edward Garrett's daughter? I'm Detective Madden."

The woman on the porch above them blinked in response. She might have been in her forties, short and muscular with a sun-brushed look that came from spending a lot of time outdoors. Her hair was blond and she wore it long, like a veil that curled over the shoulders of her shirt. Eyes the same blue as the shirt, and intense. She lifted a hand in greeting. "You'd better come up."

Father John followed Madden up the steps. The woman shifted her gaze to Father John. He could feel her eyes apprising him: cowboy hat, blue jeans, plaid shirt. "You some kind of clergy?"

"Father John O'Malley," he said, "St. Francis Mission." He put out his hand. The woman took his hand for a moment, then glanced at Madden and moved along the porch railing, as if she wanted to open some space around her. "How did it happen?"

"You've heard?" Madden said. News traveled fast across the rez on the moccasin telegraph, Father John was thinking. Up here, outside of town, it was the internet. "I'm sorry. Your father was shot."

She tossed her head and let out a squeal that might have come from a tiny, trapped animal. She clasped her arms over her chest and hugged herself. "I knew it would happen."

"You knew your father would be shot?" Madden had pulled the notepad and pen out of his shirt pocket.

"Call it a premonition, if you like," she said. "I had a vision." She pivoted toward Father John. "Arapahos know all about visions. I went to the theater last night to hear Custer, that is, my father channeling Custer. He gave his glorious victory speech from after he had routed Jeb Stuart at Gettysburg, saving the Union army, and practically winning the whole damn Civil War. He even bragged about his victories against the so-called savages on the plains." She pushed herself off the railing, stepped across the porch and dropped onto the wide armrest of a wood chair. "On the drive home, the sky was gray, thick with clouds, and the road was dark. My headlights barely picked out the way. I remember leaning over the steering wheel, watching for deer or antelope. The clouds started to part, making a black, star-filled trail across the sky. The trail climbed over a ridge, and the clouds on either side looked like hills. I saw my father on horseback galloping along the trail, over the ridge, away from me. The clouds closed around him, and the sky turned gray again. I knew he would die. And you know what else? I had the feeling that maybe he deserved to die. I didn't go to the parade. I didn't want to see it happen."

Madden scratched something in the notepad, then looked up and cleared his throat. "Anyone threaten your father? Any altercations he told you about? Enemies in the area?"

She shrugged and stared at the floor planks. "Indians," she said. "Arapahos, whatever. Two of them came to the theater. They sat in the back row across the aisle from me. Stoic-faced and still as statues. I watched them the whole time Custer . . ." She broke off and lifted her eyes. "Sometimes I don't know who he was, my father or Custer. He went on and on about his glorious victory at the battle of the Washita against the murderous Cheyennes, one of his favorite themes. From what I've read, Washita was a massacre of a camp of peaceful Cheyennes. Women, children, and old men. Somehow the great Custer had missed the large camp of hostile warriors nearby. If he had waded into them, it probably would have ended his career eight years earlier. The whole time he was bragging about Washita, I kept my eye on those Indians. Half expected one of them to jump up and shoot him. He switched to the Little Bighorn, how it should've been his crowning glory. Would have made him president, except for the treachery of his subordinates, Reno and Benteen. They deserted him, he said. Nothing about Crazy Horse and his warriors, as if they didn't matter." She shook her head, and Father John wondered if she was speaking of Custer or of her father. "Those Indians didn't even blink."

"Would you recognize them if you saw them?" Madden asked.

"They looked Arapaho. Long faces, prominent cheekbones, hooked noses."

Father John took a moment, trying to piece together a reason for anyone to come to Indian country, pretend to be Custer, and brag about fighting the Plains Indians. He asked if she had called her father and told him about the vision.

She nodded. "I called his cell the minute I got home and pleaded with him to cancel the parade. He laughed. What would the Seventh Cavalry do? Troopers from all over the country. The beginning of the season. He made one excuse after the other. Dozens of parades and rodeos scheduled across the West. Montana on June twenty-fifth for the reenactment of the Battle of the Little Bighorn. Should they just cancel everything and go home? 'Remember, Dottie'—he called me Dottie. He used that deep Custer-like voice he put on whenever he gave a speech. 'To die in the saddle is a worthy death.' I'd heard him talk like that before. It was what Custer believed."

Dorothy stared out across the yard as if she were expecting another vision. The dirt driveway stretched between mounds of sagebrush and brown sand hills. Gusts of wind swept off the hills and knocked against the logs of the house. The floor planks squeaked. After a moment, Father John asked if she might like him to call other family members.

"Others? There's no one but Dad and me," she said, pulling her gaze away from the yard. "Mom died ten years ago. Dad stayed in the army a few years, then retired. After that, Dad became crazy obsessed with Custer. He no longer had any life of his own, so he decided to live Custer's." She gave a little laugh that sounded as if she were choking. "He'd always been an amateur historian. Loved the Civil War. He could quote Lincoln word for word. But he was always drawn to Custer, and pretty soon he moved on to the Indian Wars. Following Custer around, I guess. It was like he was reborn. He was Custer. You believe in reincarnation, Father?"

"I believe we continue our journey after this life. We're in the hands of God."

Dorothy stood up and walked back to the railing. The wind

caught her hair and blew it across her face. She looked out at the yard through the flailing strands of hair a moment before sweeping it aside and tucking it behind her ears. "I believe in reincarnation." She swung around, light flashing in the blue eyes. "I saw it in my father. He changed into somebody I'd never known and couldn't understand. As if Custer never died at the Little Bighorn, like it was all some terrible mistake for him to have been cut down at thirty-seven years old. So my father was reliving Custer's life, giving him more time."

"I understood your father had a wife," Madden said.

"Wife?" Dorothy tipped her head back and gave a forced laugh, as if the idea was preposterous. "Custer had a wife. The indomitable Libbie. The only reason my father married the woman was because she channeled Elizabeth Custer. Custer needed Libbie. Crazy."

"How can I get in touch with her?" Madden asked.

"I wouldn't know. I met her once. That was enough. In her little calico frock and sunbonnet and lace-up boots, staring adoringly at my father. She was a big hit with the crowds at the Bighorn reenactment. The grieving widow."

"Where was home?"

"For Custer? On the plains, galloping here to there. Oh, you mean my father. He traveled in his RV."

"I've spoken with Nicholas Veraggi and Philip Osborne," the detective went on. "They told me your father was buying a ranch outside Dubois."

"Marcus Reno and Frederick Benteen." The woman rolled her eyes. "Not exactly Custer's favorite people. I believe he detested them. Maybe he was just jealous. After all, they survived the Little Bighorn."

"What about Veraggi and Osborne?" Father John said. "Did your father detest them?"

This seemed to stump her. She walked back to the chair and plopped down on the seat. "It's hard to say, isn't it? Where my father left off and Custer began?"

"Did your father close on the ranch?" Madden went on.

"I have no idea," she said. "He and Mom had a ranch outside Laramie. Who knows when he was last there. He came to see me a couple of days ago and said he'd sold the ranch and intended to buy one near Dubois. He said he had invested the money he'd made off the ranch and expected to pay cash for the Dubois place. It would be for me, he said, when his time came. I told him it wasn't necessary. 'You want to be a father now?'" She gave a sharp laugh. "A little too late, I told him. Besides, my divorce settlement left me just fine, thank you very much. Ronny Winslow may have been a womanizing sonofabitch, but he was a rich one. You ask me, the RV was Dad's permanent home. I don't think he had any intention of settling down again on a ranch. Do you really think Custer could have settled down?"

"Do you know the location?"

"He called it the old Stockton place."

Madden's pen scratched at the notepad. "You've been very helpful," he said, fishing a small wallet from his shirt pocket. He removed a card and handed it to Dorothy Winslow. "Call me if you think of anything else. Anything at all."

THE HIGHWAY MELTED into a shimmering white light under the blazing afternoon sun. Detective Madden peered through the sunglasses he'd pushed onto his face, both hands on the wheel.

Knuckles popped like white pebbles. He hunched forward to see beneath the rim of the lowered visor. "A real mess on our hands," he said. "Indians fighting whites. Not good for Lander or the rez. We've been trying to work together for years now. Something like this comes along and blows everything out of the water."

Father John didn't say anything. He watched the light moving ahead like the mirage of a white-capped river. As long as Madden assumed one of the Indians had shot Garrett, there would be tension between Indians on the rez and whites in Lander and Riverton. Chances were, someone at the theater would identify the Arapahos Dorothy had seen, and Madden would start with them. Father John could almost hear Lou Morningside's voice: "Easy to blame us. Indians just waiting to go to town and shoot a white man. Makes sense to white people."

"Until the investigation is over," Father John said, "we don't know what really happened."

"I get it, Father. You're holding out for the Indians, like you're one of them. You gotta admit Indians hated Custer back in history, and Indians don't forget. The way I see it, this was their chance to bring Custer down a second time." He wiggled his shoulders as if to work out a cramp and went back to staring ahead under the visor.

Outside the land rolled away from the highway like waves on a brown ocean with debris of sagebrush and clumps of wild grasses floating on the surface. The sky dropped all around, the color of a blue wildflower. "Garrett could have had enemies."

"Don't get me wrong," Madden said, shooting him another glance. "I'm not the kind of investigator that starts with a theory of who's guilty and overlooks any evidence that proves otherwise. Those guys exist. Give a bad name to every detective in the

country. We'll take a close look at Garrett's private life, business dealings. But we also have to talk to those Indians in the
parade. Bureau of Indian Affairs Police will cooperate. They'll
bring them in. Somebody saw something, and we have to find that
person."

Father John watched the rolling brown hills flatten into the
outskirts of Lander. Sagebrush and wild grasses gave way to a
string of warehouses, trailer parks, gas stations, and motels. Garrett's murder was the kind of case that crossed jurisdictions and
involved police on both sides of the reservation's border. "This big
an area, we have to cooperate," the BIA Police chief had told him
once. "Otherwise the bad guys could step across a line and disappear. Police can't cross the lines, so nobody would be looking for
them."

"You can help us, Father."

"How's that?"

"Talk to the Arapahos at St. Francis. Any Shoshones on the rez
you know. A murderer's on the loose, and it's to everybody's
advantage—Indian and white—to bring him to justice. Tell them
we're investigating everybody, not just Indians."

Father John hoped that was true. He wanted to believe the
man. But he'd been at St. Francis long enough to know how easy
it was, despite all good intentions, to fall into the old mind-set: A
crime committed in town? Indian must be guilty. Guilty of being
Indian. "I'll tell them," he said. He wasn't sure he could convince
them.

Madden slowed down and pulled into the curb behind the red
Toyota pickup. Everyone in the area knew the old pickup that
Father John had driven since he'd arrived at St. Francis. Old then,
and that was ten years ago. He had to smile at the idea that he

couldn't go anywhere without someone spotting the pickup. "You can hear it coming," Vicky Holden had once told him.

He thanked the detective, got out, and was about to shut the door when Madden held up a hand. "You'll call me if you hear anything, right?" he said.

"How about I call the BIA Police?" Father John said.

FATHER JOHN FOLLOWED the curve of the highway into Hudson, then crossed the border onto Rendezvous Road and headed into the reservation. Clouds drifting across the sun cut some of the glare. Still he drove with the visor down against the bright sky, his cowboy hat pulled low. To the west were the small white houses of Arapahoe, and in the distance the blue, snow-streaked peaks of the Wind River range. He stopped at the sign on Seventeen-Mile Road, then made a right and headed for the blue billboard with the words *St. Francis Indian Mission.* Another right past the billboard and he was in the tunnel of cottonwoods. Mounds of fluffy white cotton lay like snow under the trees.

A sense of peace usually came over him as he drove into the mission, but not this afternoon. The mission was quiet, yet he couldn't shake the sense that the quiet was temporary, the quiet on a hillside before the battle. A knot of apprehension tightened inside him as he turned onto Circle Drive and drove past the yellow stucco administration building, the wide driveway that led to Eagle Hall and the guesthouse, the white stucco church with geometric symbols of the Arapaho painted in red, blue, and yellow, the old gray stone school that was now the Arapaho Museum. In front of the redbrick residence was a small tan two-door sedan. Someone with long black hair in the driver's seat.

Father John pulled in next to the car and got out. By the time he'd walked around the front of the Toyota, Darleen Longshot was leaning on the top of the open door of her car. She looked shaky and pale, reluctant to let go of the door.

"You okay?" he said.

"I gotta talk to you, Father."

4

DARLEEN LONGSHOT WAS small with nervous hands that ran up and down the thighs of her blue jeans. Her eyes were dark, red-rimmed, and sore-looking, as if she hadn't been able to stop crying. "I've been waiting for you, Father," she said in a husky, smoke-ravaged voice. "I'm going crazy."

"Come in." Father John ushered her up the front sidewalk to the concrete stoop at the front door. He reached past her, pushed open the door, and followed her inside. The quiet of late afternoon suffused the residence. No sounds of Walks-On, the golden retriever he'd found by the side of Seventeen-Mile Road five years ago, scrambling down the hallway on three legs. No music, no television voices. This was the time of day the bishop and Walks-On walked down to the Little Wind River at the edge of the mission.

"We can talk in the study." He nodded the woman into the small room on the left. After she had settled in one of the visitor's chairs, he walked around and sat down in the old leather chair behind the desk. Stacks of papers, folders, envelopes spilled across the surface, nearly burying the laptop. He tried to keep up with the routines of the mission—bills to pay, thank-you notes to write for checks that spilled out of envelopes from people he had never heard of, phone calls to return, elders to check on, parishioners to visit in the hospitals—but it was like riding across the plains, topping each bluff only to spot a higher bluff ahead.

The chair creaked as he leaned back. He grasped the armrests and waited while the woman across from him dabbed a tissue at her eyes and blew her nose.

"I'm sorry," she said, leaning sideways to stuff the tissue into her jeans pocket. "I don't mean to be a nuisance."

"You're not a nuisance. Tell me what's going on."

"It's Mikey." She drew in a long breath and held it a moment before blowing it out like smoke. "You remember my kid?"

"Of course." A small kid with a wedge of black hair that hung in his eyes. Not much good at batting or throwing the ball, but he could run like the wind. If a pitcher put him on base, the Eagles could count on Mikey scoring a run. It had been several years since Mike Longshot had come around the mission. On those Sundays when Darleen came to Mass, she came alone.

"Mikey never came home from the parade this morning," Darleen said. Her voice so small he had to lean forward to catch the words. "I been waiting for him all afternoon. I'm so worried I don't know what to do."

"You expected him home right away?" Father John tried to keep his own voice soft, like a blanket that might absorb the woman's fear.

"I didn't know what to expect after . . ." She clasped and

unclasped her hands, then dipped her mouth against her fist. "I was there. I seen what happened to Custer. I seen what the warriors did."

Father John looked away a moment. He could see it still: warriors galloping around, cavalry stalled, horses plunging. "Are you worried that Mike had some part in it?" he said.

She looked up. Her dark eyes were clouded with fear. "He didn't have anything to do with it. Mikey would never be part of murder. He's not dead inside. He couldn't kill anybody. He can't even stomp on a spider. He likes watching all kinds of living things, just watching and seeing how pretty they are."

"What worries you, Darleen?"

"They're going to say he did it."

"Who?"

"The warriors. I know how their minds work. The cops start coming around, asking a lot of questions, getting too close, one of them will swear he saw Mikey pull out a pistol and shoot Custer. All the others will back him up, and the cops are going to be so happy they solved the case. Big newspaper headlines about how clever they are. Another Indian thrown in prison. Who cares?"

"What's going on, Darleen?"

Her hands were kneading the air above her lap. She opened her mouth and emitted a muffled strangling noise, as if she were choking. Father John jumped to his feet, but she threw out one hand. "You know . . ." she began, then sank back against the chair and dropped her eyes in a gesture of defeat. "Mikey's different. He was never like other boys."

Father John nodded.

"He's special, my Mikey. Rob and I knew we'd been given a special child almost from the time he was born. And we were grateful that the Creator had trusted him to us. He's sensitive. When his daddy died in that car wreck, I thought Mikey was going to lay down and die, too. It was a long time before I could get him interested in doing anything. You remember how you came to the house and talked him into playing with the Eagles?" She had started crying, blurring the words and running her palms over her eyes. "Best thing ever happened to Mikey," she managed. "He started coming out of it. Made friends. But as he got older, boys turned on him. They saw he was different. They forgot. Lots of Raps forgot the Old Time. The ancestors would've treated Mikey like a holy person. They would have respected and admired him because the Creator gave him two spirits. Male and female."

Father John waited for the woman to go on. He had counseled hundreds. He had lost track of the numbers of parishioners stopping by the office—Father, you have a minute? He could see Mikey Longshot stretching his legs for home, scoring the winning run, and the rest of the team crowding around, hoisting him up and carrying him around like the trophy they'd just won. When had that changed? When had the kids decided he was different?

"You don't know how it's been," Darleen went on. "The bullying. Anything happen, the other boys ganged up and swore Mikey did it. Like the time somebody stole the seventh-grade teacher's purse. The other kids swore they saw Mikey take it, so he ended up with a juvi record. He really wanted to play basketball in high school. The other guys tripped him, pushed him down, did everything they could to make him look like he couldn't handle the ball, so he sat on the bench. Wouldn't go back to school after that."

"I'm sorry," he said.

"Two years ago, he got shot. You remember?"

Father John said he remembered. He had sat with Mike at Riverton Memorial after the doctors had dug a bullet out of his ribs.

"White guy shot him in the park in Riverton. Lied to the police. Said Mikey was coming on to him. That wasn't Mikey's way, but some of his so-called Arapaho friends backed up the white guy. Raps backing up the white guy, saying that's what they'd seen, so the cops said it was self-defense. Now they can say he had a motive to shoot a white man."

She ran her fingers over her eyes and squeezed the rim of her nose. Then she looked at him and tried for a smile. "He can handle horses better than anybody on the rez. Been training mustangs since he was sixteen. He walks right out into the corral. Horse can be going crazy, pawing the dirt with fire in his eyes, and Mikey starts talking to him. Pretty soon, the horse calms down. Gets all gentle. Mikey saddles him up and rides him around. I've seen it happen a hundred times. He's . . . what you call it? A horse whisperer. He can ride any horse and make it do what he wants. Horses love him. They have a sixth sense, you know. They see he's special. Blessed by the Creator."

Darleen leaned forward and clasped her hands in her lap. "That's why they came to the house last week."

"Who came to the house?"

"Colin Morningside and a couple other Raps. Said they wanted to talk to Mikey. I was about to tell them to get lost, but Mikey came down the hall and said, 'What's up?' They went outside. I kept watch at the window. They hung around the pickup and talked for fifteen minutes, then Colin and the others drove off. Mikey came inside and told me they heard that Custer and the Seventh Cavalry were going to ride in the rodeo parade in Lander. They said they were getting warriors to ride. They wanted Mikey. Bad feeling came over me right then. I tried to talk him out of it."

"You said he's a great horseman."

She nodded. "They needed him. When I saw what they did

today, riding around the cavalry, racing toward one another. A dare ride, like in the Old Time. Mikey knew how to keep his horse under control and get the other horses to follow. Horses know who's the leader, and they do what the leader does."

"What are you saying, Darleen? You think one of the Indians killed Garrett?"

"They all killed him." Her voice reached for hysteria. "That was the plan. Race around like an attack, dare the cavalry to do something. Scream. Yell. Make a big commotion so nobody sees Custer fall off his horse. They'll get away with it, too. The cops start getting too close, the warriors will give them Mikey." She jerked a little sideways, as if her own words had sent a shock through her. "Oh, my God, Father. He'll go to prison for the rest of his life."

"Look, Darleen," Father John began. "Nobody knows yet what happened this morning."

"Oh, Father." She dropped her face into her hands. "Everybody knows." Her voice was teary and blurred. "There isn't anybody on this rez that didn't want Custer dead." Looking up, she seemed to make an effort to pull herself together. "That man thought he was Custer. He stood for everything Custer did to Indian people. Now they've killed him."

THE SUN HAD disappeared behind the high mountain peaks, and a dusty yellow light slanted over the mission grounds. After helping Darleen into her car and watching the jerky way she drove around Circle Drive into the cottonwood tunnel, Father John started toward the Little Wind River. In the stillness, the mission seemed frozen in time. He could imagine Jesuits from the past, those of the austere photographs that lined the corridor in the administration building, walking to the river. The feeling that he was part of something larger than himself, the latest in a parade that would continue on, never left him. The past inhabited the reservation and clung to the mission like the invisible wind.

He headed through the coolness of the shadows between the administration building and the church. Little spits of dust rose around his boots and turned the toes gray. What Darleen had said made no sense, and yet, there was a sense of the past here, as if General George Armstrong Custer still rode across the plains, attacking villages, burning tipis and food supplies, shooting the picketed ponies. There were people on the rez whose ancestors had died in Custer's attacks. Darleen was right about one thing: No Indian would mourn Custer's death. Except that the man who'd died this morning wasn't Custer.

And what about the rest of it? A plan the warriors had hatched and carried out? Under the leadership of Colin Morningside, dressed and painted like Crazy Horse, the Oglala chief who had defeated Custer? Detective Madden suspected an Indian had shot Garrett. Eventually he would focus the investigation on the Indian impersonating Crazy Horse. But the plan had covered that possibility. The warriors would give up Mike, someone dispensable because he was different.

Help us, Dear Lord. Guide us. Show us the way.

Walks-On came bounding toward him, stick in his mouth. Coming around a bend behind the golden retriever was the bishop. Baseball cap shading half his face, gray hair standing out below the rim. Father John sank onto his haunches, took hold of the dog and scratched behind his ears, then ran his hands over the back of his coat. When Walks-On dropped the stick, he scooped it up and tossed it ahead. Walks-On bounded after it as Father John stood up and fell in beside the bishop. They headed back the way Father John had just come. "What about the rodeo?" he said, trying for a lighter tone.

"I thanked Lou for the offer of tickets, but . . ." The bishop stopped walking and drew in two or three breaths before he started off again. "I'm afraid it would be too dispiriting. A man dead. Indians and cavalry impersonators pulled from the program. Everyone will be sad, I think." He waited, then added: "And worried. But Lou said the purses are pretty big, so the rodeo will go on."

Father John didn't say anything. Cowboys and Indians came from across the West to compete in the rodeos. Bronco and bull riding, calf roping, dozens of events, once known as cowboy fun. Rodeos were the way rodeo riders made their living.

They walked in silence. Blue-black shadows had begun to drape the guesthouse and Eagle Hall. Walks-On raced ahead, the stick balanced between his jaws. They were crossing Circle Drive when Father John told the old man what Darleen had said, thinking how good it was to have an older priest to talk to. There wasn't much Bishop Harry hadn't seen as the bishop of Patma. Horrendous experiences that came up from time to time, as if the past were always present. Young girls taken from the mission school, sold into marriage, burned to death. Young boys with hands and legs amputated by their own parents to make them more successful street beggars.

"What do you think, John?"

Father John took a moment to marshal his thoughts into a logical sequence. There must be logic that deals with the present, explains the causes and effects that have nothing to do with the past. He shook his head. "It's not logical for someone to shoot a man who had nothing to do with what happened in the past," he said.

The bishop stopped. He was half a head shorter than Father John with a rounded stoop to his shoulders. He started up the steps to the residence, then turned and looked Father John in the eye. "Still, it might be true," he said. "Events move across time according to their own pathways. What will you do?"

Walks-On had dropped the stick at his feet. Father John picked it up, tossed it across the front yard, and watched the dog lope with surprising grace on two front legs and one hind leg. There was a logic here. Toss stick. Dog runs. Dog retrieves stick. But anything might intervene and stop the sequence. Nothing was inevitable.

"I don't know," he said.

From the time I was a boy, I knew I wanted to portray Custer, a great and noble American, courageous and daring. I wanted to follow in his footsteps.

Father John sipped at the hot coffee he had brewed and read through the black text on the screen. When he had typed "reenactments" in the search box, a page of Web sites had materialized, and he had clicked on "My Life as Custer, a biography of Edward Garrett." The first pages had been a travelogue of the cities and counties, parades, rodeos, and county fairs where Garrett had appeared as Custer. Sometimes with 7th Cavalry reenactors; sometimes with his wife, Belinda Clark, dressed like Libbie Custer; sometimes alone. Photographs dotted the text. Garrett, in buckskins and wide-brimmed hat, squinting in the sun, aiming a rifle at some distant point, serious-looking and straight-shouldered, a man in command.

I found an old buckskin jacket in the thrift store where we used to shop and begged Mother to buy it for me. It was perfect. Could have been worn by the great man himself. Mother wasn't happy about laying out the money on what she called my wild dreams, but I promised to pay her back. I gave her every dime I made off my paper route until I had paid off that debt, and I was proud. I was sure Custer was the type of man who never welshed on a debt. From somewhere else, I got a wide-brimmed hat that looked like Custer's. That was the beginning. I read everything about Custer. I knew how to walk and talk like him. Some of his famous Custer luck rubbed off on me, and I started acting like Custer in school shows. I talked myself into parades. Soon as I got out of the army, I found other reenactors as inspired by Custer and the 7th Cavalry as I was, and we started putting on mock battles based on the Little Bighorn battle.

"From those beginnings," the article went on, "Edward Garrett has become the foremost interpreter of General George Armstrong Custer in the nation. He has appeared before crowds of thousands who no doubt wish that the fate of the great general might have been different. Look for Garrett at the reenactments of the Battle of the Little Bighorn . . ."

Father John closed the site. A wave of senselessness washed over him. Edward Garrett, alive on the Web site, reminiscing about how the larger-than-life image of Custer had taken hold of him as a kid, how he had wanted to be like Custer. Year after year, reenacting the Battle of the Little Bighorn, where Custer's luck had run out. Now Garrett was dead.

He read down the next page of Web sites and clicked on "Reenactments—Living History." The text that popped up on the screen explained that hundreds of men and women participated in reenactments of famous military battles across the country. Most reenacted Civil War battles, such as Fredericksburg, the Battle of the Wilderness, Gettysburg. But reenactments were also staged of famous battles in World War I and World War II. The only reenactments on the plains, it seemed, were those of the Battle of the Little Bighorn.

Those who dedicate time, energies, and money to reenactments do so out of a love of history and the desire to bring history alive. "We are educators," explained Herb Finer, part of the reenactment of the Battle of Bull Run. "We are living interpreters of the past, and our goal is to help people understand major historical events that shaped the present. When you see a soldier shot from his horse, it is real. The image stays in your mind, and you never think of history again as dull, dry, and unimportant."

While it is true that reenactors portray battles in which many men died horrible deaths, the battles took place between armed combatants. The results might have gone either way because the combatants were equal. Civil War battles were fought between armed warriors, unlike the massacres of unarmed civilians by soldiers that occurred during the Indian Wars. Such massacres as Sand Creek and the Washita were hardly equal fights, and are unworthy of reenactment.

Father John closed the site, then typed in a new search: "Battle of the Little Bighorn reenactment." Dozens of sites appeared. He clicked on "Historical Interpretation Video." A panoramic view of the Little Bighorn River Valley swept across the screen. Bluffs, narrow ravines, slopes of tall grass surrounding the blue-green river that twisted through a valley at the base of sandy cliffs. The sound of drums and the *Hi yi hi* cries of the Indians coming from a distance, moving closer. The faint outlines of white tipis materializing alongside the river, like ghosts. Dozens of tipis at first. Hundreds. Thousands.

He tried to remember what he had once taught his American history classes about the Battle of the Little Bighorn. Fifteen years ago, a different lifetime, and even then, he remembered, Custer and the Bighorn had seemed remote, a footnote. Now he had the sense of watching the actual camp come alive. Sioux, Cheyenne, Arapaho under the leadership of Sitting Bull, the spiritual leader, and Crazy Horse, the war chief. The largest Indian camp ever assembled. Four thousand Indians. What a sight the village must have presented to Custer's scouts when they topped a bluff high above the village.

Cutting through the drums and the cries was the sound of a bugle playing the jaunty, familiar melody of "Garry Owen." A column of troopers rode across the grassy slopes. Blue uniforms and a mixture of blue caps and gray wide-brimmed hats, rifles strapped on backs, metal harnesses and stirrups clanking with the music. Riding ahead were officers, Benteen and Reno. Father John recognized Osborne and Veraggi. Edward Garrett in the lead, blond hair almost hidden under a wide-brimmed hat, dressed in buckskin shirt and trousers with fringe running down the arms and legs.

He shut down the video. It was like watching men riding to their deaths.

5

ANGELA RUNNING BEAR concentrated on the man's voice coming from the radio on the dashboard. The Honda shimmied. Engine humming, exhaust smells drifting. The news still seemed incredible. Edward Garrett shot to death at the rodeo parade yesterday while she had been curled on a lounge chair on the balcony of the condo in Jackson waiting for Skip to finish his meeting. They were going to dinner, fancy restaurant in a hotel. They would be seated on the patio, waiters hurrying about, wine stewards bowing to Skip Burrows, bringing the best wine. He was important. She felt important when she was with him. They had driven back to Lander in silence, music playing softly on the radio. Then the interruption, the news. A murder on Main Street.

Now the radio voice droned on with more details as she backed down the graveled driveway that led from the rental house—a one-room shack, really—past the old two-story where busybody

Betty Black lived. Probably a hundred years old, with nothing to do but watch Angela's coming and going and who she came and went with. Skip always parked a block away and walked down the back alley. She let him in the side door. It wasn't good business for the town to know he was having an affair with his secretary. Half his age, Arapaho. People would talk, and one thing about Skip she had learned over the last months was that he liked to control the gossip about himself. Last night he had walked her down the alley. Stayed for an hour before he had swung out of bed, saying he had to get to the office early this morning.

It bothered her, a prick of discomfort in the happiness. He had broken off with his old girlfriend. Why did they have to sneak around, walk down alleys, spend weekends in Jackson where Skip said no one cared if they were having an affair? Why couldn't they live like a normal couple, love each other in the open? Friday afternoon, she had left the office before he did—they never left at the same time. She had waited at her apartment. At every muffled sound from outside—the squeal of a tire, the sound of an engine cutting off or a dog barking—she had thought, He's here. Except she knew he would walk to her place. Finally he was there, filling up the living room, taking up all the space, breathing all the air. And something different about him, she had thought. Something on his mind as they had driven to Jackson making small talk.

She had dreamed about the house he was building on the beach in Cabo. They could live like other people there. Morning swims, afternoon siestas, cozy dinners with the last of the sunlight splayed on the water, and the nights alone, just the two of them. She wondered when they would move to Mexico. *Trust me*, he always said. He had made some big investments that would pay off soon. Money never seemed a problem for Skip. Big house in Lander, the silver BMW. She had seen the stacks of cash in the briefcase he had brought to Jackson this weekend.

Angela turned into the street, shifted into drive and took a side street to Main. The radio voice was like background noise. "It is believed the murder occurred when about thirty Arapahos broke ranks and started galloping around the cavalry. Hundreds of on-lookers were on the curbs, and police have asked anyone who may have seen the shooting or noticed anything unusual to contact them."

She hit the off button, dragged her bag onto her lap, and bur-rowed inside, steering with her knees to avoid the cars parked at the curb. She pulled out the cell and punched in Skip's number. Everybody would be stopping by today. Edward Garrett—*Call me General*—murdered in the street! She could picture the man strid-ing into the office in his fringed buckskins, like those worn by the Rendezvous guys who dressed up like traders and camped on the Wind River outside Riverton like it was the 1800s and the Indians were about to show up and trade buffalo hides for sugar and cof-fee. Living in the past, like the general. She wished she could do that, turn back the clock.

The familiar voice, low in her ear. "This is Skip Burrows. Sorry you've missed me. Leave your number. *Chou!*" She hit the end key, realizing she should have called the office. Skip always came in early. Brewed coffee. Answered e-mails, dictated letters, and read documents, the mundane work of a law practice that he couldn't get done during the day with the phone ringing and people drop-ping by.

She called the office. "You've reached the law offices of Skip Burrows, attorney at law." It was her own voice. She tapped the off button again and tossed the phone onto the passenger seat.

How many times had the general stopped by? Two? Three? Never an appointment. "My buddy Skip in?" he'd say, and Skip would appear in the doorway and beckon the man into his private office. Everybody in town knew they could stop in and chat with Skip whenever the notion struck them. Coffee always hot. But the general wasn't a townie. She had no idea where he came from, only that he would show up from time to time.

Angela drove through the residential street, swung right, and worked her way down the block toward the white-painted brick building that faced Main Street. They had argued, Skip and the general, the last time Garrett had dropped by. Tuesday? Wednesday? She used to jot the names of drop-ins in the appointment book, until Skip told her not to bother.

She turned into the parking lot behind the building and pulled into the vacant spot with Burrows Law Firm painted on the curb. Skip's slot next to her was empty. Odd, she thought. He was always in the office before she arrived.

She got out into the warm breeze that swept across the pavement. Sunlight bounced off the chrome on the other parked cars. A new thought hit her, rose out of nowhere, and she knew it was part of the uneasiness she had been trying to ignore: Where had Skip gone last night after he'd left her? The ex-girlfriend's place in Riverton, Deborah something? A little pain sliced through her. She wanted to trust him. Why didn't she trust him? She fixed the strap of her bag across her shoulder and tried to steady her footsteps on the pavement, images of Skip floating ahead. Dark blond hair tousled on her pillow, sleep-logged eyes blinking at her, the slow smile when he said "Good morning, beautiful." Oh God, she loved the man.

The back door swung open as she reached for the knob. She

had to swerve sideways as Bob Peters, the accountant across the hall, plunged outside. "Sorry, Angela," he said, holding the door for her. "Heard about Custer?"

"General Garrett? Yeah, I heard."

"Who could have done it?"

"I have no idea."

"They're your people," heading toward the car parked at the curb.

"You have some inside information?" She called over her shoulder. She felt a mixture of anger and puzzlement as she headed down the hallway. Something was missing: the familiar smell of hot, brewed coffee that usually floated toward her.

She grabbed the doorknob beneath the pebbly glass window with two rows of painted black letters: Skip Burrows, JD, Attorney at Law. The knob jammed in her hand.

There was the swish of the back door opening and closing, the sound of footsteps pounding down the hallway. "Didn't see him come in this morning." Peters was holding a brown envelope. He leaned into his own door, pushed it open, and disappeared.

Angela knocked on the glass and waited for the sound of Skip pushing himself away from his desk, crossing the office, muttering out loud, "Use your key!" She wanted to talk about Garrett getting shot, go over what they knew, try to digest the information. She wouldn't mention the argument between Garrett and Skip. She didn't want to watch the confident expression dissolve at the edges as he digested the implications. He'd argued with a murder victim!

She swung her bag around and dug into an inside pocket past the comb, lipstick, package of gum, and assorted receipts. Squeezing the key between her thumb and index finger, she dragged it out of the bag and stuck it into the lock. She stepped into the office and stopped, feeling as if she had hit an invisible wall. Drawers hung open; batches of papers and files littered the floor. Motes of dust floated in the sunlight drifting past the blinds. The surface of her desk was clear, just as she had left it Friday evening with Skip urging her to hurry. He'd see her at her place later, he'd said. She had tried to hurry, which had made her drop a glass of water, which bounced off the edge of the desk and took up more time—picking up the pieces of glass, patting paper towels against the carpet.

The little table next to her desk was vacant. Her computer was gone!

An eerie quiet hung over the office. She dropped the bag on her desk and walked to the side door. A car passed outside, a door slammed somewhere in the building. Her hand trembled as she opened the door.

She stood frozen in place. A tornado? Bomb? Vandals? Skip's desk overturned, drawers hanging open. File folders and papers strewn over the floor, books tossed off the shelves. No sign of his computer. The neatness, the everything-in-its-place that Skip insisted upon, had been desecrated, Skip's personality obliterated. Someone was screaming. She jammed her fist into her mouth to stop the noise and forced herself to walk into the office, her mind a jumble of thoughts. Skip could be lying behind the desk, hurt, dead. It was a crime scene, and his voice went round and round in her head: *Damn fools! Don't know better than to touch anything at a crime scene.*

Only the blizzard of papers littered the floor behind the desk. She used the ends of her blouse to turn the knob on the bathroom door and peered inside. Empty, and as clean and groomed as Skip himself. He wasn't here, and a faint sensation of relief trickled through her. Then she saw the opened window, the right pane pushed across the left, leaving a gaping hole that overlooked the parking lot. And here was something—a trail of blood drops on the windowsill. When she looked closer, she saw the drops of blood among the papers between the desk and the window. Outside, the window screen lay in the branches of the bush below.

She swung around, threw herself toward the door and across the outer office. She managed to yank the cell out of her bag, her fingers skittering like butterflies as she punched in 911. "Your emergency?" The woman sounded half-asleep. "Something terrible has happened," Angela heard herself saying. "Somebody broke into Skip Burrows's office on Main Street. Something's happened to Skip."

"Your name?"

Angela gave her name, then heard a disembodied voice rambling on about how she was Skip's secretary and had just gotten into the office and found the chaos.

"Officers are on the way."

At the edge of her view: a shadow moving across the glass door. "He's back!" she shouted.

"Who's back?"

"Whoever did this. He's in the hallway!"

"Angela?" It was Bob Peters's voice, his fist pounding the wood paneling.

"It's okay," she said. Her legs felt rubbery; she propped herself against the edge of the desk to keep from falling. "It's the accountant from across the hall."

"Don't let anyone in. Understood?"

Angela said she understood, then pushed the end key.

"Angela!" Peters had already let himself in. "Are you all right? I heard somebody scream."

She tried to swallow, but her mouth had turned to sandpaper.

"Good heavens." Peters started across the outer office toward the opened door that framed an oblong view of Skip's office.

She lunged for his arm. "You can't go in there. Police are on the way."

When he turned toward her, she saw her own shock mirrored in his eyes.

"Skip's gone," she managed.

"What do you mean, he's gone?" He wrinkled his nose and turned his head, sampling the air. "I don't smell any coffee."

Angela had to stop herself from grabbing hold of Peters's white shirt and shaking him. "You must have heard something. What did you hear? How could anyone trash the office and force Skip out the window and you not hear a thing?"

Peters was shaking his head. "Sorry, Angela. Only thing I heard was you screaming."

THE TWO UNIFORMED officers stepped around the office, craned their necks outside the window, apprised the parking lot. The cars, people hurrying over. Angela looked away. She leaned against the door frame and watched the officers moving about like robots, silent, lips pressed together. Finally they started toward her, and she backed into her own office. Peters was bent forward in a side chair, hands clasped between the knees of his khaki trousers. He looked up as the officers planted themselves in the center of the room.

"He's hurt," she said. "You have to find him."

No one spoke. The tall, blond officer started scribbling something in a notepad and took a couple of steps toward Peters. "What time did you arrive?"

"Just before eight." Peters straightened his shoulders and gripped the armrests. "Skip comes in early most days, like me. His car wasn't in the parking lot."

"How well did you know him?"

"Know him? Not well. 'How's it going? Another hot day.' The kind of stuff we talked about. Skip was never very serious, if you get what I mean."

"Why don't you tell us?" The other officer tossed the question over his shoulder and moved closer to Angela. She felt as if she might jump out of her skin. Skip was out there someplace, hurt. He could be dying. They should do something! She squeezed her eyes shut against the tears.

"Hey, Angela here will tell you. Skip's everybody's friend. Always got a friendly hello, how-you-doing for folks. People love the guy. Isn't that right?" Peters glanced at Angela, as if he'd stumbled out onto the edge of a cliff, and it was up to her to pull him away. "Isn't that right?" he said again.

"Right," she managed. Skip Burrows, the best-liked man in town. He knew everybody. Everybody knew him. Want to hear a new joke? Need a laugh? Need a friendly clap on the back? Stop in and see Skip Burrows. It was a wonder he ever got any work done. How many times had she apologized to his scheduled appointments, left flipping through magazines while Skip and one of his friends told jokes in his office?

The officer with the notepad gave her a long, narrow-eyed look. "What's his license plate?"

"Ten something," she said. "I don't know. He drives a silver BMW."

The officer nodded; the pen scratched the notepad.

"When did you say you last saw him?"

Angela pulled her lips between her teeth. She hadn't said. No one knew about her and Skip. It was their secret. She wiped a palm across the moisture blossoming on her face.

"He was at his desk when I left at 5 o'clock Friday," she said, and the officer jotted in the notepad and didn't push her, didn't inquire if she and Skip had a relationship outside the office.

When he looked up, he asked if Skip had any family.

"He was married once," Angela said. This caught both officers' attention. Eyebrows shot up in unison. "He told me they had been divorced for twenty years. She left him after he got back from Desert Storm. He said she married a college professor who would never join the military and moved to Alabama."

Scribbling. Scribbling. The officer flipped over a page in the notepad and continued writing. "Any enemies?" he said without looking up. "All these fine people stopping in to shoot the breeze and drink coffee. Anybody not so friendly?"

Peters let out a short guffaw, as if the idea of Skip Burrows having an enemy was as unlikely as . . .

Angela closed her eyes against the rest of it: as unlikely as someone shooting Custer in the middle of Main Street.

"What is it?" the dark-haired officer said.

"I heard him arguing with a friend last week." She had no idea what had pushed her to say it. She loved the man; such a thin line between trust and distrust. "The man stomped out. 'Win some, lose some,' Skip said."

"You have a name?"

Yes. She had a name. Colonel Edward Garrett. She had called him "General," because Skip said the man liked that.

6

THE LONG VIEW of Main Street, wide-laned and lined with hanging baskets of flowers, took Vicky Holden by surprise, it looked so peaceful. Except for the yellow police tape that fluttered in the street a half block away. Vicky had stopped in the doorway of the coffee shop, barely aware of the pressure of Adam Lone Eagle's hand on the small of her back, ushering her outside. Shadows and sunlight mingled in wide rectangles on the sidewalks, a robin's egg blue sky all around, not a cloud in sight. And yet, a man had been shot to death not twenty-four hours ago. A thin line of pickups and cars moved slowly toward the tape before turning onto a side street.

Adam guided her onto the sidewalk and pulled the glass door closed behind them. In the distance, sirens rose and fell like a memory. Adam's hand felt firmer, more protective, against her back. "Probably an accident," he said.

They had grabbed coffee and scones and carried them to a small metal table against the brick wall. The shop was always crowded in the morning. People coming and going, the little bell on the door jingling nonstop, conversations buzzing. Snippets of conversation cut through the noise: *We were right there. Saw the whole thing. You saw him go down? Saw him laying there soon's the Indians rode ahead. One of them shot him, poor man. Just because he pretended to be Custer.*

Vicky had squeezed her eyes shut for a moment against the earnest faces bending toward one another, theorizing, guessing. An image swept over her. She was a child begging Mama to take her to the movie theater in Lander. One of the fairy tales, maybe *Snow White*, and Mama saying, *Not in town. We're not welcome in town.*

She lived here now. In an apartment building filled with whites. She chatted with them on the elevator, waved in the parking lot. Once, when she had the flu, the widow next door had brought chicken soup. Her office was here. A small bungalow on a corner in a residential neighborhood. She and Annie, her secretary, the only Arapahos within blocks. But Arapahos drove to her office every day from the rez. No one bothered them or called them names. She remembered that, too: The rodeo grounds outside town, and white kids saying, *What're you doing here, Injun. Go back where you belong.*

"Don't let them bother you." Adam had leaned across the table toward her. "Nobody knows what really happened yesterday. There will be a major investigation, you can bet on it."

"An investigation into every Arapaho in the parade? Turning their lives upside down? Assuming one is guilty? The only question is, which one to pin it on?" She had felt a sharp prick of annoyance. Adam seemed distant, removed from what had happened, and yet it was his people who had defeated Custer and the 7th Cavalry, his people who were the heroes—Sitting Bull and Crazy Horse. Some Arapahos had ridden north to join Sitting Bull, the chief who refused to be ordered around by white people. Arapahos had wanted to be like him, free on the plains with the buffalo and the sky and the endless expanse of prairie like a grassy sea around them.

"Is that what you believe?" She had challenged him. "An Indian killed Custer again?"

Adam had sipped at his mug of coffee, eyeing her over the brim. Finally he'd said, "You're not making sense. Somebody shot a man named Edward Garrett. An actor. He could have been playing Shakespeare."

"But he wasn't. He came here as Custer. Custer, in Indian country!" Vicky had taken a bite of scone and washed it down with a drink of coffee. "You know what this means to White-Indian relations here."

"It doesn't have to mean anything." God, he was so sure of himself, so handsome and confident, with strands of gray shining through the thick black hair that he wore short, neatly trimmed around his ears. And his hands: the long brown fingers and manicured nails. A Lakota who walked into the high-rise offices of oil and gas and coal companies around the country and faced down lawyers from the biggest and richest firms. Never doubting that they would both continue to come and go in town without worry. To live as they had lived. That no one would toss a brick through the window of the house he'd bought last winter. That he would practice natural resources law from the study that overlooked the quiet, tree-lined street where kids played kickball and neighbors pushed strollers along the sidewalk. Her stomach churned. The killing could change everything.

In the distance, the sound of sirens. She tried to concentrate on what Adam was saying. Something about letting things go, the investigation taking its course. She finished her coffee, wrapped the scone in a napkin, and got to her feet. She dropped both the empty cup and the scone into the trash receptacle and headed for the door, aware of the scrape of Adam's chair behind her, the tap tap of his boots on the hard floor. Now she found it hard to take her eyes away from the street flowing into the horizon. The sirens were coming closer.

"Accident on the highway," Adam said, his hand still on her back. "I'll drive you to the office."

She turned toward him, thoughts jamming together like snarled traffic. "I'll walk." She tried to ignore the puzzled look in his black eyes.

"You're worried about a change in White-Indian relationships, yet you insist upon walking?"

She watched him swallow back the rest of the thought that worked through his expression: I'll never understand you.

She lifted herself on her toes, brushed his lips, and started down the sidewalk toward the yellow tape. Two police cars whipped past, racing toward some point farther down Main Street, sirens blasting.

In a couple of minutes, she was in front of the gift shop where she and Adam had been watching the parade when the commotion began. Up ahead, shouts, screaming, running. The parade had marched past: the blare of brass from the high school bands, the tissue-and-flower-covered floats, the beautiful teenage girls tossing flowers and kisses. But something had changed. It was hard to see the end of the parade past the crowds swirling along the curb. She had glanced at the program she'd cut out of the *Gazette*. The 7th Cavalry followed by Arapaho warriors. She had waited for the

7th Cavalry to march into view, listened for the buglers blowing "Garry Owen." The troopers hadn't appeared.

She had started weaving through the crowds, making her way up the block. Adam beside her, shouldering past a couple of cowboys with hats pushed back, squinting toward the congealing bodies in the middle of the street. A voice, one of the cowboys, had slurred the words around the chunk of tobacco that protruded like a tumor in his cheek: *By God, Custer's down.*

They had pushed past, she and Adam, but she had heard the reluctance in his footsteps, as if whatever had happened to an actor playing Custer was no concern of theirs. It was finished, settled in the Old Time. She had wedged herself beside a family and peered up the street. A riot had erupted, with police officers waving at the crowd, shouting, "Stay back. Stay back." A blur of blue uniforms and horses bucking and plunging, the sounds of men shouting. The crowd pressed forward, and she caught a glimpse of a figure in buckskins and black boots sprawled on the pavement. Sirens swelled in the air. And nervous rumors rippled through the crowd: Custer's been shot.

Vicky crossed Main alongside the yellow police tape that wrapped around a large, wet place where blood had been hosed from the pavement. A couple of cops in jeans, white shirts, and vests patrolled inside the tape, heads bent, eyes scouring the pavement. Looking for what? she wondered. A lost button? An eagle feather? Prints of horse hooves? Some obscure object that the forensic team had overlooked yesterday that would point to the Indian who had shot Custer?

She hurried down the sidewalks through the residential area. Rows of brick bungalows sheltered behind bushy pine trees and cottonwoods dusted with whispery clumps of cotton. Her office was on the corner ahead, a redbrick bungalow with a porch that stretched between the two front windows and a small sign in front that said, Vicky Holden, Attorney at Law. Annie's black Pontiac stood at the curb behind the pickup driven by Roger Hurst, the lawyer she and Adam had hired to handle what Adam called the little cases. When she and Adam had been partners. Vicky crossed the street and slowed her pace, giving her heart a chance to stop hammering. The sirens had cut off. An accident, Adam had said. Still, the sound had unnerved her, an echo of the chaos of yesterday. By the time she let herself into the bungalow, her heart was slowing to a steady, almost normal pace.

Annie was on the phone, the perfect image of a no-nonsense librarian—shoulder-length black hair, quick, dark eyes, silver beads at her neck—except that she was a no-nonsense secretary, personal assistant, and, Vicky had to admit, close friend. Annie reminded her of herself. Making her own way in the world, a woman alone, with an ex-husband in the state prison at Rawlins and two almost-teenage kids. One day she had appeared in Vicky's office. "I hear you're looking for a secretary," she'd said, "and I'm a good one."

At the time, Vicky hadn't been sure she was looking for a secretary. Business was slow. How would she handle the extra expense? She had been about to tell this young woman, who had driven in from the rez in an old pickup that laid down so much exhaust Vicky had smelled it in the office, that she wasn't hiring. Then Annie said she had kids to feed, and that had gotten Vicky's attention. Vicky had been on her own and still alive after ten years with Ben Holden and his fists and accusations. Trying to support two kids, Susan and Lucas, while she went to college and law school in Denver, looking toward the future, when she wouldn't have to beg for a job. She had never found the way to do it all. The waitressing

jobs that hardly covered the rent and left her exhausted and sleeping in class; the night shift at a brewery that paid for the babysitter
but not much else. In the end, she'd brought the kids back to her
own parents on the rez. When the future finally arrived, the kids
were grown and on their own. She had hired Annie on the spot.

Vicky closed the beveled glass doors on the sound of Annie's
voice and dropped into the chair at her desk. The computer made
tiny gyrating noises when she turned it on. She watched the icons
dance into place, then clicked on her calendar. Two appointments
this morning, canceled. Will and Mary Whiteman, hoping to final-
ize the adoption of their granddaughter, and Bonner LeBois, needing a new will, now that he had married Beverly. All from Ethete,
which meant a long drive south on 287, across the reservation
border into Lander. She checked the afternoon schedule. More
cancellations. Only Donna Red Cloud still on the schedule, but
she lived in town with her white husband.

Someone was watching. Vicky felt the eyes boring into her like
laser beams. She swung her chair toward the door where Annie,
blanched and wide-eyed, stood in the opening. She gripped the
door handle and leaned against the edge, as if she were leaning
into the wind out on the plains.

"What is it?"

"Skip Burrows."

"What about him?"

"He's gone."

Vicky was quiet for a moment before she repeated the word:
"Gone?"

"I just got off the phone with my cousin, Andrew. He was having breakfast at the café across the street from Skip's office when
police cars pulled into the parking lot."

"I heard the sirens," Vicky said. So it hadn't been an accident on the highway.

"Lot of people showing up, and Andrew went to see what was going on. Somebody trashed Skip Burrows's office, and he's missing. The police are forming a search party. Roger is taking the morning off to help."

Vicky leaned back against her chair. Law office trashed, lawyer missing? And Skip Burrows: likeable, friendly, always time to stop and chat. Remembered everyone's name and the names of their kids. He had opened the office about two years ago, and last year, he had hired Angela Running Bear as his secretary, which made the office a friendly place for Arapahos. For a while, Vicky's own practice had slowed down, her own people finding their way to the office in the white-brick building at the far end of Main Street. Skip had taken to stopping in unannounced, assuring her he had no intention of taking her clients, suggesting that they might work together. He and Roger had become friendly, walking into town for coffee some mornings. Gradually things had returned to normal, as if the novelty of another Arapaho in a law office had worn off.

"Angela called 911 when she got to work this morning."

Vicky took a moment, letting the news settle, find a place in reality. She was about to turn back to the computer when Annie gave a little cough, as if to clear the way for more news. "I checked the phone messages for the weekend," she said. "You had a call on Friday at 6:03 in the evening. No message, but the ID said the call came from Skip Burrows."

7

FATHER JOHN HAD taken the early Mass. A dozen parishioners, missals propped open on the pews in front, rosary beads threaded through gnarled, brown fingers, lips moving silently. The sun slanted through the stained-glass windows and cast arrows of red, yellow, and blue light across the church—a small chapel, really—built by the Arapahos after the leaders had asked the Jesuits to come and teach their children. He offered the Mass for the soul of Edward Garrett, a stranger killed in their midst. And he prayed for the Arapahos who had ridden in the parade and for their families, all of whom would be waiting for the tornado about to touch down.

After Mass, he stood in front and shook hands with the people filing past. The old faithfuls, he called them, who drove battered pickups across the reservation to the morning Mass at St. Francis Mission almost every day. Mason Walking Horse had held on to his hand for a long moment. He had black, watery eyes that shone like pebbles at the bottom of a creek. "Who else they gonna investigate except the warriors?" He hurried on without waiting for an answer. "Tell that white detective we're watching him. Raps weren't the only people at the parade."

Father John gave the old man what he hoped was a reassuring nod. He'd do his best, he said. It was true that hundreds of people had lined the curbs yesterday. But the fact remained that Garrett had died while the warriors raced around the cavalry. Logic could be implacable.

Walks-On bounced down the hallway when Father John let himself into the residence. He tossed his cowboy hat on the bench, then stooped over and scratched behind the dog's ears before following him into the kitchen. The bishop's chair was vacant, his breakfast dishes cleared. Already in the office, Father John thought. Waiting for the onslaught of calls begging the priests—the white priests—to talk to the white cops in Lander. He could imagine the pleas. Just because the warriors were there didn't mean they were guilty of murder. Guilty of being there was all.

Elena was swishing dishes at the sink, her back to him. He shook a little more dried food into the dog's dish in the corner and poured himself a cup of coffee. He was about to help himself to a bowl of the hot oatmeal on the stove when Elena said, "I'll get it, Father." She still didn't turn around. Somewhere in her seventies; he had no idea how old she was. Ageless, really. Keeping house and cooking for the priests at St. Francis Mission for more years than anyone remembered. But she remembered everything. Pastors whose portraits now lined the front corridor of the administration building, watching him every day past rimless glasses, sometimes smiling, he had imagined, often frowning. Oh, Elena remembered the stories. How Father Peter quoted Shakespeare. A Shakespearean quote for everything. How Father Michael had run straight for Eagle Hall when he thought AIM had occupied the building. How Father Barry had kept the elderly Father Benson at the mission after he lost his eyesight.

Father John sat down at the table and sipped at the coffee, watching the old woman dry her hands, toss aside the towel, and ladle scoops of oatmeal into a bowl before she faced him. Eyes red-rimmed and sunken, as if she'd spent the night crying. Red blotches dotted her neck and cheeks.

"Sit down and tell me what's going on," he said as she set a bowl of oatmeal in front of him.

Elena filled a coffee mug, slid onto the chair, and patted a strand of gray hair into place. "I should have stopped the killing," she said.

The statement took him by surprise. He was about to take a spoonful of oatmeal, but he set the spoon down and waited.

"It's still going on." Her voice cracked. She blinked hard against the tears shining in her eyes. "The killing and hatred. God help me. I could have stopped it."

"Elena." He reached over and took her hand. It felt small inside his own, her palm warm and smoothed with age. "Is this about yesterday?"

She stared at him a moment before she nodded. "I had a dream vision Saturday night."

Father John understood. Men went off by themselves, fasted and prayed for three days for a vision, but women received visions in their dreams. "Do you want to tell me about it?"

"A lot of horses circling around soldiers. Around and around, the warriors shouting and yelling. I saw the white chief with the big hat fall off his horse. I knew he was dead." She took in a gulp of air. "I thought I should go and find him, tell him not to march in the parade. Tell him to leave our land."

"Do you think it would have done any good? Do you think he would have left?"

"Yes." Elena bent her head into her hands. "I heard my grandfather's stories running through my head. How his father was camped with Chief Black Kettle at the Washita River. It was 1868, four years after the fool soldiers killed the people at Sand Creek. Killed both Cheyennes and Arapahos, women, children, old people. Everyone they could shoot. After that, Black Kettle kept leading the people around the plains, trying to stay out of the way of the soldiers, waiting for the government to tell them where they should go and live. Then Custer brought more soldiers to the village, and it happened again. Killed Black Kettle and his wife, Woman To Be Hereafter. Left their bodies floating in the river. So many people lying on the ground, crying with pain. They shot my great-grandfather in the hip and left him for dead. Grandfather said he never walked right after that. Custer took his hostages. Children and old people and many beautiful women. He gave the women to his men for whores. The warriors scouted him after that. They vowed to kill him. I would have told him that, and he would have known to leave."

"I understand," Father John said. "But Edward Garrett was not Custer."

"He thought Custer was brave and honorable." Elena swallowed hard and looked down at her hands wrapped around the coffee mug. "Now he's dead. More killings will come. Just like after Bighorn, soldiers dropped out of the sky and flooded our lands and killed the ancestors. Cops are gonna flood the rez, and the tribal cops will help them, just like they helped kill Crazy Horse. I should've found the white man and told him."

"Listen to me, Elena." Father John had let go of her hand, but now he took it again between his own. "I'm a white man. I'm telling you that the chances are very small, probably nonexistent, that Garrett would have given your dream vision any thought at all. His own daughter had a vision. She pleaded with him not to ride in the parade, and he rode anyway."

"No good will come of this." She sat back against her chair and stared past him a long moment. "I wish I could go to the ancestors."

"What about the people who need you here? What about the mission? What would we do without you?"

"I don't have good feelings."

"Yes, I know."

"You'd starve to death."

That was true, he told her.

IT WAS ALMOST noon before the phones stopped ringing. What will happen to the warriors? Will they all be arrested? Charged with murder? He had tried to convince people not to worry too much. The investigation had just started. The voice of the bishop saying much the same floated from the back office. After a fifteen-minute lull, he'd walked down the hallway and told the bishop he was going out for a short while. The old man had looked up from the book open on his desk, given him a little wave, and said what he usually said. He would hold down the fort.

Traffic was light on Seventeen-Mile Road, a few old pickups and sedans, sun glinting on the windshields. The brown humpbacked foothills rose into the sky ahead. An odd silence hung over the plains around him. Wind rippled the wild grasses and knocked against the pickup. In the distance, he could see horses grazing in a pasture. It reminded him of a still-life painting, everything stopped and waiting.

He swung right and fifteen minutes later pulled into the dirt lot behind a convenience store in Ethete. Light traffic moving through town, people pumping gas in front of the store, others going in and out. Almost normal, he thought, and yet a heaviness in the air, as if a storm were gathering. He parked and walked through the shade dropping from the building toward the entrance, waved to Ernest Featherstone, about to jam a gas nozzle into the tank of his truck, then held the door for a woman and two toddlers. Inside, cool air washed over him from the air conditioner that buzzed overhead. A small crowd bunched around the food counter on the left.

"How you doing, Father?" Mike Longshot stood behind the counter, crooking his neck to peer past a heavyset woman with a thick, black braid that curled down the back of her white tee shirt. Father John waited while Mike poured coffee into a Styrofoam cup, straightened out the wrinkled bills the woman handed him, and swung toward the cash register. He was thin, with ropey arms and a blue vein that pulsed in the middle of his forehead. He wore a light blue shirt buttoned down the front with a nametag clipped to his chest that said, Mike. About five foot eight, Father John guessed, but he loomed taller from the platform behind the counter, absorbed in counting change into the woman's outstretched hand, as if the rest of the store, the people sipping coffee and Cokes and eating hot dogs in the blue plastic booths behind them and wandering up and down the aisles with wire baskets hooked on their arms, didn't exist.

"Got a minute?" Father John said after the woman had walked away.

Mike slid his eyes toward a large man at the far end of the counter, the buttons of his uniform shirt popping over his stomach. "Not supposed to visit with customers," he said. "But . . ." He held up a hand, palm out in the Arapaho gesture of peace. "Break in ten minutes, you want to hang around."

Father John ordered coffee and carried the cup over to a booth that a couple of teenage girls had just vacated. He pushed their glasses and squashed napkins to the back of the table, sat down, and sipped at the coffee. Strong and bitter, probably sitting in the coffeepot all morning. Jason Smidge and Leticia Yellowman walked over. "Good to see you, Father," they said, a duet in different keys. "What brings you to Ethete?"

"Visiting parishioners." He shrugged, smiling off any further questions. One of the things that had struck him when he first came to St. Francis was the way the parishioners kept track of the priests. Where they went, who they saw, what they said. Days after he had visited someone in the hospital, another parishioner would stop him and recount his conversation with the patient. It was the way news moved across the rez. Nobody wanted to be left out. Like the Old Time, he thought, when criers walked through the villages crying out the news. He asked about Jason's new baby and Leticia's daughter, who had joined the army and was on her way to Afghanistan. "Pray for her," Leticia said, and he said he would pray for both of their families.

Jason gave a small salute and headed toward the front door. Leticia made small talk for a couple of minutes—too bad about that guy getting killed in Lander; what was he thinking? Showing up like Custer?—then ducked back into the aisles as Mike set another cup on the table and slid into the booth. "You here about yesterday?"

"Your mom came to see me. She's very worried."

"Yeah? Isn't everybody?" Mike dropped his eyes and studied the brown liquid in the Styrofoam cup. "They'll blame us warriors."

Father John took another drink and studied the young man across from him. He wondered if Mike had any idea that his mother feared the other warriors would offer him up, the sacrificial lamb. "The police are going to talk to all of you," he said.

"How they gonna find us? We were painted and wearing regalia. How they gonna know who was there?"

"They're going to start with the two Arapahos at Garrett's performance Saturday night," Father John said. At that, the complacent expression on the Arapaho's face dissolved into a look of shock, as if he had been sleepwalking and had awakened at the edge of an abyss.

"What's that prove?" he said. "We can't go to a theater in town and watch a white man make a fool of himself? I went along with Colin to see for myself if Custer was as stupid as Colin said."

"His name was Edward Garrett."

"He's still stupid." Mike took a gulp of coffee and stared past Father John's shoulder. "Okay, you want the whole story?" He hurried on without waiting for a response. "Colin and some of the other guys came out to the house last week and asked if I would show them some riding tricks. They had an idea to make a dare ride at the parade, you know, gallop around the guys pretending to be the Seventh Cavalry. I said, 'What the hell? Why not?'"

"You weren't concerned?"

Mike leaned over the table and locked eyes with him. "I'm always concerned. But they needed me. Nobody else knows how to gallop thirty horses in a tight, double circle without one of the horses getting spooked and bucking off the rider. So I went to Colin's pasture and we went through the routine about ten times until all the warriors could have kept the horses under control in their sleep. Colin said, 'You want to ride with us?' I said, 'No thanks.' I didn't have a beef with Custer. I didn't give a damn if he paraded down Main Street. 'Well, you should hear the guy talk,' he said. I guess he'd watched a video on YouTube. So I went."

"Is that what made you decide to ride?"

"You could say that. White man up on the stage, looked just like Custer. I'm sitting in the back row thinking, He's come back. Like an evil spirit nobody can kill. Strolling across the stage, bragging about clearing the land for civilization, killing the savages. A lot of white people clapping and laughing at his stupid jokes. We walked out early, 'cause we'd both had enough. 'I'm in,' I told Colin."

Father John waited a moment. This was worse than he'd feared. Probably thirty warriors in a conspiracy to commit murder. Dear Lord, the whole area—rez and towns and the fragile peace built across borders over more than a century—would break apart. "They were planning to kill him?" he said.

"Kill him?" Mike shook his head and gave a snort of laughter. "It was like Custer's spirit was living inside Garrett. Like I said, you can't kill an evil spirit. We wanted to show him what we could do. Show the Seventh Cavalry and all the white people watching the parade. Gallop around and fall into columns ahead of the troops. Take our rightful place. Remind folks that a bunch of so-called savages defeated the mighty U.S. Army."

"What do you think happened?"

"Nothing happened, far as I saw. I was concentrating on riding, making sure all the riders kept tight turns. I wasn't watching the bastard and the other officers leading the cavalry."

"It might be a good idea"—Father John hesitated, then plunged on—"to talk to Vicky Holden before you talk to the police."

"I'm not talking to any cops."

"They'll find you, Mike. Take my advice. Call Vicky."

8

THE RINGING STARTED as Vicky got into the Ford Escape. She found the cell in her black leather bag and checked the readout: Vicky Holden, Law Office. "I'm here," she said, clamping the phone close to her ear against the sound of the wind whipping about the parking lot at the senior citizens center. She left the door open to allow the heat inside the SUV to escape.

"You have someone waiting to see you." Annie's voice was so clear, she might have been sitting in the passenger seat.

"I thought the schedule was open," Vicky said. She had spent the last two hours at a corner table that overlooked the gray asphalt ribbon of Ethete Road, sipping at a cup of coffee one of the grandmothers, Myra Red Horse, insisted upon refilling, while she met with clients who, as they had told Annie, preferred not to come into town today. First, explaining the adoption process to Will and Mary Whiteman. She had watched them cross the senior center, dodge the empty tables, and slip outside past the wood door, shaking their heads at the complications of adopting their own granddaughter. Not like in the Old Time, Mary had said. "We would've raised her then. No judge telling us what to do, no social workers inspecting the tipi."

"You want the adoption to be legal and final," Vicky had told them. What she had left unsaid was the hard reason: so your meth-addicted daughter and whoever her current boyfriend might be cannot take her away from you.

She had waited ten minutes before Bonner LeBois came through the door. Apologizing for making her drive across the border and north through the empty spaces of the reservation. She had spent another hour working out the details for the will that Bonner wanted.

"You won't believe this." Annie was whispering now. "She says she's Elizabeth Custer."

"Where is she?"

"In the outer office. I'm calling from Roger's office so she can't hear me. Roger said he'd be glad to talk to her, but he's been out all morning with the search party looking for Skip Burrows. Seventy, eighty people showed up. They walked the riverbanks, the dry creek beds, all the fields. No sign of Skip. Roger's trying to get ready for Jake Withers's court appearance this afternoon."

Vicky didn't say anything. She was thinking about Jake Withers and the DUI charge, the kind of case Adam had insisted should go to Roger, leaving them free for important cases. When she and Adam had been a team.

"She said she'll wait however long it takes," Annie was saying. "You want me to tell her you're out for the day? I can say you're not accepting new clients."

Vicky found the keys in the outside pocket of her bag and turned on the ignition. Elizabeth Custer. Probably one of the reenactors. "Tell her I'll be there in thirty minutes," she said, pulling the door shut. Then she slipped the cell back into her bag. The airconditioning hummed above the hiss of warm air spilling from the vents. She lowered the windows, backed into the lot, and swung out onto the road.

ELIZABETH CUSTER WAS a small woman in her thirties with the toned look of an athlete, a waist about the circumference of a dinner plate, and short, curly brown hair that stood out around the edges of her blue bonnet. She wore the kind of flowing, ankle-length dress Vicky had seen in photos of suffragettes in the early 1900s. Pale yellow, long sleeves, white lace cuffs and collar. She was pretty in a plain and unsmiling way.

"We can talk in my office," Vicky said, opening the beveled glass doors and waving the woman through. From behind the desk, Annie shrugged and gave her a raised-eyebrow look.

"Let's begin by telling me your legal name." Vicky closed the doors, made her way around the desk, and sat down. She waited while the woman gathered her long skirt in one hand and dropped onto the edge of a side chair. Crossing her legs, she dangled a white boot into the space between the chair and the edge of the desk.

"Belinda Clark may be the way the world"—she gestured with her head toward the doors and the world beyond—"knows me. But I think of myself as Elizabeth Custer." Her mouth stretched into a smile that seemed awkward, unaccustomed. "Libbie," she said. "I have been Libbie since high school, when I first read about her. Enormously strong, powerful, and dedicated woman. She never stopped protecting the reputation of her dear husband. Cut down so early in his brilliant life, only thirty-seven." She shook her head at the injustice, and for a instant, Vicky thought she detected moisture brimming in the woman's light-colored eyes. "Libbie was not daunted. No matter what lies Benteen and Reno told, she countered them with the truth. Autie—that's what she called him—was a true military genius."

"You're a reenactor?" Vicky said.

"For fifteen years now. You see . . ." She leaned forward and laid a palm on the surface of the desk. "I believe my body is a vessel in which Libbie's spirit continues on. Let's be honest, a powerful spirit like hers would want to live. I believe she chose me. Do you think I'm a lunatic?" She let both hands flutter in front of her. "It doesn't matter. It is as it is." She spoke calmly, as if she were commenting on the warm, sunny day.

"How can I help you?" Vicky wasn't sure what to think. The woman believed she was the embodiment of a dead woman's spirit. She seemed harmless.

"My husband was shot to death yesterday."

"Edward Garrett was shot to death."

"He was my husband."

"I'm very sorry," Vicky said. "Were you at the parade?"

"I was driving to Denver to visit my sister. I had planned to spend a couple of weeks with her, then meet Edward at the Little Bighorn for the reenactment. Naturally, the instant I heard the news on the radio I turned around and drove here. I found our RV parked in the lot where we always park when we visit the area. They had moved his body to the morgue in the basement of an old court building, but after great persuasion on my part, the police allowed me to see him. To say good-bye." She hesitated, her features calm, reflective. Belinda Clark, Elizabeth Custer—whoever she was, Vicky was thinking—had shown more emotion over the death of George Armstrong Custer.

"The police didn't believe we were married," the woman went on. "I don't exactly carry my marriage certificate around in my bag." She held up the string bag she cradled like a cushion on her lap. "We've been married two years. Kept it a secret for a while, since Edward wasn't keen on letting his daughter know. Eventually he spilled the beans. Dorothy Garrett Winslow did not approve of me. Well, that's a laugh." There was no amusement in her voice or in the light gray eyes. "Little Dorothy, as Autie—I mean, Edward—called her, didn't approve of her father, either. All that traveling around the West, riding in parades and rodeos, giving presentations to Rotary Clubs and Lions Clubs and Kiwanis Clubs and dusty run-down theaters on the main street of Western towns that don't know they've already died and should be buried."

She paused, tilted her head back, and stared past the brim of her bonnet at the ceiling fan, circling, circling. "It wasn't so odd, what we did. Look at all the great actors, the way they become whatever character they're playing. They become inspirited! It was the same for Edward and me." She hurried on. "The point is, I am Edward's legal wife, entitled to his assets. Isn't that correct?"

"It depends," Vicky said. "Did he have a will?"

"No."

"What is your legal domicile?"

"Excuse me?"

"Where do you live?"

"The RV. We've lived in the RV since we got married. Edward had a ranch outside Laramie, but he sold it last year. The owner of the adjacent ranch offered Edward half a million dollars, so he took it. He told me he put the money in a bank. It was my job to trust him, the way Libbie trusted Autie. Believe in him, no matter what. But when I went to the bank, I was told the account was closed. I remember Edward talking about a great investment that would increase his money by thirty percent. What I want is to make sure that whatever money my husband had will come to me and not his greedy, mean-spirited daughter."

"I'm going to need documentation," Vicky said. "I'll need your marriage certificate. Bank records, brokers' records. Anything that can help me locate your husband's assets. I can ask the district court to open a probate action and appoint an administrator to determine your husband's assets. I'll get a subpoena to check the records. I will also need your power of attorney."

The woman allowed the words to hang between them a moment. Then she rummaged in the floppy woven bag, pulled out a handful of papers, and handed them across the desk. "It's all there. I spent last night in the RV going through the important documents Edward kept in a small safe."

Vicky laid the papers in front of her. Marriage certificate, Laramie, Wyoming, two scrawled signatures. A bank statement from Wyoming Central Bank on Main Street. She looked up at the woman across from her. "Zero balance," she said.

"Nothing in an account that should have at least five hundred thousand dollars. When I saw that, I started asking people in town to recommend a lawyer. Stopped people on the street. In the restaurant. They recommended you. I want you to find out where the money went. It's true that Edward found a ranch near Dubois that he wanted to buy. I believe that is why he was so eager to increase his money. Some Realtor in Riverton, Deborah Boynton, was helping him. Very annoying, I must say. After calling the ranch outside Laramie a metal halter around his neck and finally dumping it, he couldn't wait to buy another one. Close to Little Dorothy, he said. They could get to know each other again. But the freedom we had with the RV! Travel across the plains, Texas to North Dakota, Kansas, Colorado. Always moving about. It was glorious. Libbie was never so happy than when she traveled with Autie. All those quiet, lovely evenings alone in their tent on the prairie. Autie writing his memoirs, Libbie stretched on a couch beside him, reading."

"Where is the ranch? Perhaps the sale went through."

"You ask me, Little Dorothy got her hands on it."

"Not unless Edward gave her the money."

The woman's face settled into a hard, angry mask. "He had no right. You'll help me? I'll sign whatever you need."

Vicky stood up, walked over, and pushed open the beveled doors. She told Annie to draw up a power of attorney and prepare the documents to file a probate action to get a subpoena for the financial records of Belinda Clark and Edward Garrett. Then she asked her to arrange an appointment with an officer at Wyoming Central Bank.

When she turned back, Belinda Clark was on her feet, pleating her skirt between her fingers. "Dorothy Winslow is his daughter's name. I suspect you'll find the money went to her." Holding her head high, the brim of her bonnet pointed forward, she moved past Vicky like a prairie schooner sailing over the plains.

9

ANGELA NOSED THE blue sedan against the pasture fence and got out
into the wind, which whipped her skirt and blew her hair across
her face. The smell of burnt things, like a distant fire, was in the
air. She pulled her hair back and stood looking out over the pasture. Five Appaloosas grazing and swishing flies with their tails.
No sign of Colin. She leaned through the open window and pushed
on the horn. Sharp, loud blasts ricocheted between the barn and
the small, white house with a fresh coat of paint glinting in the
sun. A horse neighed. It wasn't polite to announce her presence,
demand that someone take notice. But she didn't live on the rez
anymore.

"Colin!"

The barn door squeaked open. Colin—six feet tall with deep-
set black eyes and slicked-back black hair, hooked nose and full
lips, so handsome it made her feel unsteady—came walking out,

wiping his hands on an oil-smudged rag. "What're you trying to do?" he called. "Spook the ponies?"

"I have to talk to you." Angela threw another glance around the ranch. The pastures running into the sky, the log fence, the horses and buildings. Hers for the taking, had she wanted it. Marry Colin and be stuck on the rez until she turned into a bent, old grandmother, clacking her dentures. If he had been willing to come with her, how wonderful it would have been. Such a big world, so many places to see. "Leave here?" Colin had said, and the look he'd given her! As if she'd suggested they run off and join a circus. "My grandfather got this land from his father. If my father hadn't gotten cancer and died, the ranch would have been his. Someday it will be mine, and I'll pass it onto a son. Stay with me, Angela."

She had left her sister's house and moved into Lander, as far away as the pitiful savings she'd managed to stash away would take her. On the other side of the border was what mattered. She'd seen the ad on the internet in the library. Law firm secretary. Apply online. She had e-mailed her application and checked her cell for two weeks before the call came. The minute she'd set foot in Skip Burrows's office, she knew she was where she belonged. Skip had liked her résumé. Two years' experience as a secretary in the Wind River school district; two-year certificate from the tribal college. He could see she was ambitious, he'd told her, and he liked that. Later he told her how he had liked even more the way she looked: black hair; lively, intelligent eyes; and curves in the right places.

"Let's find some shade," Colin said, walking along the side of the house to the back stoop. He could be infuriatingly matter-of-fact, as if she were the pizza delivery girl showing up with a pizza. He unfolded two webbed chairs that had been leaning against the house and set them facing each other in a column of shade. "Water? Coke?"

"Coke. Why not?" Angela dropped into one of the chairs and waited. From inside the house came the sucking noise of a refrigerator door opening and closing, the sound of a can popping, and the scuff of Colin's boots on the linoleum floor. The screen door swung open. Colin came down the steps holding Cokes. He handed her an icy, sweating can and sat down across from her.

A long moment passed, Colin sipping, not taking his eyes from her, before he said, "You here about your"—the slightest hesitation, his Adam's apple working up and down—"boss?" he said.

"What the hell have you done?"

Colin took a long drink of Coke, then wedged the bottom of the can into the hard-packed ground. "I'm not following."

"It's not enough you and your so-called warriors shot that crazy guy . . ."

"Hold on." Colin rose a little off the webbed seat and dropped back down. "You sound like the cops. Lander detective shows up here this morning with a couple of tribal cops. Minds already made up. Waiting for me to confess, give them the names of the warriors riding with me. They're going to make our lives miserable. Drag us in for interviews, keep threatening to have paroles revoked or bring charges for crimes we didn't commit. I'm telling you what I told them. My boys had nothing to do with that white man getting shot."

"Nobody believes that, Colin. You told me you had it all planned. You were going to show Custer and the Seventh Cavalry something. You didn't tell me you planned to kill him!"

He pulled his lips into a tight line and fixed his eyes on her, as if he might imprint the words into her skull. "I never ordered anybody killed. What we did was symbolic. A dare run. We galloped around the Seventh Cavalry, surrounded them before they knew what was happening, same as at the Little Bighorn. Warriors appeared all of a sudden, rose up out of the grass. Custer knew he and his cavalry were dead men. We wanted to show them we're still here. We're still strong. We defeated Custer."

"You're lying." For an instant, Angela thought he might rise up again. Toss the chair across the dirt yard, stomp off into the barn, and leave her sitting here with no answers, nothing. He had a quick temper. It had exploded on her more than once, but now she could see him struggling with himself, a dark flush in his cheeks.

She pushed on. "You told me you would be in charge, like Crazy Horse. You gave the orders. Kill. Kill. Kill."

"Crazy Horse wasn't stupid," he said. "Nobody's stupid enough to shoot some guy in front of hundreds of people. You know what I think? The shooter was up there." He jammed a fist at the sky. "Shooting out of a window. Easy for the police to say killer must be an Indian. They have a real narrow theory that works for them." He leaned forward, so close she could smell the Coke-sweet odor of his breath. "You don't give a damn about that Custer fellow. You think I have something to do with your boyfriend going missing."

"They were friends, Skip and the guy that got killed. He came around the office a few times. They got into an argument. Cops are going to put it together, start thinking somebody was after both of them. Soon as they find out about us, they're going to say you wanted Skip out of the way. Dead, like Custer."

"You forget, Angela. There's no us. Not anymore."

She looked out across the pasture. The wind made the soft noise of a calf sucking a teat. Colin was right. There was no longer anything between them. What had she heard on the moccasin telegraph? He'd been seen around the rez with different women. What did she care? She had Skip.

Except that Skip was gone.

She bit at her lower lip and looked back at Colin. Full of himself, legs spread apart, boots dug into the dirt. "What is it?"

Colin took a few seconds before he said: "You ask me, you're in a lot of trouble. Did he finally dump you? That would make the cops think you had something to do with his disappearance."

"He didn't dump me."

"He was planning to."

"You're lying."

Colin leaned forward and clasped his hands between his knees. "You want the truth? After you broke things off and took up with Skip Burrows, I started paying attention. Checking up on him. I did it for you, Angela. You ask me, he's a big phony. Everybody's good friend. Just don't turn your back on him. Followed him to Riverton a couple times, straight to the house of a white filly. You want her name?"

"Shut up! Shut up!" Angela jumped out of the chair and stomped to the corner of the house. She forced herself to turn back. Is that where Skip had gone after he left her last night? Head buried in the pillow against the sounds of his footsteps in the alley, the faraway roar of the BMW's motor.

"The Realtor?" she managed.

"You sure you want to know?"

"Maybe she knows where he is."

"Deborah Boynton. Works in a real-estate office off Federal. Red hair and green eyes that stop traffic. You'd better forget her. If she knows anything about Skip disappearing, you don't want to get involved."

"You don't get it," Angela said. "I love Skip. I'll do anything to help him." She swung around and hurried to the hatchback. In ten minutes she was driving east on Seventeen-Mile Road with the sun lingering over the mountains behind her, the plains lit in gold and magenta, Riverton ahead.

ANGELA TURNED INTO the narrow parking lot in front of the strip mall with doors and plate-glass windows stuck in a yellowish frame building. Slowing across the lot, peering at the signs on the plate glass. Nails, Tai Chi, Best Tacos in Town, Coffee and Donuts, Barber, Take-Out Chinese, Hometown Realtors. Even before she got out of the hatchback, she could see the real-estate office was closed. Photos of houses and apartment buildings plastered on the plate-glass window stood out in relief against the dark interior. Painted across the glass door was Open 8 a.m. to 5 p.m.

She stepped in close and started banging on the door. The glass shimmered under her fist. She peered inside willing someone to emerge from the shadows in back, wind past the wood reception counter and metal chairs lined against the side walls, and fling open the door. *Deborah Boynton?* the person would say. *Not here. No one's here. Gone home for the day. And where's home?* she would ask. *Well, that depends on who wants to know.*

"I want to know." Angela realized she was screaming at the glass door and the emptiness on the other side. She leaned her forehead against the glass. Why hadn't she asked Colin where this white woman lived? Her legs felt like liquid. She had to prop herself against the doorjamb to keep from falling. What good was any of this? What did it matter who the white woman was or where she lived? Skip mattered.

She pushed herself off the prickly wood jamb and headed back to the car, feeling wobbly and disoriented in the dusk coming on, drifting across the parking lot like a dust storm. She pulled into the thin line of traffic on Federal and turned south onto Highway 789, driving past the warehouses, garages, and drive-through liquor stores swallowed in shadows.

Her thoughts were filled with Skip. Sunday evening at her apartment, so tall and forceful and handsome she had thought her heart might stop beating, standing in the middle of what passed for a living room in the day and the bedroom with the sofa bed pulled out at night, saying something about having to turn in early, a busy day tomorrow, something might come up. She remembered having a hard time following the words. She typed his memos and letters, prepared the legal documents and all those stupid reports. Everything. She didn't remember anything unusual that might have come up, except that his army buddy had been killed. Skip had brushed his lips against her cheek and said . . . What was it he had said? The last words he had spoken to her: *Remember the good times, little girl.*

What had come up? A change in plans he hadn't thought to mention? An ex-girlfriend named Deborah Boynton back in the picture? Angela had never stopped wondering if Skip might be seeing *her.* She had tried to believe him when he told her it was over.

For a moment after he left, she'd had to stop herself from running down the outside steps, banging behind her the carry-on she had taken to Jackson, racing the half block to where Skip usually left the car, and climbing into the passenger seat, Skip at the wheel, taking them away. What else could matter?

The lights of Lander twinkled ahead. She drove toward Main Street and turned right, the car heading toward her place on its own, like a horse returning to the barn. Then she passed her turn and kept going toward the white-brick, two-story building at the end of town. The last place Skip had been.

The building looked dark and deserted, a lone streetlamp flaring over a corner of the parking lot. She turned into the empty stretch of asphalt that melted into the shadows. It was when she pulled a U-turn to drive back into the street that she saw the light flickering in the office windows.

She slammed on the brakes, jumped out, and ran to the door, struggling to pull her keys from the inside pocket of her bag as she ran. She jammed the key into the lock, pushed the door open, and darted down the dark corridor for the office. "Skip!" she shouted. "Skip. Skip. Skip."

The key wedged itself into the lock, past the strip of yellow police tape, and she pounded on the door. Shouting, her own voice rising around her. The door swung open and she threw herself inside, barely aware of the dim emptiness engulfing her, the shadow of her own desk floating like a ghost against the light from the street that filtered past the window. Barely aware of the large, black force at the edge of her vision until it crashed against her, driving her into the hard surface of the floor. She could hear the crack of her ribs. She couldn't breathe, and the blackness enveloped her like a heavy blanket.

10

BLUE-UNIFORMED OFFICERS MILLED about the office. Overhead, fluorescent lights buzzed and blinked. Angela sat at her desk listening to the pounding in her head. No, she had told the officers, she did not need an ambulance. She had managed to pick herself off the floor to the noise of boots retreating in the corridor, the door still open. She had found her bag sprawled under the desk, dragged out her cell, and called 911. Then sirens had blared in the distance and intruded upon the quiet.

"This is still a crime scene." The detective in blue jeans, leather vest, and white shirt, walked out of Skip's office. He had introduced himself as Detective Madden. "Why were you here? Again?" He had asked the same question at least three times.

"I told you," Angela said. "I saw a light in the windows. I thought Skip was back."

"You were just driving by and you saw a light." He shrugged. "Did you get a look at the man who hit you?"

"He wore a black ski mask." Angela shook her head. "It happened so fast. He must have yanked the door open, because I stumbled inside and he hit me. I blacked out. When I came to, I was on the floor. I heard him running away."

"What made you think Skip was here?" Detective Madden ignored the two uniforms on their haunches, peering at the piles of papers around them.

"I hoped it was Skip. I thought maybe they let him go . . ."

Madden lifted one hand, as if that might make sense. "Could be the same guy here this morning. Trashed the place. Didn't find what he wanted on the computers, so he came back."

"He took Skip!" She realized she was shouting. "All that blood, Skip could be dead by now. Why aren't you out looking for him?"

"What do you suppose the intruder was looking for?" Madden said, ignoring the outburst. He moved his big head side to side, taking in the papers cluttering the floor and trailing from Skip's office. More papers and file folders than littered the floor this morning. The intruder had emptied more drawers.

"How should I know?" Her heart had turned into a drum.

"You're Skip's secretary. You handle mail, letters, e-mails, files. Correct? Type the office business into the computer?"

Angela waited a beat, willing the pounding in her temples to stop. "I type what he tells me to type. I'm not a lawyer. Most of it doesn't make any sense to me." She tilted her head toward the computer. "Some things he handles himself, what he calls confidential lawyer-client stuff. I do routine stuff: documents he files with the courts, thank-you-for-your-business letters, a bunch of reports. I answer the phone, make appointments, and try to keep Skip on schedule. Visitors are always dropping in." She could feel the balloon of tears expanding behind her eyes, and she swiveled toward the window and tried to focus on the dim haze of the streetlight in the blackness. Skip was out there somewhere, in the blackness.

When she turned back, Detective Madden had pulled a chair over closer. He sat hunched over, big red fists clasped on her desk. "What else did you do for Skip Burrows?"

Angela felt her breath stop in her throat. The pounding in her head speeded up. She stared at the bulky, big-chested man taking up most of the space in front of her, the curve of his shoulders, the office blurring at the edges. They had been so careful. Parking down the street, taking trips out of town. Except that people did know, she realized. That busybody landlady probably knew. Colin. Everybody on the moccasin telegraph. It was a joke, when she thought about it. All that sneaking around, and for what? People in town were talking anyway. She closed her eyes and stared at the image of Skip, hurt, bleeding, forced out the window, landing in the prickly bush below, thrown into the BMW.

Madden pushed on, saying something about an intimate relationship that might throw light on Skip's disappearance.

"I don't understand," she heard herself say. "I don't know anything about his disappearance."

"You were in an intimate relationship?"

She waited a long moment before she nodded.

"The landlady says you left Friday night and didn't return until last night. Where did you spend the weekend?"

"Jackson," she said. "Skip had business there."

"Did he tell you what it was?"

Angela dipped her face into her hands a minute, then made herself look up at the detective. "It wasn't my business. I did what he told me. Why are you asking me these questions? Why aren't you looking for him?"

"According to the landlady, your boyfriend left sooner than usual last night. Makes me think you might have had an argument. Maybe he broke things off. Is that what happened?" Madden hurried on. "Told you he didn't need you anymore? Didn't want you anymore? That would be harsh, break a girl's heart."

"Shut up!" Angela jumped up and kicked the chair back. "It's not true!"

"Maybe you called Colin Morningside, your old boyfriend." He shrugged. "What would make me think that? Because you had a habit of calling him from time to time. I have the record of calls on your mobile. Maybe you talked him into teaching your lover a lesson."

"You're crazy." The other officers strolled out of Skip's office and stood like statues behind Madden.

The detective got to his feet and moved to the edge of the desk, blocking her path to the door. "You know what I think? I think your Arapaho boyfriend believes he's Crazy Horse. I think he knows what happened to Garrett at the parade yesterday. I think he planned the whole thing. And I'm having a hard time swallowing your story. Like trying to swallow a fat robin that keeps flapping its wings. You don't know anything. Skip Burrows's secretary and lover completely in the dark, marching to orders." He leaned toward her. The sour, coffee-soaked odor of his breath hit her in the face. "I think you know what happened to the money."

Angela held herself perfectly still. Her breath lodged in her throat.

"Skip cleaned out his bank account Friday. Four hundred thousand, a nice haul. Arranged ahead of time to get cash. What did he intend to do with all that cash? I think that, after he broke up with you, you called Colin and told him about the money. Maybe you saw it. Maybe Skip told you about it." He shrugged. "I don't know, but I'm going to find out. Problem is, there wasn't any money in this office. Officers were here most the day looking through drawers and files. You and Colin planning to divide the money?"

Angela could feel the hot flush in her cheeks. Four hundred thousand dollars! She had caught a glimpse of money—piles and piles of money—when he had opened the briefcase in the trunk. As if he wanted to make sure the money was still there. But four hundred thousand! She couldn't imagine that kind of money. She remembered Skip going out Friday afternoon. So like him, go for a cup of coffee and return hours later full of gossip. When he came back, he was carrying the briefcase. She could see Skip strolling across her office, calling out, "Anybody looking for me?" She had followed him into his office. Two clients had called for appointments. The crazy Custer guy, Garrett, had called and wanted to know when Skip would be back, but she had evaded the question. One thing she had learned working for Skip was how to evade questions.

She made herself look straight at the detective. The man's eyes were lit with accusations. Somebody knew Skip had that kind of money on him and had come looking for him. And Detective Madden thought she was involved. "I don't have to answer your questions." She spoke slowly, pounding in each word. Another thing she had learned from Skip: Nobody had to talk to the cops. Tell them so and make them understand. "I'm leaving now," she said. "You can talk to my lawyer."

For the briefest moment, she thought he wasn't going to move, then he hoisted himself to one side and she brushed past him toward the two uniforms stationed like guards on either side of her path across the carpet. She made no effort to avoid the papers that crunched under her feet. Skip, how upset he would be to see his organized files littering the floor. She yanked open the door and flung herself into the corridor. The tears had started spilling down her cheeks, blurring her vision. This was worse than she had feared. She hadn't known Skip had withdrawn money from the bank. A man walking around with four hundred thousand dollars, like a neon sign flashing: take me, take me. She wiped at her eyes, let herself out the main door, and hurried toward the hatchback, tripping on the lip of the sidewalk, wiping at her eyes to see where she was going. Skip. Skip. Where are you? What were you doing?

She slid into the car, turned on the ignition, and shot backward out of the parking space. Then she drove onto the street, tires squealing around her like a wild, hurt animal. Scattered papers flashed in front of her. The office trashed this morning, and trashed again this evening. What was the guy looking for? Everything was on the computers, and he had taken the computers when he took Skip. He had what he wanted. Except . . .

Angela gripped the steering wheel to keep from veering into one of the cars parked at the curb. It was so obvious. She should have realized this morning that whoever took Skip hadn't gotten all of it. He hadn't gotten the back-up flash drive that dangled from her keychain and clanked against the dashboard. A remnant from her job at the Wind River school district when her computer had crashed and everything was lost. And her boss—she could still see the fat woman with the red rash that looked like a magic marker had been slashed across her cheeks advancing on her desk, sputtering and gasping for air, angry because the computer had crashed. Angela had feared the woman would fall over, and all she could think of was, how would she ever be able to lift her off the floor? That evening she had gone out and bought a flash drive. Every day, the same routine—back up with the flash drive before she left the office.

Totally unnecessary. Skip had laughed at her. There was a backup attached to his computer, and their two computers were linked. But the computers were gone, and so was the backup.

Now the man in the black mask wanted her flash drive. In an instant, she understood. The slim, pocketknife-size flash drive that pinged and jangled with her keys was the ransom she would use to save Skip. The man would figure out that she had the flash drive and call her. When he did, she would tell him what he had to do. She felt herself begin to relax. She was in control.

ANGELA DROVE THROUGH the dark shadows of bungalows sheltering among pine trees, in and out of globes of yellow light from the streetlamps. A light-colored car had materialized in the rearview mirror. She turned right onto another residential street and laughed into the muffled buzz of the tires. In control? In control of nothing. Skip could be dead. Detective Madden could talk to her lawyer? She didn't have a lawyer. At the corner was an all-night Laundromat. She pulled into the parking lot, fished her cell from the bottom of her bag, and punched in the number for information. The car had stopped at the corner. The driver—dark face; God, he was wearing a ski mask—was staring at her hatchback.

She rammed the gear into reverse and spun backward across the lot. Forward, turning onto the street, gas pedal pressed hard,

odometer needle swinging. Right at the next corner; the car in
the mirror making a U-turn. Left into an alley, plunging toward
the end, then another left onto the street. Racing, turning, until the
side-view mirror was clear. She pulled into a driveway and parked
next to a brick house. No lights in the windows, darkness falling
around her.

She realized the call had ended, and she punched the number
for information again, half-turned in the front seat, watching the
street. It took a moment before she had the number and heard
Annie's voice on the other end.

VICKY STOOD AT the stove running the spoon around chunks of beef
and vegetables that sizzled and popped in the hot oil. The softness
of evening settled in the apartment, the comfort of ordinary things.
Behind her, she could hear Adam setting plates on the table, laying
out knives, forks, and spoons.

Then he was behind her. The weight of his hands moving
around her waist. He leaned in close and kissed her neck. "You
smell good," he said.

"I smell like onions and garlic." She tried to ignore the little
shivers running through her. Thinking this was as it should be.
They could move forward, and she would not look back and she
would not think of what could never be. She hadn't seen John
O'Malley in months, but she'd heard of him. Helping somebody
on the rez. Moving the Black Horse family into the guesthouse
at the mission after their house burned down. Getting a scholar-
ship for the Redman kid to Creighton University. Her people, all
of them. Sometimes it seemed he did more for her people than
she did.

"I like onions and garlic." Adam started to move her around, and she had to set the spoon on the counter.

He was kissing her then, and the ringing noise sounded far away, in some other apartment perhaps, except that part of her knew the ringing came from her cell on the counter. "Leave it," he said, and kissed her again, but she felt herself backing away, pushing against the strength of his arms. A ringing phone always made her uneasy. Someone might need help.

She held up a hand and tried to ignore the mixture of hurt and acceptance that crossed his face. "It'll just take a minute," she said, swinging toward the phone.

Annie's voice at the other end. Racing on about Skip Burrows's secretary and a lot of money missing and a man in a black mask.

"Hold on," Vicky said. "Who are you talking about?"

"Angela Running Bear. She's scared to death. She was attacked tonight at Skip's office, and the detective thinks she's involved in his disappearance. Will you see her?"

"Tell her to come in tomorrow."

"I mean now, Vicky. She's hysterical. She thinks the cops will arrest her. She's afraid to go home. I told her to go to the rez, but she says the cops there are working with the Lander cops. They're all working together. They'll find her wherever she goes."

Vicky held her breath and studied the way the light ran around the edge of the counter, aware of the heat of Adam's gaze boring into her. Finally she said, "Where is she?"

"On her way to my place."

"I'll meet her there in ten minutes."

Vicky set the phone down and turned toward Adam. "I'm sorry," she said. "Skip Burrows's secretary may be in trouble." When he didn't say anything, she went on: "She's alone in town, scared to go to the rez. She doesn't know what to do. The cops think she knows what happened to Skip. I'll be back in a hour, and we can eat then."

"I don't think so," Adam said. His mouth drew in the familiar rigid line of the old argument. Everything came first, he'd told her—how many times? Any Arapaho in trouble came first. Always ahead of him.

He walked past her and took hold of the doorknob. "Call me when you have some time," he said. "I won't be sitting by the phone."

"Don't go, Adam," she said. "I'll be back within the hour."

It was a moment before his hand relaxed on the knob and he turned toward her. She could see the concentrated effort going on inside him, like the effort of a cowboy trying to stay on a bronco. "If you want me to be with you," she said, "you have to let me go."

11

THE FRONT DOOR of the small brick house flew open. Annie stood in the doorway backlit by the light inside. She motioned Vicky past her.

From somewhere came a low, anguished moaning. "Thanks for coming," Annie said. Her voice was shaky.

"What did Angela tell you?" Vicky waited while Annie closed the door, taking her time as if a sudden jolt might aggravate the moaning. The living room had a lived-in look, cushions crumpled on the sofa and easy chair, an array of mugs and plates scattered over the coffee table, a vase of drooping, dying flowers, a pair of men's loafers in front of the chair.

"She's not making a lot of sense." A grid of worry lines creased Annie's forehead. She looked strained and thin in blue jeans and a pink tee shirt. "She thinks the attacker followed her."

"Followed her here?"

"She says she lost him." Annie gave a noncommittal shrug, as if the story might be true, or only partly true, or a figment of Angela's imagination.

The sound of footsteps cut through the moaning. Roger Hurst emerged in the living room. "Sorry you had to come out," he said, fixing Vicky with a tired smile. "Annie and I have been trying to get her to calm down, but she's convinced somebody killed her boss and wants to kill her. I've been trying to tell her there's no evidence Skip is dead. This morning, the search party checked the alleys, fields, and creek banks. The fact that we didn't find anything is a good sign, you ask me. I can't convince her. She wanted to talk to you. Only an Arapaho lawyer can help her." His expression froze for an instant, as if he wished he'd reined in what he'd said. He threw out his hand, like an usher, and motioned her into a hallway.

Angela lay curled into the pillows on top of a bed, legs drawn beneath her, sandals half falling off her feet. A fist was jammed into her mouth, against the eerie sounds erupting from her throat. Her eyes were wild and unfocused. Vicky dropped onto the edge of the bed. The girl was probably in her early twenties, younger, Vicky thought, than her own kids, Lucas and Susan. Fragile and vulnerable looking, the way Susan had been at that age, before she'd found a way to plant her feet firmly on the earth and walk forward.

"You wanted to see me," Vicky said.

The girl was crying softly. She clasped her hands on her head and buried her face into the pillow. Shaking so hard Vicky could feel the mattress moving. She set a hand on the girl's shoulder. "Try to take a deep breath." She was thinking the girl might need a doctor. "I knew your grandparents before they died." She stopped herself from saying she had gone to school with Angela's mother.

Stabbed to death in a bar in South Dakota. "I know your family. You can trust me."

After a moment, Vicky felt the shuddering subside. The girl began to push herself upright, unfolding her legs and dropping them over the edge of the bed. "I love him," she said, sitting up, clasping and unclasping a piece of bedspread. "I love Skip. He lied to me. Cheated on me, and the cops think I know what happened to him. They think I'm responsible."

Vicky was quiet. They must have hidden the affair, Skip and his secretary. She hadn't heard any gossip, but she knew she missed a lot of the gossip. Not everything on the moccasin telegraph reached her. She said, "What happened tonight?"

Angela let out another stuttering moan, like that of an animal in pain, and looked at Vicky. There was the wild, uncontrolled stare in her eyes. "I was attacked."

Before Vicky could say anything, the girl hurried on: "I saw a light in the office. I thought Skip had come back. I ran inside, and someone knocked me down."

"Who?"

"He was big, all in black, a black mask. I blacked out, and he ran off. The office was even more of a mess than this morning."

"What was he looking for?"

The girl hesitated, gathering the answer, eyes clouded, as if she were looking inside herself. A vein in the center of her forehead throbbed. "Money," she said finally.

"Skip kept money in the office?" Odd. Maybe petty cash to buy coffee and donuts, but the kind of money that would lead someone to abduct Burrows and search the office?

"Four hundred thousand dollars! He cleaned out his bank account. The cops think I know about it."

Vicky didn't say anything. Her thoughts ran to the blue-bonneted woman in her office who thought she was Libbie Custer. Who might have preferred to be Libbie Custer, but had found herself in the twenty-first century. And had married Edward Garrett, who thought he was Custer. Garrett had also withdrawn a lot of money from a bank account.

"Why do you think Skip took out so much money?" she said.

"He didn't tell me." Angela paused. "He didn't tell me anything. He didn't tell me about his girlfriend in Riverton. All he said last night—the last time I saw him—was that something had come up. He had a busy day today. The cops think he broke up with me, but he didn't."

A man with four hundred thousand dollars? What if the cops were right and Skip had broken up with her? No wonder they thought Angela might know more than she let on.

More than she let on. The thought stuck, like a broken record. Something about the girl was vacant, closed off, as if there was more that she didn't want to talk about. *Listen to your instincts, Grandmother always said. Listen to what feels right*. Something about Angela Running Bear did not feel right.

The girl had started sobbing. "I suspected he was cheating on me," she managed. "I didn't want to know, you understand?"

Vicky nodded. Easier to look away from the lipstick smudges and the perfume smells. She had looked away from Ben Holden, even from Adam. Easier not to know.

"I believed his lies. I found out today he was still seeing an ex-girlfriend, Deborah Boynton in Riverton. White woman, Realtor. Whenever she called the office, I told myself she was another client." She shuddered and emitted a little laugh that sounded like a cry.

Deborah Boynton. The Realtor who had helped Edward Garrett locate a ranch in Dubois. Vicky was barely aware that the girl had grabbed her arm. "The man in the black mask killed Skip." Angela was shouting. "He thinks I know where the money is, so he followed me tonight. He's going to kill me."

"Skip is missing," Vicky said, trying for the soothing voice she used in the courtroom to gain the trust of a reluctant witness on cross-examination, hoping the witness might open a door into the hidden places. "It doesn't mean he's dead."

Angela stared at her, wide-eyed. "You didn't see the blood. I saw the blood on the carpet. On the windowsill. He was hurt. Someone took him. The search party looked everywhere in case his body had been dropped in a field or by the river. Seventy, eighty people spent hours looking for Skip. Everybody loved him. Who would hurt him? Who would do that?"

"Listen to me, Angela. We have to think about your safety. Can you go to rez, stay with family?"

The girl was shaking her head. "He'll know where to find me."

"If he's not Arapaho, he won't know."

Angela stared straight ahead, unblinking. "How do I know who he is?"

True, Vicky thought. The man from the office could be anyone. She forced herself to focus on what the girl was saying, something about Colin Morningside. "We were together until Skip came along. The cops think I told Colin about the money." She started shaking again. "They think Colin shot that Custer guy, so what difference would it make if he killed Skip?"

Vicky remained quiet. A skein of thoughts crossed one another, like yarn in a weft. A pattern started to emerge. The connections, the touch points. Two white men, both with zero bank balances. One shot to death in a parade, the other abducted from his office, leaving a trail of blood behind, and the police thinking the incidents could be related. "Tell me," she said. "Did Skip know Edward Garrett?"

A shadow of surprise and consternation came over the girl's face. "I told the cops," she said. "Far as I know, they weren't exactly friends, just army buddies from a long time ago. The first Iraq war, Skip told me, like I should care. I was just getting born. Garrett showed up when he was in town. They sat around and talked about the old days. Sometimes they went out for coffee."

"Did Garrett come to the office last week before the parade?"

"Like I told the cops, the general—that's what he liked to be called—showed up, walked right past me, and let himself into Skip's office. I saw Skip get up and shut the door. Usually he didn't care if I heard him shooting the breeze with somebody."

"When was this?"

Angela rolled her eyes and contemplated the ceiling. "Thursday, I think. I heard them arguing. The door opened and Garrett—he looked like Custer, you ask me—came flying out. Fists clenched and face red as a beet."

An uneasy feeling gripped Vicky. She could still see the prim, Victorian woman on the other side of her desk. Her client. If the cases turned out to be connected, she would have a conflict of interest if she were to agree to represent the girl.

"He slammed the door behind him," Angela was saying. "I got up and went into Skip's office. He was sitting with his back to the desk, looking at the wall. 'Everything okay?' I asked. He said everything was okay. Misunderstanding with an old buddy. Nothing for me to worry about. He said I should go back to typing the reports he wanted to get out."

Vicky stood up and walked over to the window. She pushed the flowery patterned curtain away from the frame and looked out through the slim opening. A forest of bright stars filled the sky, and a circle of faint light flared over the sidewalk and street. Her Ford parked at the curb, a hatchback sedan in the driveway that probably belonged to Angela. She turned back. "You live in town?" She could guess the answer before the girl nodded. She had known other Arapaho girls like Angela, eager to escape the rez, work in the outside world, blend in, be part of something bigger. Skip Burrows would have been the answer to her dreams. She would never go back to the rez. It would mean erasing part of herself, the part that had found the courage to move away.

"I rent a place," Angela said. Then she told Vicky the address, as if the address made it real.

"Would you be comfortable going home if a police officer kept an eye on your neighborhood tonight?"

"Where else am I going to go?" The girl gave Vicky a long, pleading look. "You'll help me?"

"I can give you some advice, probably the same advice Roger gave you. Don't talk to the cops again without a lawyer present."

"You'll be my lawyer?" Vicky felt her muscles tense at the sharp hope in the girl's voice.

"I can't promise. I may have a conflict." She started to recommend Roger, but the girl had already rejected a nonnative lawyer. In any case, Roger was part of her firm, part of the conflict. And Adam Long Eagle was part of her. She looked away from the disappointment in the girl's eyes and headed toward the hallway, then turned back. "Who's the cop who questioned you?"

"Detective Madden," Angela said, her voice barely a whisper.

Vicky found Roger and Annie seated on the sofa in the living room, an air of expectation about them. "Do you think she's in danger?" Roger said.

It was possible, she told him. More than possible, she was

thinking, with four hundred thousand dollars involved. "Will you see her home?"

They both nodded. "I'll drive her car," Roger said. "Annie can follow us." They both got to their feet and disappeared into the hallway.

Vicky lifted her bag off the small table where she had dropped it and extracted her mobile. In a moment she was connected with the Lander Police Department, asking to speak with Detective Madden. Several seconds passed, a deadness in the phone pressed to her ear. She had decided she'd been cut off just as the loud, gruff voice erupted on the other end.

"Madden," he said.

Vicky told him who she was and that she had been talking to Angela Running Bear. She told him someone had followed the girl after she left the office this evening.

"She get the plate? Make of car?" Angela walked into the living room, gripping a bag to her chest, flanked by Roger and Annie.

"I don't think so. She was too scared. Can you see that an officer patrols her neighborhood tonight?"

The detective said he'd do what he could in view of the attack she had sustained in the office. "I'll want to talk to her again," he said.

"She'll have representation," Vicky said before thanking him and ending the call.

The others stood at the opened door waiting for her. She followed them outside. "The cops will keep an eye on your place," she told Angela. She wondered if it made any difference. The girl would have gone there anyway. Anyplace but the rez.

12

FATHER JOHN STOOD at the window and watched Lou Morningside lift himself out of the pickup. He looked older than his years, bent with worry, face half hidden by the wide brim of his cowboy hat. He walked slowly and did a little hip-hop motion coming up the concrete steps. The old front door squealed on its hinges. Father John went out into the corridor. "How are you, Grandfather?" he said. "Just brewed some coffee. Would you like a cup?"

Lou nodded as he walked into the office. Father John stopped at the small metal table next to the doorway and poured two mugs of coffee. Out of the corner of his eye, he saw the old man sink into a side chair and take hold of the armrests, as if to keep himself from falling out.

He handed Lou a mug, carried the other mug around the desk, and dropped into the old leather chair that squeaked and settled around him. He waited. It wasn't polite to make inane remarks, especially when the old man's worry was as obvious as his denim shirt and jeans and scuffed boots. *Cosi fan tutte* played in the background.

Lou had set his cowboy hat on the floor next to him. A band of gray hair was sweat-plastered to his scalp. He bent his head toward the mug and sipped at the coffee. "Cops came around yesterday," he said, looking up. "BIA officer and Detective Madden. Asked Colin a lot of stupid questions. Did he own a weapon? A twenty-two, by chance? You ask me, they already made up their minds. They think he shot that white man 'cause he looked like Custer, and Colin looked like Crazy Horse. Had his hair tied up with grass and rubbed his face with dirt, like Crazy Horse. Colin's relatives at Pine Ridge gave him their stories passed down from ancestors at the Little Bighorn. Crazy Horse hated Custer. All the Indians hated Custer, except for the traitors and scouts that led him to the villages. They thought he was a fine white man." He shrugged and gave a bark of laughter.

"You know what is really nuts?" Lou went on. "Crazy Horse didn't shoot Custer. The old Indians said Rain in the Face was the one that shot him. And there were other Indians that took credit. Blows up the cops' theory like a firecracker, only they won't listen. They just ask questions and don't hear answers." He laughed again. "Indians stuck awls in Custer's ears after he was dead, because he never listened to what they had tried to tell him. How they didn't want to fight anymore."

Father John took a long drink of his own coffee, trying to put the pieces together. Coming to Indian country, throwing what Custer had done into the faces of the people whose ancestors had suffered the consequences, didn't make a lot of sense. But Edward Garrett had been traveling the plains for years dressed like Custer, talking to audiences as if he were Custer, glorifying the massacre at the Washita River, the takeover of the Black Hills, the brilliance of the campaign that led to the death of his entire command. Sooner or later—maybe it was inevitable—somebody would have shot him.

And that was interesting. As if the man, Edward Garrett, had wanted to die, shot by an Indian like his hero.

"How's Colin?" he said.

Lou shook his head. "Old girlfriend of his, Angela Running Bear, came around late yesterday. Accused him of shooting Custer and taking her boss off someplace."

Father John took another sip of coffee. "Skip Burrows?" he said. Odd that the girl assumed a connection between the death of one white man and the disappearance of another.

"What made her think Colin was responsible for her boss's disappearance?"

"He wasn't just her boss."

Father John leaned back, pieces clicking into place now. "Do the cops know about Angela and Colin?" He was thinking Colin could be in a lot of trouble.

"Cops have ways of finding out things. Colin was pretty upset after she left, like she had turned a knife in him. Wouldn't eat. Laid around on the sofa all night. Finally got up this morning and went out to feed the horses."

"Where is he now?" Father John said. The boy needed a lawyer. He would talk to him, urge him to call Vicky.

"Gone." Lou shook his head and stared down into the mug. "I told him he had to forget the girl and think of himself. I told him to get out of here, go to Pine Ridge and hide with his Crazy Horse relatives. Colin didn't have anything to do with Garrett's death, but they're gonna blame him anyway. Him and Mike Longshot, 'cause it was Mike that drilled the warriors on the dare run. Case solved."

Father John tried to bring the picture into focus. The cops might make a case that Colin had a motive to kill Garrett, but it was shaky. Built on a hard-to-prove theory that two men acted as if they believed they had lived in the past and were intent on playing out past lives. Motives to abduct Skip Burrows might be easier to construct, based on jealousy, revenge. The oldest motives in the world.

"Detective Madden might think Colin left because he's guilty," he said.

Lou was quiet, as if what Father John had said was obvious, but Colin had to leave anyway—before he could be arrested.

Father John could sense the terror in the old man. Crazy Horse had been killed by policemen after he had been arrested. "How can I help?" he said.

Lou cleared his throat. His mouth worked silently around the words. "Talk to that white cop, Detective Madden. He's the one that's got the BIA cops all stirred up, trying to identify the Indians in the parade so they can question them. Looking for somebody that says, 'Yeah, I saw Crazy Horse shoot Custer.' Indians weren't the only ones that hated Custer. Tell that to the detective."

"HEY, FATHER JOHN." The big man straddled the corridor, gun holstered in the black harness that crossed the chest of his white shirt. "Just about to pay you a visit. Come on in."

Detective Madden swung around, and Father John followed him past a row of closed doors and into a small office so tidy, it that might have been vacated weeks ago. Desktop gleaming in the fluorescent ceiling light, computer screen dark, keyboard squared with the edge of the desk, pencils and pens gathered in a blue coffee mug. Filing cabinets against the walls, drawers neatly shut. A philodendron with shiny, healthy leaves spread over the top of one cabinet.

Father John took a side chair and waited while Madden hoisted himself around the desk and dropped into a swivel chair. "I'm thinking one of those warriors knows what happened to Garrett," he said. "Either pulled the trigger himself or saw the Indian that did."

It was like being hit with a fastball, Father John was thinking. No time for polite preliminaries, for settling in and connecting. This wasn't the rez. "What makes you so sure it was an Indian?" he said.

The detective heaved his bulky chest over the desk. Nodding, the beginning of a smile at his lips. "Dressed up like Custer! Got up on the stage and bragged about his brave exploits conquering the West for civilization. Audience ate it up, clapped and cheered. I was there. Tell you the truth," he said, exhaling a long breath, "we were expecting trouble. Maybe a riot. Only two Arapahos showed up. Colin Morningside and Mike Longshot. BIA Police have been real cooperative. We talked to both men. Funny thing, they don't know who was in the parade. Won't even admit they were in the parade. Oh, we can prove they were there," he went on. "Morningside likes to dress up and play Crazy Horse. Weaves grass in his hair, smudges dirt on his face. He's done it before for parades and powwows. I have a dozen witnesses who will swear Morningside was in the parade. Longshot? The kid's a basket case. Didn't take much leaning on him before he started to talk. Then clammed up and said he was going to get a lawyer. Sooner or later we'll have the names of all those warriors. Somebody's bound to have priors, be on probation or parole. That's the guy who will confirm what happened."

"Confirm? You already know?"

"We have two white men attacked one day apart. Garrett killed and Skip Burrows abducted. Who knows if he's still alive. Connection is Colin Morningside. Hated Custer, hated Skip for taking off with his girlfriend. I'd say that's a pretty good connection."

"Look, Madden." Father John leaned forward. "I've known Colin and Mike since they were kids. They're not capable of murder."

"No? In my line of work, I have to think everybody's capable of murder." He held Father John's eyes a moment, then looked away, considering. "There's money involved," he said, looking back. "A lot of money. Both Garrett and Burrows had cleaned out their bank accounts recently. Money's disappeared."

"How would Colin or Mike know anything about that?" Enough money, he was thinking, to convince Colin Morningside to get involved in murder? Flee to Pine Ridge? He could feel the muscles tightening in his chest. Madden didn't seem to know that Colin had left the area. It wouldn't look good for Colin when he found out.

"Then there's the girl," Madden said. "Worked for Burrows. Says Garrett and Burrows were old army buddies, had themselves a disagreement last week. I suspect she knows a lot more than she's saying. You know her?"

He knew the family, Father John told him. Parents killed in a bar fight in South Dakota. A sister, Claire, and her boy. The boy played on the Eagles, the baseball team Father John had started his first summer at St. Francis. He tried to think when he had last seen Angela at any of the powwows or celebrations.

"I'm going to level with you, Father," Madden said. He leaned back into his chair, relaxed looking. "We have one or more killers walking around, and we're chasing our tails trying to figure out who they are. We'd like your help. Talk to those Indians, let them know we want justice for a murdered man. Garrett was shot up close with a twenty-two. A powerful revolver, like a Ruger LCR twenty-two. We've eliminated every other possibility. No gunshot from the curb. No gunshot from a window somewhere. We want to find Burrows before he's a dead man. We're not looking to hang anybody. We're looking for the truth."

"They think you've made up your mind an Indian killed Garrett," Father John said. "If they thought . . ."

"Yeah, yeah, yeah." Madden threw up both hands. "You tell them we're looking at every angle. Right now we're looking at everybody with a connection to Garrett or Burrows. We're talking to everybody on Main Street. Somebody might remember seeing something. Tell them that."

OUTSIDE, FATHER JOHN rolled down the windows and switched on the ignition. The pickup spurted into life. A hot, dry wind blew through the cab. He flipped on the CD player on the seat beside him and turned up the volume. *Di scrivermi ogni giorno* burst around him. He pulled away from the curb, made a U-turn, and headed toward Main Street, trying to work the syllogisms into a logical sequence. Something was missing. Where was the evidence that Garrett's murder and Skip's disappearance were connected? It could be nothing but coincidence, and coincidences happened. He turned onto Main, heading back to the rez, then changed his mind. Lou Morningside's voice running through his head now. *Indians weren't the only ones that hated Custer.*

13

THE RV CAMP looked busy and permanent, a small town inventing itself at the edge of Lander. People moving about and lounging in outdoor recliners close to the front stoops. Men bent over barbecue grills, smoke spiraling above their heads. Cars were parked at angles here and there; horse trailers stood beyond the RVs. Father John drove slowly down the dirt path that served as a main street looking for a familiar face. Clouds of dust swirled upward and smudged the windshield. He'd rolled up the windows halfway, but he could taste the tiny, dry granules. The CD player was playing *Soave sia il vento*. Ahead were a couple of men in the blue uniforms of the 7th Cavalry, antique looking with brass buttons and high stiff collars. He stopped beside them. "Where can I find Nicholas Veraggi and Philip Osborne?" He hoped he had the names right.

The men squinted at him through the blowing dust. Sergeants, standing straight and confident, as if Father John were a superior officer. "Beg your pardon, sir," one of them said. "I'm afraid I don't know who you're referring to."

"Benteen and Reno," Father John said. If this was the game, he would play it. He felt as if he'd crossed a border into a past time resurrected and come to life around him.

"Last two RVs." The sergeant held out his hand like a traffic patrolman.

Father John thanked him and drove on. Curious: in this past time, there were no children. Only men and a few women bustling about in long skirts with bonnets tied on their heads, and flushed, sunburned faces. He stopped next to the RVs at the end of the road. *Outback* was plastered in black along the side of the beige RV. The other RV was larger, with swirls of brown and white paint that, he guessed, were meant to suggest the wind whipping past. On the bumper was a large, white sticker with thick red type that said: Custer Lives.

As far as he knew, the RV camp had materialized about two weeks ago. Each time he'd driven past, the camp had seemed larger. This was powwow and rodeo season in Fremont County, and he suspected a lot of the Little Bighorn reenactors were passing through. He wondered how long they would stay now that Garrett was dead.

He parked behind a dark blue, dust-smeared sedan lined up next to the two RVs. The instant he switched off the ignition, he heard the voices, angry and shrill, over the opera music. He hit stop on the CD player. The voices were louder, as if they came over a loudspeaker. He got out, slammed the door, and waited a moment before heading toward the metal stoop that slanted sideways at the door to the brown-and-white RV. His boots smashed the dried brush that poked through the dirt.

The voices stopped. The metal door slammed open, jingling and shaking on its hinges. A woman who looked to be in her fifties, with dark, curly hair that poked out of her blue bonnet, and a long, cotton dress with sleeves pushed above her elbows, flung herself down the wobbly steps. Picking up her skirt, she swished past him, as if he were part of the landscape, and hurried across the road. She stomped up the steps into a compact-looking RV with *Adventure* painted on the side. The sound of the door slamming reverberated in the wind.

Philip Osborne stood on the top of the steps and stared after the woman. He looked remarkably like the photos of Frederick Benteen, Father John thought. Silver hair mussed, as if he perpetually ran his fingers through it; light eyes narrowed into laser slits. He came down the steps, boots clanging on the metal. Behind him was Nicholas Veraggi, a big man with dark hair and black eyes shadowed beneath thick, black eyebrows. He had a small, black mustache. Uncanny how much he resembled Marcus Reno.

Veraggi leaned heavily on the flimsy metal railing as he came down the steps. Both men were in the uniforms of the 7th Cavalry. The smell of beer floated around them.

"Father John, isn't it? Guess you heard that," Osborne said. He seemed to be the leader of the two, even though Veraggi, quiet and brooding on the bottom step, probably outranked him here in the trailer park. Benteen had been a captain, Father John was thinking; Reno, a major.

Osborne had an older, more mature look, and when Veraggi stepped down alongside him, Father John could see the puffed redness around his eyes, the bleary way he tried to focus. The look of a drinker. They were both drinkers. Father John could spot the truth a mile away, feel it in his bones before it was obvious to everyone else. Veraggi, the sloppy drunk who slurred and staggered. Osborne, the gentleman drunk who planted his feet carefully and gripped the railing, as if he always gripped railings to keep from toppling over.

The kind of drunk he had been, Father John thought. Smug, congratulating himself on pulling off another binge, planting his footsteps one after the other into the classroom, sure no one could tell. What a fool he'd been, an alcoholic fool. Everyone had known.

"Who is she?" he said, tossing his head toward the trailer across the road.

"Libbie." Veraggi made a slurping noise with his lips.

"Name's Belinda Clark," Osborne said in a careful, controlled tone. "Edward's wife. Taking his murder real hard."

"I wouldn't say that, Captain," Veraggi said. "The one she's mourning is the general. That's a blow you don't recover from, man like that, cut down in his prime. He would've done great things, had he lived. Would have been elected president." He laid his head to one side and spit out a wad of phlegm.

"Yeah, and the moon would have evaporated," Osborne said. "Sooner or later, Custer was going to lead the Seventh to disaster. He was a hothead. Thought about himself and his reputation first. The men whispered about it all the time. They were always worried. You didn't like him any more than anybody else."

"You forget Libbie. Beer, Father?" Veraggi said.

"No, thanks," Father John said. The man had already walked around the stoop and was rooting among the chunks of ice in a cooler. He lifted himself up with some difficulty, as if he were lifting a bale of hay, tossed a can to Osborne and popped open another can. He raised it to his mouth and gulped probably half the contents. Strands of white foam trickled down his chin. The smell of beer hit Father John in his rib cage, like an arrow shot from nowhere.

"That woman over there," Osborne said, popping his own can, "is in love with money. Met up with Edward at the Little Bighorn reenactment couple years ago and latched on to him. Found out he had a big ranch outside Laramie. Married him two months later and started working on him to sell the ranch. Wants the money now. All she cares about."

"She seemed very upset."

"Blames us for Edward getting shot," Veraggi said. He took another long drink of beer and belched. "Says we should've protected him from the wild Indians, come to his rescue. Backed him up. Says we let him die."

Osborne gave a bark of laughter. "How were we supposed to protect him? Indians rose up out of nowhere. Raced around our command, double column of riders, whooping and hollering. All we could do to stay mounted, the horses were so spooked. Then the Indians rode in front, got back into formation, and kept going down Main. That's when I saw Edward on the street. Figured he got thrown. Reno and I"—he paused a moment, then went on— "we knelt over him. Telling him not to die. We was gonna get the medics. I saw that big hole in his chest, and it was like a vision, like I was back at the Little Bighorn on the hillside, staring down at the general's body."

"Was his wife there?" Father John was thinking that, at least, Libbie Custer had been waiting for her husband at Fort Lincoln when he was killed. There was mercy in that.

Osborne and Veraggi were both shaking their heads. "Showed up yesterday," Veraggi said. "Tore through the trailer looking for the money. Stomped over here and started blaming us. The woman is certifiably nuts."

"Why would she blame you?"

"She's talking about Custer! Libbie never stopped blaming us for not coming to Custer's defense. Well, we were pinned down by Indians. All we could do to stay alive." Osborne leaned forward and cleared his throat. Then he took another drink of beer, as if he'd had second thoughts. "Problem with being a reenactor," he said finally, "you forget who you are. Riding in parades and arenas, reenacting the battle, I'm Benteen. You understand? The rest of the world, a hundred and thirty-some years, fades away like it never happened. I'm Benteen, and I have to follow orders and kill Indians." He looked off into space a moment. "I pretty much am Benteen the whole season. First of October, the powwows, parades, reenactments stop, and I get in the trailer and go back to Tennessee and work in a bar until the season starts up again. I get into my own life. Philip Osborne, best therapist bartender in the state. Ask any drunk. He'll tell you. But it's like Benteen's in the next room, waiting to come out again."

"You're saying Edward's wife is upset Custer was killed?" It seemed preposterous, but everything about the reenactors was preposterous and mysterious. He had a sense he was talking to ghosts.

"Edward's wife," Osborne said, emphasizing the words, "is upset 'cause the money's gone." He shrugged. "Says Edward withdrew the money he got from the ranch, and now it's disappeared. Says we took it. Hell, we didn't even know he'd withdrawn it."

"Did anybody in the command know?"

Osborne was staring into space again, and Veraggi said, "Kept pretty much to himself. You heard of actors that get into the part and live the part for weeks and months at a time? That was Edward. He got into the part. He was Custer for the whole season, so he never showed up to drink beer or eat barbecue with the troopers."

"Is that the same for you?'

"Nah." Veraggi said, bringing his eyes back to Father John's, as if he had hoisted himself again into the present. "I can put Reno away long enough for a couple beers with the guys. Sometimes it's the same with Osborne here. Right?" He leaned toward the man in the captain's uniform. Neither one had missed many drinking bouts, Father John was thinking. "But I understand Edward. He was the best Custer impersonator ever. He was . . ." He hesitated, his eyes focused on the distances. "He was Custer."

"Daughter hated all of it," Osborne said. "Thought the old man was crazy. Didn't want anything to do with him."

"She was the part of Edward that he wanted to hold on to," Veraggi said. "You see her after her old man got killed?"

Father John told them that he'd driven out to the woman's ranch with Detective Madden to give her the bad news. "She mentioned that her father had intended to buy a ranch close by."

"You ask me," Osborne said, "that's where the money went. He put it down on a ranch, and that crazy wife of his wants it back. Last thing she wanted was another ranch."

Father John took a step backward, away from the stench of sour beer. "The cops think one of the Indians shot Edward," he said.

Osborne nodded. "That's what happened, all right."

"Did you see it?"

"I told you, we couldn't see anything. It was like a tornado hit us. We were trying to survive."

"I don't think any of the Indians were responsible."

"Come on, Father," Osborne said. "How long you been on the rez? Too long, you ask me. You want to think they're innocent victims. Well, you should've seen what those innocent victims did to our troops at the Little Bighorn. Scalped them, cut off private parts and stuffed them in their mouths, rammed stakes and awls in them. Jesus, there was no cause for that."

Except desperation, Father John was thinking. And mindless anger at troops that had attacked their villages, killed and captured their women and children, burned their tipis and stores of food.

"It was a hard time on all sides," he said. "What about your feelings toward Edward?"

"You accusing us?" Veraggi squeezed the empty can in one fist and tossed it under the metal steps.

"I'm not accusing anybody." He kept his eyes on Osborne.

"You said some of the men in Custer's command didn't have much use for him. Anyone in the command feel that way about Edward?"

"Like I said," Osborne began, "Edward kept to himself. He didn't socialize enough to get under anybody's skin. Only one that got to know him was his wife." He gave a quick nod in the direction of the trailer. "Look, Father." The man took a step closer. "Edward was an officer. He was a full bird colonel in Desert Storm. The first Iraq war. That's how we met him, Veraggi and me. He was the commander. Won medals for bravery. Took a bullet in his thigh. After the war, we kept an eye out for each other, you might say. Then a few years ago, we saw Edward was impersonating Custer, so we decided to join the Seventh Cavalry. Ride with the general. Let me tell you"—he leaned forward, stabbing each word into the air—"officers like Custer keep in their own tents. Sometimes he'd call the troops together and give them a pep talk, like tomorrow we'll meet the enemy and he will be ours. That kind of thing. But he wasn't kicking back and joking and drinking with the troops. I told you, Edward was Custer."

14

FATHER JOHN LEFT Osborne and Veraggi sunk in webbed folding chairs, sipping beer and staring into space. He fished his keys out of his jeans pocket, got into the pickup, and slammed the door. Nothing they had said changed anything or would send Detective Madden onto a different track, away from the Arapahos. Edward Garrett was a loner. Not much chance for a loner to antagonize people.

The engine coughed into life. He looked across the hood and along the dirt road to the white trailer on the right, trying to grasp the shadowy thought at the edge of his mind. Edward Garrett, who had thought he was Custer, had fought in the first Iraq war. He'd been wounded. Father John had counseled vets from wars in Iraq and Afghanistan with post-traumatic stress disorder. Men and women who spent sleepless nights watching the horror movies in their own heads, looping through the fear and terror and exploding roadside bombs and pieces of their buddies pasted all over them. He wondered about Garrett and what he had gone through. Maybe it was easier to be George Armstrong Custer, cushioned by the years, than it was to be Edward Garrett.

He shifted into first and started down the road, then swung right and jerked to a stop on the dirt apron in front of the white RV. Even if Garrett had found a way to deal with his nightmares, that didn't explain the other troopers here. All veterans? All suffering from post-traumatic stress disorder? Unlikely. He walked up the metal steps and knocked on the green door that bisected the trailer. A thin-lipped woman with brown curls escaping around a blue bonnet flung open the door and beckoned him inside.

"Been watching you with those drunks," she said. "I got you figured for the priest that was with Edward at the end." She nodded toward the red plastic benchlike sofa attached to the wall and sat down on a wooden chair.

"Father John O'Malley," Father John said. He perched on the bench. The trailer was small and closed-in with faint smells of roses mixed with odors of coffee. "I'm sorry about your husband."

The woman gave a noncommittal shrug. She wore a yellow dress with puffed sleeves that camouflaged the narrow shoulders and the wide hips spreading over the sides of the chair. "Everybody calls me Libbie."

"Is that your name?"

"On my birth certificate?" She shook her head. "Belinda Clark is the so-called legal name, but we all name ourselves in a way, wouldn't you agree? We all wear a mask and pretend to be whoever we want to be. I happen to be comfortable in the role of Libbie Custer. Such a strong, confident, and tenacious woman! Oh, if she lived today, she would be president." The woman stared off into space, as if the thought had taken her somewhere else. "I should thank you," she said, bringing her eyes back to his, "for your efforts on Edward's behalf. I heard you brought the news to his horrible daughter. What I wouldn't have given to have seen her face! Now everyone will know the truth."

"I'm not following," Father John said.

"Isn't it obvious? She wanted him dead. How else could she get her hands on his money? She arranged this whole charade. I'm sure she's in cahoots with the Indians." She leaned forward, one hand gripping the edge of the table. "I'm surprised you didn't see it in her, you being a priest and all. You must talk to all kinds of people. Listen to their sins. Seems to me you should've seen her for what she is, a scheming, grasping witch."

"She seemed shocked by her father's death."

"She's a very good actress." Belinda Clark threw her head back and laughed at the ceiling. "Ironic, wouldn't you say? She detested what Edward did, running around the country impersonating Custer. And so good at it! Why, one newspaper reporter at a reenactment of the Little Bighorn asked him if, in some way, he believed he was Custer. Reincarnated." She smiled at the memory. "That's how good an actor he was."

The woman dipped her head toward the door and the RVs across the road. "They're almost as good as he was. Playing their roles, both of them. How they hated my husband! They could have saved him, but they refused. Just sat on their horses and let my husband die! Their commander. The man they had sworn to follow and obey and protect!"

For a second, Father John wondered who she was talking about. Edward Garrett or George Armstrong Custer? "You're saying that Veraggi and Osborne hated Edward?"

"Yes, of course. They were always jealous, because he out-ranked them. My husband was the commander, the big cheese. Nobody could measure up to the general."

"You mean Edward? I understood he was a colonel."

She squared herself toward him and gave him a slowly develop-ing smile that made the muscles around her mouth resemble spreading glue. "The difference between outsiders, like yourself," she said, "and reenactors is that we can move back and forth. In and out of characters, if you like, or historical persons. We can come back any time we like, or we can stay where we feel the most comfortable. Where we belong. It's as if we were born in the wrong time. As if some cosmic catastrophe occurred that kept us away from our own, natural time and thrust us here." She opened her arms and waved them about, as if she could take in the whole universe. "You're a philosopher."

"I'm a priest," he said.

"Whatever. Priest, philosopher." She leaned forward and shook a schoolteacherish finger at him. "You live with invisible realities every day, the things that can't be seen under a microscope. You must understand what I'm talking about."

"You believe that in some way you are Libbie Custer? And Edward was Custer?"

"It's not that simple." She was shaking her head, rolling her eyes. A particularly dense student! "What I know is that I could have been Libbie, and maybe"—she stumbled over the rest of it—"maybe I was. But I'm fully aware that I can step back into Belinda Clark and the present any time I wish. That is what outsiders don't understand. You think we're all a bit crazy. Edward's daughter thought her father was a nut. She didn't have the capacity to real-ize he was different. He could move from one person to another.

He had a great capacity to imagine Custer. He could bring him back to life. Is that really so hard to understand? So impossible?"

Father John was quiet. Pavarotti as Calaf, becoming the character, singing him to life in *Nessun dorma*. Caruso as Pagliacci. He had listened to the recording of *Vesti la giubba* a hundred times, caught up in the imaginary world. So many plays and movies with great actors. Laurence Olivier as Hamlet, the prince of Denmark himself stalking the halls of Elsinore, alive. Meryl Streep becoming Margaret Thatcher.

He got to his feet, cowboy hat in one hand. There was barely room to step toward the door past the woman's white boots crossed in the middle of the aisle. "I stopped by to see if there was anything I could do for you," he said.

"You can tell that detective to release my husband's body." She rose alongside him. "I intend to have his body cremated, then I'll spread his ashes across the plains in the unspoiled spaces he loved. Wyoming, Colorado, Montana, South Dakota. All the places where he felt most at home. Free."

Father John wondered again who she was. The wife of Edward Garrett or a very good actress playing a role. "I can ask him when the body will be released."

"You do that," she said. "Maybe the detective has figured out that Dorothy stole her father's money. Ask him what he intends to do about it."

Father John waited for her to go on, something he had learned from counseling. People seemed to throw away something important, then went after it because they hadn't really meant to throw it away. All he had to do was wait.

"Edward sold his ranch in Laramie," she said, spitting out the words. "He had a lot of money in the bank account. A half million dollars. He was set to buy another ranch near Dubois, though for the life of me I never understood why. Edward preferred to roam." She shrugged. "'Why do you want another ranch?' I asked him. 'You just got rid of one. Let's go off, live in the trailer, sit outside under the sunshade, and read and write. You can write your memoirs. *My Life on the Plains with Custer* by Edward Garrett.' Oh, for a while I thought I had convinced him. I could tell he liked the idea of having his name on a book, connected to Custer forever. Next thing I knew, he announced he found a ranch he really liked. Close to Dorothy. My God! Dorothy, who hated his guts and only wanted his money."

"What makes you think she took his money?"

"It's gone. Disappeared into thin air. Who else could have gotten hold of it? That conniving witch talked him out of every last cent." She was still standing so close that she had to tilt her head back to look up at him. The brim of her bonnet cast a faint shadow across her eyes. "Detective Madden should investigate the theft of Edward's money."

"Have you told him about this?"

She gave him another slow smile. "Naturally. It did little good. It's so simple, I don't know how he could miss it. Like shooting at a bull's-eye as broad as a barn and hitting the trees a hundred feet away. Dorothy got hold of his money somehow, and hired those Indians to create a disturbance at the parade and shoot Edward while nobody could make out what was going on. Brilliant, when you think about it. I'm sure she didn't have to work too hard to convince them. Flashed a little money around. Besides, they hated Custer, all the Indians did. They could sense something about Edward, sense Custer in him. They were happy to do her bidding. She still has the bulk of the money."

She stepped back and tilted her head even further. "Make him understand," she said.

"Look, Mrs. Garrett . . ."

She interrupted. "You can call me Libbie, or Belinda, if you insist."

"Belinda," he said, "Madden is investigating anybody who might have wanted your husband dead. If the money is part of it, he'll find out. We have to wait until the investigation is complete."

"We? We? It wasn't your husband who was shot by those filthy, marauding Indians who should have been chased back to the reservation. What were they doing off the reservation, anyway?"

Father John stared at her a moment, unsure of what she was talking about. Custer, sent out with the 7th Cavalry to round up Indians and force them onto a reservation? Edward Garrett, pretending to be Custer? "They're not captives," he said. "They're free to move about like any other U.S. citizen."

She shook her head. "Well, some things about the present do not make sense. We must agree to disagree, but I can tell you that my husband . . ."

"Edward," he said.

"Yes, Edward, and Custer, both believed there was a place for Indians and a place for whites. They should be separate, free to go about their own lives on different sides of a border."

"Edward believed that?" Father John was thinking that the man had imbibed nineteenth-century prejudices. Playing the role of Custer. Thinking like Custer. Maybe they went together.

"I can see that you don't." She was shaking her head hard. "It doesn't matter. What I want is justice. I want the Indians that killed my husband and the woman who put them up to it to pay for what they've done. Do you understand? I want them to pay!"

* * *

FATHER JOHN DROVE back through the RV camp, past troopers sitting about on canvas stools, smoking cigars and drinking beer out of aluminum cans, then turned onto a paved road. In a couple of minutes he was on Main Street. It was as if he had stepped out of a time machine. People sauntering about, some with Styrofoam cups of coffee. Everybody dressed in jeans or shorts and tee shirts and high-soled running shoes. Tourists and townspeople, and all of them from the present. He didn't spot any Indians.

He swung onto 789 and followed the curves along the Popo Agie River into Hudson, then crossed the border into the reservation and drove down Rendezvous Road, trying to make logical sense out of what Belinda Clark had said. A daughter who hated what her father did for a living, willing to have him killed for his money? It was difficult to reconcile the Dorothy Winslow he had talked to—the sadness and reflection in her eyes—and the picture her stepmother painted. People could assume roles, play parts. He had heard enough confessions and counseled enough people to know the roles people played. Some were better than others. Some were professionals. But Garrett's daughter was not a professional actress. Even so, that didn't mean she couldn't be very good.

He stopped at the sign on Seventeen-Mile Road, then turned right. Ahead, the blue billboard with St. Francis Mission in large white letters winked in the glare of the sun. Something Belinda had said nagged at him. Veraggi and Osborne had hated her husband. They were jealous of him. Why? Did he make more money playing Custer? Get more attention? No doubt that was true, but was that enough to cause them to hate him?

The logical conclusion spun in his mind like a tumbleweed in the wind. Logic, so relentless, so unforgiving. Hatred could lead to action. If Veraggi and Osborne hated Garrett, what action might they have taken?

Father John turned into the cottonwoods, the thick branches blocking out the sun and leaving the road in deep shadow. He shook off the conclusion. Sometimes logic only made sense in a syllogism, not in the actual world. Hatred enough to kill the man who made their own roles possible? Without Garrett, Veraggi and Osborne would have to wait for another Custer impersonator to take part in the Battle of the Little Bighorn reenactment.

Without Custer, there were no roles for Benteen and Reno.

15

THE REAL-ESTATE OFFICE sat between a barbershop and a Chinese take-out in a low-slung building with yellowing white paint. Plastered across the plate-glass windows were white cards with photos of houses and lines of black text. Above the cards, black letters spelled out Hometown Realtors.

Vicky parked in the middle of the lot and threaded her way around the other parked cars to the sidewalk. The burning asphalt worked through the soles of her sandals, the sun beat through the cotton of her blouse, and a dry wind whipped at her skirt. Sounds of traffic from Federal drifted on the wind. She let herself through the glass door. It was like stepping into a refrigerator, and she fought the impulse to grab her arms and hug herself against the cold air blowing out of vents in the white tiled ceiling.

"Howdy!" The man with the wide grin and mop of curly black hair behind the reception desk looked about thirty, close to Lucas's age, she thought. But there was something unfinished about him: thin shouldered and long necked, skinny arms that protruded from his blue short-sleeve shirt, and long fingers that grasped a ballpoint pen, which he tapped on a pile of papers. "How can we be of service?" he said, hope and curiosity in his tone. The metal nameplate at the front of the desk read Eugene Carmody.

Vicky walked over. "I'm here to see Deborah Boynton."

"You have an appointment?"

"I'm afraid not." She slipped the small leather envelope out of her bag, extracted a business card, and laid it on the pile of papers.

The grin dissolved as Eugene Carmody studied her business card. "Lawyer? Any problem?

"I'm here on behalf of a client," Vicky said. "Is Deborah in?"

The man stared at her a long moment. "Sorry. I haven't seen her today. She comes and goes. You know how it is in the real-estate business. Half your time is spent out showing properties. I can leave her a message."

"Perhaps you can help me," Vicky said. "I represent the widow of Edward Garrett. She needs to know whether her husband closed on a ranch he was interested in before he was killed."

Eugene Carmody rolled his chair back and jackknifed to his feet, long arms and long legs in motion like a puppet's. "You'd better talk to our broker." He stumbled around the side of the desk. "Linda Lewin," he said over one shoulder as he disappeared through a door into the rest of the office. Footsteps reverberated off the thin-partition walls. A door opened and closed, followed by the muffled noise of voices that sounded strained and deliberately low pitched.

Vicky walked across the reception area and studied the portraits on the wall. Deborah Boynton, third photo, second row: red curly hair that brushed the shoulders of a blue blazer, green eyes, and a wide smile turned toward the camera. Thirty or thirty-five, Vicky guessed, confident and wary looking at the same time. So this was Skip Burrows's former girlfriend. The same Realtor who had represented Edward Garrett.

Several minutes passed before the footsteps pounded again, coming closer, and the door swung open. Eugene Carmody stood with one arm extended, urging her forward. "Second cubicle on the right," he said.

Vicky stepped past him into a narrow corridor that resembled a maze through the warren of small cubicles with half-glass walls. Inside the cubicles, Realtors sat at desks that looked like counters, heads curled over computer screens, phones jammed against ears. The tap tap of keyboards punctuated the soft buzzing undercurrent. Ahead, standing in a doorway, was a tall woman with brown hair smoothed back into a bun with strands that flowed down her neck. The smile that creased her face was filled with impatience, as if she hoped the interview would be brief.

"Linda Lewin." She held out a hand with red-tipped fingers.

Vicky shook her hand, then followed her into the small cubicle. With one foot, the woman guided a chair across the floor until it stood at a right angle to the narrow desk. "Have a seat." She perched on the chair in front of the computer screen.

"I was hoping to speak with Deborah Boynton."

The woman gave a slow, understanding nod. "Deborah's been very busy lately. What is it you want to know?"

"I represent Belinda Clark. I'm sure you know her husband, Edward Garrett, was shot to death Sunday afternoon in Lander."

"In front of hundreds of people! Who would have thought the Indians would be so bold."

Vicky could feel her skin prickling, her cheeks flushing. She waited a beat before she said, "The killer hasn't been identified."

"Well, excuse me," Linda Lewin said, the smile frozen on her face. "You ask me, Garrett took a big chance coming to Indian country pretending to be Custer."

"The investigation is still open." Vicky emphasized each word. "My client needs to know if her husband completed the purchase of a ranch near Dubois."

"Deborah would be the one . . ."

Vicky held up one hand. "You're the broker, and Deborah isn't here. I have Mrs. Garrett's power of attorney and I have filed a probate action."

Linda Lewin lifted a hand and turned toward the computer. Head down, hunting for the keys, fingers crossing one another. Finally, she looked up at the monitor. "The Stockton Ranch. One thousand acres, twenty-five-hundred-square-foot ranch house, one story, three bedrooms, two baths, barn and two outbuildings, fenced corral. Very well priced at five hundred and fifty thousand dollars. Garrett made a cash offer, which the owners accepted. Sale contingent on buyer producing payment." She made a quarter turn toward Vicky. "Appears the sale was not final. Too bad the poor man was killed."

"Cash offer?" That tallied with what Belinda Clark had said. Her husband had sold the ranch near Laramie. The money had been in the bank, unless he had invested it somewhere else. "Did Deborah say why the sale was delayed?"

"This is a busy place." Linda Lewin waved a hand at the cubicles around her and the low rumble of noise and ringing phones. "Realtors work on lots of deals at once. No one has time to stand around and jawbone about the details."

"When do you expect Deborah?"

"I never expect Deborah or any other agent." The woman gave

a quick shrug. "They're here when they're here. Deborah often works at home. I believe she plans to work at home all week. On the other hand, she could pop in at any minute, but I wouldn't suggest you wait."

"Where can I find her?

"You expect me to give you her address?"

"My client has the right to know the exact status of the real-estate deal and why it didn't close," Vicky said. Running through her head were the words of Belinda Clark: *Five hundred thousand dollars. Where is the money?* "I can get a subpoena . . ."

"No. No. No." The woman lifted both hands, then let them fall against the edge of the desk. "No subpoenas. Pardon me, but we don't need lawyers, either. Deborah lives three blocks west of here. Turn left at the corner. White house with wrought iron fence in front. Keep ringing the bell. Sometimes she gets so engrossed in work she doesn't hear it."

VICKY WAITED FOR a line of pickups and SUVs to lumber past before she pulled onto Federal. Air rushing across the opened windows battled the stifling heat inside the Ford. The voice of LeAnn Rimes rose over the hum of tires on asphalt. *Through the laughter and the madness and every moment in between. Oh, I want you with me.* She took a left into a neighborhood of identical houses. Bungalows painted white with front door stoops that mimicked small porches. In the middle of the block was the house with the wrougt iron fence and flowers spilling out of window boxes and a ragged sidewalk with grass growing in the cracks. A large elm threw shadows over the lawn.

She pulled to the curb, let herself through the small iron gate that whistled on its hinges. She picked her way up the sidewalk to the porch. The doorbell button felt limp and unattached when she pushed it. No sounds inside, only stillness. She knocked hard and listened for a disturbance of some kind, footsteps or scraping chairs. Nothing. She knocked again, then glanced around. The neighborhood was almost as still as the house. Branches of the elm swayed in the wind, causing the shadows to ripple like water in a creek.

Vicky turned back and knocked again, a perfunctory rap, like an exclamation point that merely emphasized she was there. She didn't expect an answer. If Deborah Boynton was inside, she had remained quiet, answering the intrusion by ignoring it.

Vicky retraced her route down the uneven sidewalk and through the gate. A young woman behind a baby stroller stood at the corner of the wrought iron fence. Small, fat white legs protruded from the stroller. Inside, Vicky could see the blond head drooped in sleep.

"Hello," she said, walking over. "Do you know Deborah Boynton?"

The woman was probably in her mid-twenties, serious and nervous looking at the same time, with long, blond hair that straggled over the front of her black tee shirt, and thin white legs below cutoff jeans. She wore flip-flops that made a little squishing noise as she stepped from one foot to the other. "We live next door." She shrugged toward the rectangular house that looked like a clone of the Boynton house.

"I understand she often works at home," Vicky said. "I was hoping to find her."

"She's gone."

"Gone? When?" She might have just missed her. On the other

hand, if Deborah Boynton had been gone awhile, she might return soon. Vicky looked back at the quiet house, a sense of emptiness about it, debating whether to wait or come back later.

"She left Sunday." The baby started to stir and made little crying sounds. The fat white leg bucked up and down.

"She hasn't been back since then?"

"She went on vacation," the woman said, jiggling the stroller back and forth. "I seen her wheel her suitcase out and put it in the trunk of her car. She drove off and hasn't come back. I been picking up her mail and keeping it for her."

"How long will she be away?" It struck Vicky as odd that the broker hadn't seemed to know about any vacation plans.

"It's not like we're best friends," the woman said, a hint of regret in her tone. "We visit sometimes. She picks up our mail when we leave. Me and Dale don't go away much, only to see his folks in Cheyenne. I get Deborah's mail when she goes off. Usually just for a weekend. Don't blame her none for wanting to get away. Clients calling all the time, expect her to drop whatever she's doing and take them around. I hear her phone ringing all day. Been ringing since she left Sunday. Like I say, can't blame her for getting out of here."

"Did she happen to mention where she was going?"

The woman shook her head in a long, careful motion, as if a sudden memory might cause her to nod. "She never said. But . . ." She hesitated. "You her friend?"

"Vicky Holden," Vicky said, putting out her hand. The woman took hold of Vicky's fingers and gave them a little shake. "I'm an attorney."

"Attorney." The woman bit at her lower lip. "Is Deborah in some kind of trouble?"

"I don't believe so."

A look of relief flooded the woman's face. "Oh, that's good. You never know . . ."

"Is there some reason to believe she might be in trouble?"

"Oh no. I wasn't saying that. It's just that, you know how boyfriends can be."

"How can they be?"

The woman shrugged, then leaned over and patted the baby, who had begun to stir again. White legs jumping. "Best not to cross them," she said, looking up. "Just do what they want. Everybody gets along real good then."

"Do you know the boyfriend's name?"

"Seen him around from time to time. Don't know how serious they are. But whenever he said 'Let's go someplace,' she packed up and went. Like I say, mostly for a weekend. Never asked his name. None of my business, when it comes right down to it. Between you and me, I never liked the looks of him. One of them happy, smiling guys that'll punch you out, you say the wrong thing."

"Was he around when she left Sunday?"

"She usually went off with him, but not Sunday. She got in the car alone and drove off. Come to think of it, maybe she wanted to get away from him."

Vicky dug in her bag and extracted another business card. "If Deborah comes back," she said, handing the card across the top of the stroller, "please give her this and ask her to call me?"

"Yeah, sure." The woman stared down at the card, then folded it between her fingers.

As Vicky drove away from the curb, she watched the woman in the rearview mirror slip the card into the pocket of her cutoffs.

16

A PENCIL LINE of sharp light slid past the bottom of the curtain. Angela pulled the covers over her head, then threw them off. The bedroom was hot and stuffy; her skin felt clammy. She swung her legs over the edge of the bed and pushed herself upright. She had spent most of the day in bed. The clock on the nightstand glowed 2:14, which was probably somewhere near the correct time. The clock hadn't worked since Skip knocked it to the floor a month ago. He hadn't meant to do it, and he had been calm and thoughtful ever since.

Skip. She could feel her heart jumping. Out there somewhere beyond the window and the dirt driveway and the wide afternoon streets. Alive. *Let him be alive.* She prayed out loud to the Creator, the Great Mystery. *Behe'teiht.* So many words for God, she wondered how he knew when someone called him. All she cared about was that the Creator would keep Skip alive.

She made herself get to her feet and wandered across the glorified corridor that was the living room and bedroom into the closet-sized kitchen, drawn by her own hunger and thirst. She poured a glass of water, took a slice of bread out of the package on the counter, and flopped down on the stool, stuffing the bread into her mouth, gulping the water.

"What a mess you are." Out loud again, and the sound of her own voice gave her a start as if someone else were in the house. She was no good to herself or to Skip. She had to clear her head, be ready when the phone call came. She was sure the call would come. How long could it be before whoever had taken Skip and trashed the office twice realized there was no flash drive? It didn't take a rocket scientist to figure out who had the flash drive.

Angela reached along the short counter, grabbed her bag, and dug out her keys. Attached to the key ring was the flash drive. Hidden it in plain sight, that's what she had done. She had read a mystery novel about how the killer had hidden evidence in front of the detective's nose, and he never saw it, not until the last pages when—what do you know?—the evidence had been there all the time. It had made her laugh. So clever and smart, nobody had figured it out.

Except it didn't feel clever and smart now. The pictures in her mind of papers and files strewn about the floor, cords yanked from computers and phones—the violence in the office—made the bread and water churn in her stomach until she thought she would be sick. She should take the flash drive to the office, leave it on the middle of her desk, and drive away. Across the border to the reservation where she belonged.

She pulled out another slice of bread, hoping it would settle the bread she had already eaten. She could see more clearly now, as if she had been given a second sight. Across the border to what? There was nothing on the rez for her. Dad, whoever he was, gone before she was born. Mom and three—or was it four?—husbands. She had lost track in the midst of the boyfriends and stepdads wandering in and out and Mom being mostly drunk. Then Mom and the latest stepdad dead in a bar fight in South Dakota. She'd had grandparents once, and that had been a comfort, until, stooped and lined with disappointments and broken promises, they had faded away. One day, Grandpa didn't get out of bed, and a few weeks later, Grandma stumbled on her way to the barn and never got up. And they were gone, and all she had of herself gone with them.

There was her sister, Claire, no better than her mother, and that poor kid of hers that still had a few years before he would be old enough to escape. There had been only Colin to rely on, but Colin was stuck on the rez like a barbed wire fence. He would never leave.

She fingered the cool, shiny flash drive, black metal with a red lightning streak down the side. Her ticket, like an airline ticket to a better place. When Skip came back, they would leave all this behind, just as he had promised. *Angela, babe, you and me are going to Mexico, but first we'll hit the road and take in the sights. San Francisco, New York, London, Paris. Where do you want to go? What suits your fancy?*

Skip always said weird things like "What suits your fancy?" He made her laugh and dream. He was her ticket out of here and so far away from the reservation the border would no longer loom like a giant snake, flicking its tongue, threatening to devour her.

She had figured it out. Last night, tossing in bed, watching the starlight glow in the curtain, she had plotted out the scenario. When the man who took Skip called—he would call, she was certain—she would tell him how it had to go down. The meeting in a public place. People around, traffic driving by. An ordinary place, like Main Street. The thought of Main Street had stopped her for a moment. The Custer guy had been shot there in front of hundreds of people.

Still, Main Street, first thing in the morning, with people going to work, bustling about, would be the meeting place. She would park at the curb and the man should park across the street. Skip had to be in the car. She had to see him, be certain he was alive. She would get out and stand on the curb to show good faith. Another term Skip liked to use. Show good faith, as if everything depended on the show. You didn't actually have to have good faith, you just had to act as if you did.

She would hold up the flash drive. As soon as Skip got out of the car, walked across the street, and got into the passenger seat of her car, she would set the flash drive on the curb, calmly walk around and slide in behind the wheel, and drive away. The man should wait until she had driven off. She would make that very explicit. If she showed good faith by standing on the curb, then he must show good faith by waiting in his car.

Simple. How much she had learned from Skip. How much was in a smile, a handshake, a friendly, welcoming manner, as if you trusted the world and the world trusted you back. Good faith. It was like oil on the gears of an old truck.

Angela spun the flash drive in a little circle. What was on her computer that the man wanted? Nothing but pages and pages of boring legal jargon with columns of numbers that she didn't understand, and yet, somewhere in that jargon, there was something as big as Skip's life, something she could use to ransom him. She went back into her bedroom, picked up the laptop Skip had given her, and carried it back to the counter. She flipped open the top. A couple of keystrokes and the screen bounced into life. She inserted the flash drive and tapped her nails against the edge of the counter until the icon of a disc came up. Then she opened it.

She had never opened the flash drive. She'd had no intention of rereading the boring legal documents she spent her days with. The flash drive was her protection, that was all. A backup that could save her job if the computers crashed. She supposed she'd had some idea that if disaster struck and her computer went down, she would whip out the flash drive and prove to Skip how necessary she was, always looking ahead, paving a clear path for him.

Well, disaster had struck, and now Skip was gone, along with his computer and backup as well as her computer. All that was left was the flash drive. Whatever was on the flash drive had also been on her computer. A duplicate, worth Skip's life.

She studied the list of files. Every day for the last six months, she had backed up the files. They had grown and spread like spilled paint. Letters, briefs, requests for court orders, documents she'd downloaded and filled in the blanks. All those reports with long columns of numbers. Routine and boring. A robot could have handled the documents.

She searched for Deborah Boynton, and several letters came up. Thank-you letters for referrals. Angela scrolled quickly through them. Nothing to suggest that Skip and Boynton were anything but business friends. Lawyer and Realtor, referring clients to each other. She hadn't wanted to know.

Then, in one of the letters, she spotted the name Edward Garrett. Skip, thanking the Realtor for looking after his old army buddy Edward Garrett and helping him find suitable property. Could he take her to dinner sometime to show his appreciation?

Angela swallowed back the taste of acid and bread in her throat. She hadn't thought there was anything between Skip and Deborah Boynton. Skip took lots of people to dinner. His way of showing appreciation. He was known everywhere in Lander and Riverton and Jackson—the whole area—for treating people to breakfast, lunch, dinner, endless rounds of coffee. He practiced law in restaurants.

She closed the letter file, then did another search for Edward Garrett. The letter she had just closed came up, along with two quarterly reports, pages filled with numbers. Once she had asked Skip to explain the numbers, eager to show her good faith, how she wanted to learn so she could be more help to him. He had waved off the question, told her it was complicated, not to worry about it. Fill in the boring columns with the numbers he forwarded to her.

For a moment she thought she would start weeping, and she didn't know how she would stop. She jammed her fists against her eyelids, willing the hard knots of moisture to dissolve. Pictures of the office flashed in her mind, so neat and tidy, a welcoming place where she had felt at home. Gone. Files, papers, trash thrown around the floor, blinds knocked sideways, spots of blood on the carpet and windowsill. The smashed bush below, the sense of irretrievable loss, and the vast emptiness that had opened around her.

There were other files she forced herself to look through. Documents she had printed out and delivered to the courthouse herself, knowing they were due and Skip was out having coffee with somebody. Research documents Skip had asked her to pull off the internet. She had forwarded them to his computer. Records of incoming calls and appointments, although Skip never turned down anyone who appeared at his door without an appointment. The only thing she and Skip had disagreed about—because she had wanted to show him she was a good organizer—was how smoothly she could plan his days. He didn't want his days to run smoothly.

She closed the last documents. Routine, all of them. A record of spent days and weeks and months. She had been grateful for a way off the rez, grateful to be with Skip. The good humor man, she thought of him during the day. At night, sometimes he allowed her to see another side of him, and she was glad of that. She felt privileged that he had shown his anger and impatience, had flown off the handle once or twice and slapped her, but nothing serious. Just that other side of him that no one else ever saw, which meant she knew him better than anyone. It had made her proud and confident.

She was aware of a muffled ringing noise. How long had her mobile been ringing? She stumbled against the edge of the counter as she ran toward the sofa bed. Don't hang up! Don't hang up! She was shouting and laughing and crying at the same time. Today, Skip would be back. He would hold her again. They would be together.

She dragged the mobile out of her bag. Shaking so hard she had to hold it in both hands, she clasped it to her ear. "Hello? Hello?" she was still shouting.

"Angela Running Bear?"

A faint familiarity to the voice that she dismissed. This had to be the call. Her heart was jumping in her chest. She felt cold and clammy, legs weak and wobbly. "Yes," she managed. "This is Angela."

"Detective Madden." The voice seemed to come from another time and place that had nothing to do with the present. She forced her legs to fold her onto the bed. She was shaking. Her mouth had gone dry as crust.

"I want to interview you again. In my office, say, in an hour?"

It took a moment for the words to arrange themselves into some kind of sense. "Interview?" she said. "I've already told you everything I know."

"I have a few more questions."

Angela had the feeling she was floating overhead, looking down on the girl with mussed, black hair and puffy eyes, the short night-gown, faded yellow, with the little rip in the side seam that exposed the top of her thigh. "I can't," she said, and the sound of her own voice brought her back to herself.

"This isn't a request. I can send a car . . ."

"No." The image of the landlady's face pressed against the window, eyes as big as a horse's, watching a police car driving her down the driveway rose like a billboard over the road. "I'll be there."

17

"ANGELA'S ON THE line." Annie held up the phone and shook her head as if she had delivered bad news.

Vicky shut the front door behind her. "Ask her to wait a moment," she said, hurrying across the office and past the beveled doors to her private office. She had been expecting the call.

She slid onto her chair, dropped her bag at her feet, and picked up the phone. "Angela? What's going on?" Vicky could hear the tenseness in her own voice. She couldn't shake the feeling that somehow Garrett's murder and Skip's abduction were connected. *Look for the truth running through the coincidences*, Grandmother had said. But she had no proof. She pulled a notepad out of the desk drawer. The breeze blowing though the opened window ruffled the top page. The office was warm, but she preferred the warm summer air and the breeze to the cold blast of air-conditioning.

A gulping sob burst down the line, followed by a garble of words and shouts.

"Try to calm down." Vicky pressed the phone against her ear. "Take a deep breath and tell me what happened."

Another stifled noise. The pain in the girl's voice was so intense that Vicky closed her eyes a moment. "I want to help you," she said.

The silence went on until Vicky thought they had been disconnected. Finally the words came, shaking and blurred: "They're going to arrest me for what happened to Skip."

"What makes you believe that?"

"Detective Madden . . ." Another sob cut through the words. "He wants me to come to the police station. If I don't come, he'll send a police officer to pick me up."

She was weeping hard, and Vicky raised her own voice against the sounds. "It doesn't mean anything. It's the way investigations go. I want you to calm down and get yourself together. I'll pick you up and go with you."

The quiet on the line was almost as ominous as the crying. "Twenty minutes." Vicky waited until the girl had gulped an okay before she said, "Remember, Angela. You don't have to answer his questions or say anything."

"Why do I have to go?"

She stopped herself from saying, *Madden might come up with a reason to arrest you.* "Look, there may be something you don't realize you know that could help him find Skip."

THE GIRL SAT slumped in the passenger seat, a black veil of hair falling down the side of her face. She had been outside on the stoop of the little house behind the white, paint-peeled Victorian when Vicky drove up, and she had sauntered over like a balky pony being led out of the barn. "You'll be fine," Vicky had said when the girl crawled into the Ford. She hoped that was true.

On the drive to pick up Angela, Vicky had gone over what the girl had told her. How she had found the office on Monday morning, trashed, blood spots on the carpet, Skip Burrows missing. How she had seen the light in the window that evening and had gone inside, thinking it was Skip. How someone in a black ski mask had attacked her. Someone looking for something. And that, Vicky realized, was what Madden wanted from the girl. What had the intruder been looking for?

"Have you told me everything?" Vicky said, turning into the asphalt parking lot. The redbrick police building looked solid and substantial, an air of white authority and power in the way it claimed its space, the kind of authority that could crush a young Arapaho girl. It struck Vicky that this was why she had become a lawyer. In the Old Time, her people had had no protection from white people in substantial buildings.

She pulled into a vacant spot. Out of the corner of her eye, she could see the girl giving a slow, methodical nod, as if it were obvious she had told everything. The forced, deliberate motion gave Vicky an uncomfortable feeling.

Inside the narrow lobby was a stretch of vinyl flooring with plastic chairs along one wall. Vicky leaned close to the communicator in the window at the far end and gave her name to the thin-haired, blond officer. He looked familiar, in his twenties, smudges of sunburn on his nose and cheeks. He had probably been at the desk on other occasions when she had come in with a client, although he gave her a blank look. *All Indians look alike.* The old phrase popped into her head and made her want to smile at the idea that she and the young woman beside her resembled each other. There were times when she thought white people looked alike.

She said she was here with her client Angela Running Bear to see Detective Madden. The officer pushed a button on what looked like a radio. "Running Bear here," he said, the words muffled by the thick glass. "With her lawyer."

They waited a good ten minutes, Angela circling about, head down, letting out little intermittent sobs, squeezing a wadded tissue against her eyes. At one point she stopped and stared wide-eyed at Vicky. "Why aren't they looking for Skip? Why are they doing this to me?"

"Maybe Madden thinks you can help him find Skip." Vicky hoped that was what the interview would be about. She had started to remind the girl that she would stop any line of inappropriate questioning when the inner door swung open. Standing before them was the bulky figure and pockmarked face of Detective Madden.

"This way." He nodded them through the doorway and down a corridor flanked by closed doors with bubble-glass windows. A ringing phone cut through the buzz of muffled voices. Stale odors of coffee and closed-in spaces permeated the air. Vicky was aware of the heavy thud of Madden's footsteps behind them.

"Next door on the right," he said.

Vicky took hold of Angela's elbow and steadied her while Madden brushed past, pushed open the door, and stepped inside. The room was the size of a closet. Table in the center, empty except for a notepad, chairs on either side, and a large one-way glass taking up almost half of a wall. On the other side, Vicky knew, would be invisible detectives watching and listening. She guided Angela to a chair and sat down beside her. Madden settled himself across from them. He pulled the notepad toward him and, clicking a ballpoint pen he had extracted from his shirt pocket, looked into space. As if he were talking to himself, and not a microphone embedded somewhere, he said, "June twelfth, 3:53 p.m. Angela Running Bear and attorney Vicky Holden. Detective Madden conducting interview."

He looked at Angela. "You understand this interview will be videotaped." He nodded toward the small camera next to the ceiling.

"Videotaped?" A note of panic ran through the question. Angela shifted toward Vicky. "You didn't say anything about being videotaped."

"Standard procedure," Madden said. "Shall we get started?"

"I don't know . . ."

"It's okay." Vicky patted the girl's hand. It felt cold and clammy, and Vicky could feel the tremor beneath the skin.

Angela pulled her hand away and rounded on the detective. "What are you doing? Why haven't you found Skip? Somebody took him, and all you want to do is ask me stuff I've already told you."

The detective took a moment, smoothing out the top page in the notepad, then locked eyes with Vicky. "We have a witness who will swear she saw Skip Burrows arrive at your client's house on numerous evenings and not emerge until the next morning. She says Burrows left earlier than usual Sunday evening. She identified Burrows's photo." He shifted his gaze to Angela. "Why was that? Did you have an argument? Did he break up with you?"

"Stupid landlady. What right does she have?" Angela threw a sideways glance at Vicky. "Poking her nose into other people's business."

"As you can see, Counselor," Madden said, "the relationship between your client and the missing man certainly bears upon this investigation."

"Let me remind you," Vicky said, "my client went to the office as usual Monday morning to find Skip Burrows missing and the office ransacked. Whatever their relationship may have been has nothing to do with what happened that morning."

Madden turned his massive head toward Angela. "Burrows and Edward Garrett argued last week. What about?"

Out of the corner of her eye, Vicky watched Angela shaking her head. Burrows and Garrett again, she was thinking. The missing man and the dead man, and Detective Madden pursuing a connection.

"How would I know?" Angela said. "I thought they were friends."

"Come on, Angela. You were Skip's secretary and lover. What did Skip tell you about the argument?"

"Nothing!" Vicky felt the girl's cold fingers on her arm. "Tell him, Vicky! I don't know what they argued about."

"You heard her," Vicky said to Madden.

"How many appointments did Garrett make with your boss?"

"Appointments?" Angela gave a shriek of laughter. "People just walk in. I don't remember how many times Garrett came in. A couple of times last week."

"Before that?"

"He showed up from time to time."

"Any idea what Garrett wanted?"

"Any legal work Burrows did for Garrett would be confidential," Vicky said. "My client has already told you she doesn't know anything about it."

"Well, I'm having a hard time buying it, Counselor. It's been my experience secretaries pretty much know everything. More than the boss, lots of times." Madden looked back at Angela. "I'm thinking there was bad blood between Burrows and Garrett. Maybe your boss had reason to want Edward Garrett dead."

"That's crazy," Angela said. "How could Skip have anything to do with some guy getting shot in the parade? He was with me all weekend. In Jackson . . ."

Vicky cut in: "You don't have to say any more."

"I'm not going to let him blame Skip for something he didn't do." A steely resolve came into Angela's voice. "We were together all weekend. We didn't hear about the murder 'til we were driving back to Lander and the radio announcer said Garrett was dead. Skip was shocked. He pulled over the car and we just sat there on the side of the highway. He couldn't believe it. He kept saying, 'I don't believe it.'"

Madden took his time. Scribbling, reading what he'd written, scribbling some more. He flipped a page and smoothed out the next one. "What about the money Skip cleared out of the bank Friday afternoon? Four hundred thousand dollars. A lot of money, wouldn't you say?"

"What do I know about any money?"

Vicky could feel her stomach muscles tighten. Both Garrett and Burrows had cleaned out their bank accounts. Coincidences had a way of seeming normal, part of a regular routine, which made them easy to overlook, deadly. *All things work together*, Grandmother had said. *All things are connected.*

Madden was staring at Angela. "Did he have the money with him in Jackson?"

"How is my client supposed to know that?" Vicky said. She was thinking the girl knew a lot that she hadn't mentioned.

"Extra suitcase, briefcase he took special care of?"

Angela had gone quiet, sunk inside herself, like a little girl swallowed in the chair. "Briefcase." She exhaled the word. "He kept a briefcase in the trunk. I asked him why he'd brought work on the weekend. He laughed and said I shouldn't worry about it."

"What does any of this have to do with my client?" Vicky knew the answer even before she had finished the question. Someone who knew about the money could have arranged for Skip Burrows to be abducted. Angela was full of half-truths and evasions. If the girl had sneaked a look inside the briefcase, she would have known about the money.

WAVES OF HEAT rolled across the asphalt; the inside of the Ford was like a crematorium. Vicky could feel her heart hammering like a drum in her temples. She didn't trust herself to say anything to the girl crouched on the passenger seat until they had pulled out of the parking lot and headed down a side street through the shade of overhanging branches. "You didn't tell me about the briefcase. What else haven't you told me?" She tried for a neutral tone. Angela Running Bear wasn't the first client to conceal information.

"I didn't think it was important." The girl shifted around, and, for a moment, Vicky had the sense that if she pressed too hard, Angela would bolt. Throw open the door and jump.

"I can't help you if you don't trust me. You knew Skip had four hundred thousand dollars with him."

Angela didn't say anything.

Vicky could feel the girl's eyes lasering in on her. She tried again to swallow her anger. "Did you and Skip have plans for the future?"

"Plans to get out of here."

Vicky took a right turn. The white Victorian was halfway down the block.

"Why did Skip want to leave? He had a good practice, a life here."

"He hated it here. He wanted to be free. No clients, no phones ringing. Free as the breeze. We were gonna take off. See some of the big world. Get the hell off the rez."

"What about Deborah Boynton?"

Angela didn't say anything. She had turned away and was staring out the window.

"Skip's former girlfriend." Vicky pushed on. "Was she still in the picture?"

"No."

Vicky tapped on the brake and turned into the narrow driveway. "I think you know Skip was still seeing her. Is Madden right? Did he break up with you?"

"I told you, Skip loved me. We were going away together. We were going to live in Mexico."

"When, Angela? Did he say when that would happen?"

"When everything was ready."

Vicky pulled up close to the small house. "Do you mean when he had the money? Is that why he cleaned out his bank account? Was he getting ready to leave?"

"I don't know. I don't know anything." Angela yanked on the handle and pushed open the door.

"You need a lawyer you can trust," Vicky said.

Angela had started to get out. She turned back. "What? You're dumping me? Lawyers can't dump people whenever they want. Skip never did that."

"You're holding out on me. I can't work with secrets." God,

what did this black-eyed girl blinking back the tears know? Murder? Abduction? What was she involved in? "I'm trying to level with you. I may have a conflict of interest here. For your own good, you need another lawyer, someone you can open up with. Maybe you should think about going back to the rez for a while."

Angela jumped out and leaned down, peering into the Ford, eyes fierce and blazing. "You don't know me. You don't know anything about me. Don't tell me what to do. You're not on the rez. You got off. I'm not going back."

The girl slammed the door and marched across the patch of dried grass, head high and shoulders square. Vicky waited until she had disappeared into the little house before she backed onto the street. She was thinking she had never wanted to get off the rez and leave everything behind. Kids, parents, grandparents, the ceremonies and celebrations, the sense of home and belonging. It had just happened.

18

THE BALL FLEW high but shallow to center field. Father John watched Jimmy Feathers position under the ball, glove up and ready, eyes never leaving the ball. He had it, and with a quick crow hop, he fired it into his cutoff man, Jeremy Antelope, positioned just below the pitcher's mound. Jeremy held the ball because the runner on third base never tried to tag up and score. Had he tried, he would have been out thrown. This was the best team Father John had ever fielded. Strong, dedicated, talented kids determined to be winners. He could see himself in them: Martin Whiteman on the pitcher's mound, tall and scrawny, the way Father John had been, stars dancing in the kid's eyes about pitching for the Rockies. Father John had dreamed of pitching for the Red Sox, but the dream was the same.

"Batter up!" he called, waving over Rex Black Wolf. Today's practice was batting and fielding and keeping the eye on the ball.

The essentials never changed. So far the Eagles were 10–0, but the season was still early, and the Riverton team was out to break the winning streak on Saturday. It would be the Eagles' biggest challenge so far. "Let's see what you've got," Father John said. Then he shouted to Martin. "Don't hold back. Make him work for it."

Martin fired a couple of pitches hard and inside to Rex, who swung and missed. "Weight back! Focus!" Father John shouted. Next up in the batter's box was Lester Makepeace. Behind him should have been Ollie StandingCloud. The two boys were like twins, one always following the other. Rex connected with a loud whack and sent a single up the middle. Rex rounded first while the center fielder scrambled, then threw the ball to second base, forcing Rex to trot back, settling for a solid single.

Father John cupped his hands around his mouth and shouted out to the field. "Good work. Let's keep going. We'll show Riverton what we've got." Indian kids, he was thinking. They would get a lot of razzing in town. *Hey, Injun. How'd you get off the rez? Go back where you belong.*

He started to motion up Lester. "Where's your buddy?" he said. No sign of Ollie in the dugout. Sometimes Ollie's mom watched practice, but she wasn't there today with the other mothers scattered around the bleachers.

Lester shrugged and sprinted over to home plate, bent his knees, shifted his weight back, fidgeted with his bat, and got ready for the pitch. He tipped the first ball and sent it over the backstop. On the next pitch, he connected and drove a monster fly ball deep into right field that finally dropped into the tall grasses behind the residence. The right fielder and center fielder were chasing it while Rex rounded third base with Lester close on his heels. Rex was safe. Lester dove for home. Father John patted both boys on the back and walked them over to the dugout. "That's the kind of aggressive baserunning I want to see," he said. "Think Ollie's going to make practice?" He looked at Lester.

"He's walking over."

"Walking over?" When he'd checked the temperature before practice started, it was ninety-three degrees with a hot, dry breeze. The kid lived at least eight to ten miles out in the center of the rez. Father John motioned up the next batter.

"His mom's gone again," Lester whispered, as if he didn't want the rest to know. It wasn't anybody else's business.

"How long has she been gone?"

The kid shrugged. "I don't know. Two or three days."

"Who's looking after Ollie?"

"He looks after himself pretty good. He didn't want to miss practice."

Father John patted the kid's shoulder and walked over to the bleachers. Judy, Lester's mom, was seated between two other women. He was about to climb up through the seats when she started down, as if she'd divined that he wanted to talk to her. "Can you take over for a little while?" he said.

She nodded and jumped off the lower bench. "Keep them batting and chasing after the ball in the field," he said. "When everybody in the dugout's had another turn at bat, change them around."

She nodded. He could see the mixture of curiosity and concern working through her face, but she didn't say anything. It wasn't polite to ask for a gift, and information was always a gift. He went over to the cooler, took out a bottle of cold water, and headed down the baseline, breaking into a jog when he'd reached third base. He jogged past the residence and out across Circle Drive. The pickup was parked in front of the administration building. Two minutes later he had cleared the tunnel of cottonwoods and turned west onto Seventeen-Mile Road.

He drove hunched over the wheel, scanning both sides of the road. It was dangerous to walk along the edge of Seventeen-Mile Road. No one did it, unless he was drunk. Father John had gone about six miles when he saw the small, dark figure shimmering like a mirage ahead. Coming across the open, sunburned prairie, through the sage brush, running a little, then walking. Father John pressed down on the gas pedal and sped ahead until he'd drawn parallel with the kid. He slammed to a stop, jumped out, and ran around the pickup, waving both hands in the air. "Ollie!" he shouted. "Over here, Ollie."

The kid pulled up, like a pony reined to a stop. He looked over, waved, and then started running toward the road. Sweat glistened on his face and neck and sopped the front of his tee shirt when he got to the pickup, and Father John handed him the bottle of water. "Get in," he said, walking around to the driver's side. "I'll take you to practice."

"Thanks, Father." Ollie crawled inside and sank down, as if he might melt into the seat. He had already gulped half the bottle of water. "How'd you know?"

Father John waited for an old sedan to lumber past, then made a U-turn. He wasn't sure what Ollie would think about his friend divulging the truth. "We coaches have our ways," he said, glancing over and smiling.

The kid finished off the water and looked out the window. The sagebrush looked like rolling tumbleweeds; the plains passed like waves of a brown ocean. "Lester tell you my mom took off?"

"I heard it somewhere," Father John said. "When do you think she'll come back?"

"Soon's she runs out of money."

"You eating okay?"

Out of the corner of his eye, he saw the kid give a noncommittal shrug. "We got cereal, and I been making myself bologna sandwiches," Ollie said. The wind blowing through the open windows chopped at his voice. "Got some Coke to drink."

Father John didn't say anything. Ollie had told him enough. He could fill in the blanks. Claire was an alcoholic, a binge drinker, sober most of the time. A mom in the bleachers watching practice and the games, hugging Ollie after every win, tears of pride in her eyes. Then she was gone. Two days, three days, until, as Ollie said, the money ran out. Alcoholics were different, no two cut out of the same cloth, all drinking in their own way.

He slowed for the turn into the cottonwoods. "Anybody you can stay with for a while? Family?"

Ollie was quiet until they emerged onto Circle Drive. "My uncle went to North Dakota to work construction. I got an auntie, but she's left the rez for good."

Father John pulled up at the administration building and got out. He tried to sort out the family tree. He had known Marcia Running Bear before she died, and he knew her daughter Claire. He had heard of another daughter, but he had never met her.

The kid had jumped out and fallen in beside him as they walked back along the side of the residence to the baseball field. The sharp whack of a bat against leather and the shouts of kids broke through the wind. A hot gust spewed dust on the dirt path and slapped at Father John's face. He pulled his cowboy hat down hard. It struck him that he knew who the other daughter was. Her name had been in the *Gazette*.

"Angela?"

"She's in Lander." The kid took long strides, pulling ahead toward practice and baseball and the rest of the team as if he were coming home. "She don't want nothing to do with us," he said. "Can't blame her none." He took off running, hands in the air like a sprinter breaking past the final ribbon.

"Hey, Ollie." Judy ruffled the kid's hair. "Your turn to bat."

"How'd it go?" Father John said.

"Outfielders definitely need more work. Those Riverton kids can really hit." She stepped away from the dugout, watching him over her shoulder, and he followed her. "Lester finally told me," she said, throwing a glance over at Ollie, who was hunched over home plate, ready for the pitch. "He said Ollie didn't want anybody to know. The kid is independent as a mule. Whole family's like that. He can stay at our place until Claire gets back."

"That's good of you."

"She always comes back, you know."

FROM CIRCLE DRIVE, Father John could feel the vibrations in Eagle Hall. He rounded the corner of the church and stopped on the graveled strip that separated the church from the hall, trying Angela Running Bear's number again on his cell. The evening was hot, the front door to the hall thrown open. The loud thumping noise of what passed for music blasted the air. He stepped back a few feet and pressed the phone hard against his ear. The sky was alive with the sunset—reds, magentas, oranges, pinks streaking over the reservation. Over the faint buzz of a cell ringing somewhere in Lander, he heard the gravel crunch behind him and wheeled about. A pickup with three teenagers in the front and four in the bed shot past and slid to a stop. The kids started piling out, like puppies scrambling out of a box. Waving at him, hollering at one another, white teeth flashing in dark faces. They disappeared into the dark figures moving about inside Eagle Hall.

"Hi! This is Angela." There was a strained note of cheer in the voice. "Love to talk to you, so leave the details. Will get back ASAP."

He ended the call and slipped the phone into the back pocket of his jeans. He'd been trying to get hold of Ollie's aunt for the past couple of hours. He had memorized her message and left at least three of his own. No response. A strange feeling settled inside him. It wasn't like Arapahos to turn their backs on family. Not like an auntie to ignore her nephew. He told himself the young woman had her own troubles. He'd followed the article in the *Gazette* yesterday morning. Skip Burrows, prominent lawyer in Lander, abducted from his office. It had been Angela Running Bear, his secretary, who'd found the man gone and the office in disarray.

He headed across the gravel, drawn and repulsed by the loud noise at the same time. Last year he'd started a social evening for teenagers. Eagle Hall, all the food and soft drinks they could consume, their own music—God knows, they wouldn't have liked his—a place to be with friends. A safe place. More and more kids came each week, and he'd had to put out an SOS to the mission's donors. *Need help keeping the teenage evenings going.* It was truly amazing the amount of food they could consume.

Some of the kids were dancing at one end of the hall. The other end was set up with Ping-Pong, billiards, and a video game that one of the merchants in Lander had donated. Seated on metal chairs along the side walls, sipping Cokes, were three men he'd asked to keep an eye on the party tonight. Two were dads, the other an uncle. On the opposite wall was a table piled with food overseen by several moms and grandmothers. Usually older kids, some pushing twenty, would drop by because . . . He shook his head at the thought pulsing inside him. Because there was nothing else to do. One of the older kids was showing a younger kid how to grip a Ping-Pong paddle. Even the bishop had stopped by. Seemed the bishop enjoyed playing Ping-Pong. He was showing two kids who looked about thirteen how to play.

Father John made his way around the hall, chatting with the adults, high-fiving a couple of the kids, watching the bishop show the boy how to slam back a serve. He helped himself to a cookie and thanked the women for preparing the food—stacks of hot dogs and fry bread, chips with melted cheese, cake, cookies, and coolers of soda.

"It's good," Imelda Plenty Horses said, gripping his hand. *"Ni isini."*

He left the music pounding, the kids swaying, gathering in groups, breaking apart, moving on to other groups. The noise receded, filled in by the soft whoosh of the wind as he walked back along the graveled path. He took the concrete steps to the administration building two at a time, fished the keys out of his jeans pocket, and let himself into the coolness of the corridor.

In his office, he pulled out his cell and tried Angela's number again, dropping into the chair at his desk. The buzzing noise, the same forced cheerfulness in the voice, the familiar message only reinforced the uncomfortable feeling he couldn't shake. "Father O'Malley calling again," he said. "I thought you'd like to know your nephew Ollie is staying with the Makepeace family." He paused. He had already told her everything. "Let me know if I can be of any help." He had the sense that he was speaking into a black void.

19

FATHER JOHN OPENED the laptop on his desk, tapped the on button. The screen turned bright blue. He could feel the music vibrating through the floorboards of the old building. Finally the icons danced into place. The laptop was several years old now and slow, a relic, he supposed, but he had grown fond of it; he knew its ways.

He clicked on the browser, glanced at the silent mobile he had set next to the laptop, and tried to ignore the uneasy feeling. He forced his thoughts back to this afternoon in the RV camp. A whole camp of reenactors without a leader, no doubt wondering what might come next, which events would be canceled. A season of appearances lost. The most important event, the reenactment at the site of the Battle of the Little Bighorn—how could it take place without Custer?

And Veraggi and Osborne, slouched in webbed chairs, drinking beer. Veraggi's eyes reddened with inebriation. Osborne's mannered way of steadying himself. Across the road, Belinda Clark had been tight-lipped, shaking with anger. So much animosity toward the men who had been with her husband when he died. She had seemed to alternate between anger at the murder of Edward Garrett and anger at the death of Custer.

He wasn't sure what he was looking for, yet something about Edward Garrett's widow had stayed with him, like a sharp burr in his skin. *Just sat on their horses and let my husband die!* Veraggi and Osborne? Because they'd happened to ride side-by-side with Garrett? They said they'd had all they could do to control the bucking, rearing horses spooked by the circling Indians. It hadn't surprised them to see Garrett on the street. They assumed he had fallen. What had surprised them was that they had managed to stay mounted and weren't on the street with him.

He wondered who Belinda had been referring to. The red-eyed, inebriated men in webbed chairs, or Benteen and Reno, two men in history? A vague memory floated through his mind like a moth, hard to pin down, from the American history classes he had taught. After the battle, a short-lived, national outpouring of grief for the loss of Custer and his troops had erupted across the country. But there had been something else: hints and rumors that blamed Custer for the army's worst defeat in the Indian Wars. Then Libbie Custer had stepped into the controversy and spent the rest of her life—fifty years, if he remembered correctly—defending her husband's reputation. Father John had read that army officers who blamed Custer for the loss of his troops had backed off out of respect for another officer's widow. Custer became an American icon. The brave, faultless leader massacred by savage Indians. Libbie had never forgiven Benteen and Reno for not coming to her husband's defense. *They had let him die.*

Father John typed "Benteen and Reno, Battle of the Little Big-horn" in the search box. The thumping sounds of music had stopped. The teenage party was breaking up. He could hear engines coughing into life, tires spitting gravel, kids shouting and laughing. Dozens of Web sites materialized. It would take hours to read through them all. He clicked on a site and read how Benteen and Reno had been under siege, pinned down on Reno Hill. It had been impossible for them to come to Custer's aid.

But that wasn't the whole story, he knew. Maybe they could have joined Custer earlier, before they were pinned down. Is that what Libbie had blamed them for? Was it possible Benteen and Reno could have helped Custer, and chose not to? Could Libbie have been right?

Indians weren't the only ones that hated Custer. He could hear Lou Morningside's voice in his head. He refined the search by deleting the Battle of the Little Bighorn and adding Washita to Benteen and Reno. There it was, halfway down the first page:

Animosity developed between General Custer and his sub-commanders, especially Captain Frederick Benteen. During the battle, Benteen's friend, Major Joel Elliott, had taken sixteen men and gone after escaping warriors. The attack on the Washita raged on until the 7th had destroyed the small Cheyenne camp, burned the tipis and winter food supplies and slaughtered the pony herd—seven hundred horses. By the time Custer and the 7th pulled out, the ground was littered with bodies of dead Cheyennes. The frozen bodies of Chief Black Kettle and his wife floated in the Washita River. There was no sign of Major Elliott and his detail.

When Custer gave the order to turn the cavalry around,

Benteen inquired whether the general intended to send a detail out looking for Major Elliott and his troops. The general refused. Weeks later, Custer and his men returned to the Washita. Two miles from the site of the Cheyenne camp, in the tall grass, they found the bodies of Major Elliott and all of his men. To Benteen, Custer's abandonment of Elliott and the troops was unforgivable, a black mark on the regiment, a decision on the part of the general that he could never forgive. Later, Benteen would write that, one day, Custer's recklessness would doom the 7th Cavalry.

Father John closed the site and stared at the long list of other sites. Debates among historians, theories, conjunctures. Nothing in history was easy or clear-cut, or settled. Everything was subject to new interpretations. What had actually taken place at the Little Bighorn? What had been going on in the minds of Benteen and Reno? No one would ever know. But Libbie Custer *thought* she knew.

He shut down the computer and walked over to the window, aware for the first time of the evening quiet settling over the mission. The kids gone. The grandmothers had packed up the leftovers and driven away. They would take the food to the elders who might be running low on food. Light from the streetlamps flared over Circle Drive. It was still hot outside, he was sure, even though the thick old walls of the administration building kept his office cool. His thoughts kept running back to Belinda Clark. How much of Libbie Custer's belief about Benteen and Reno had influenced Belinda? Did she really blame Veraggi and Osborne for not coming to her husband's aid? Or was it Benteen and Reno she blamed?

My God. He was in a house of mirrors, with reflections that

twisted and turned back on themselves, bursting into the present and resolving into the past. But maybe it was simpler than he'd realized. Maybe what Veraggi and Osborne had said was closer to the truth—Belinda Clark only wanted her husband's money.

A shadow appeared at the edges of the light, moving across the field of grass in the center of Circle Drive. It was a moment before he could make out a horse and rider, the rider bent over the horse's neck, reins loosened. The horse turned left, crossed Circle Drive, and disappeared past the corner of the building. He could hear the steady, rhythmic scrape of hooves on gravel.

He left on the light in the corridor, went outside, and locked the front door. The wind gusted around him, hot and dry, crackling in the branches of the cottonwoods. He walked over to the driveway between the administration building and the church and stopped, listening for the sounds of hooves, the whinny of a horse. Nothing. Arrows of light shot from two streetlamps that stood across from each other, and a lattice of shadows fell over the driveway. The door to Eagle Hall was closed, but he walked over and tried the knob. One of the grandmothers had locked up. He headed down the driveway toward the guesthouse, windows dark and cotton-wood branches dancing against the white stucco walls. He tried that door. Also locked. Then he started back. A quick movement at the far corner of the church! He hoisted himself over the log fence that closed off a patch of wild grasses and made his way alongside the back of the building.

"Who's there?" he called. People came to the mission for all sorts of reasons. Running away from abuse. Struggling with problems—alcohol, drugs, gambling. Looking for counseling. Looking for food. Someone had ridden in here tonight and looped the reins of the brown horse around the top log of the fence. The horse shifted and stamped its feet and snorted into the wind. There was no saddle. The rider had ridden bareback, which took a lot of skill. A lot of experience and confidence with horses.

He patted the horse's shoulder. Clammy and hot. The animal needed to be brushed and cooled down. He glanced around, half expecting the rider to jump out of the shadows, but there was no sign of anyone. He retraced his steps and, at the beginning of the driveway, turned left and took the concrete steps in front of the church two at a time. The door hung open a couple of inches, and he pushed it wide open. The interior was dark except for the tiny red light flickering in front of the small, white, deerskin tipi that served as the tabernacle at the side of the altar. He waited in the vestibule a moment, listening for the sounds of movement, of breathing. The church was silent, but he could sense the presence of someone in the shadows. He moved into the church and opened the door to the confessional on the right. It was empty.

"Hello?" His voice echoed around the empty pews. The stained glass windows glowed in the dim light from outside. For an instant, he thought he heard the scuff of a boot, the rustle of someone adjusting his position. "I saw you ride in," he said, starting down the center aisle. He knew the small church—a chapel, really—by heart. The soft sound of his footsteps on the carpet, the faint smells of incense and sage. He could have found his way blindfolded. "How can I help you?"

He heard the slight movement then, like a nervous twitch. Up ahead in the front pews. He kept his pace steady, glancing along the empty pews on either side. Before he reached the third pew, he spotted the hunched shape.

"What's going on, Mike?" He stepped into the pew and sat down beside the young man crumpled beside him. He'd guessed right. Not many men on the rez could handle a horse like Mike Longshot.

The young man let out a sob that sounded like a tire deflating. Face buried in his hands, looking as if he wished he could disappear into the wooden pew.

"Mike?" Father John set his hand on the man's shoulder. He could feel the tremors rising from somewhere deep within. "What happened?"

Another sobbing noise, and the tremors turned into shivers. Father John waited. He was used to waiting for a penitent in the confessional or someone he was counseling to muster the courage to unravel the pain or grief or fear that tied them into knots.

"They're coming for me." Mike lifted his head off the pew, leaned back, and stared straight ahead, as if he were talking to himself. "Tribal cops came by the store this morning looking for me. My shift didn't start 'til three this afternoon. Lucky my buddy called, so I got out of the house before they showed up. Took Brownie out of the corral and rode up into the hills and kept going. Stopped for a couple hours to let Brownie graze some sweetgrass. Took a nap by the creek. There's nowhere for me to go. Rode back by the house and Mom told me what they said. Scared her half to death. Said they wanted to talk to me about Garrett's murder. If I didn't come in voluntarily, they would issue an arrest warrant. Conspiracy to commit murder. They can't arrest you in a church, right?"

Father John was quiet a moment. He wasn't sure that if the BIA cops got wind Mike was hiding out, they wouldn't burst through the door, march down the aisle, and handcuff him. If they had an arrest warrant. He pushed the thought aside and tried to fit Mike Longshot's dilemma into a logical sequence that might have transpired. Colin Morningside had taken off. Was that what had directed the police attention to Mike, the only other Arapaho who had gone to hear Edward Garrett speak? The BIA Police might pick him up, but it was Madden who was investigating Garrett's murder. What had Detective Madden learned that made him want to talk to Mike again?

He could still picture Darleen Longshot in his study, her voice edged with hysteria. *The cops start getting too close, the warriors will give them Mikey.*

"Have you called Vicky Holden?"

Mike started shaking his head. "I was scared. She's in Lander. No way I'm crossing the border."

"She would come to you." It was the truth, he knew. She would go wherever she could help her people. "You can stay in the guesthouse tonight," he went on, parsing the implications. Mike hadn't been arrested; technically he wasn't a fugitive, which meant Father John wouldn't be hiding a fugitive. He shunted aside the thought that the Provincial might not agree. "First thing tomorrow morning, we'll call Vicky," he said.

FATHER JOHN FOUND a brush and some rags in the storage closet, and an old bucket that surprised him by its presence. While Mike brushed Brownie and wiped her down, he filled the bucket from the water spout at the side of the administration building, sloshing water on his boots and the legs of his blue jeans. He hopped the log fence again and lifted the bucket over. Mike dropped it in front of the horse. "Plenty of good grass here," he said, rubbing the rags across the horse's back as tenderly as if she were a child. "Good girl, good girl." He might have been singing a lullaby. "She's gonna be all right until morning."

They left the horse drinking out of the bucket and headed over to the guesthouse. Hopping the fence, walking down the driveway, boots scraping the gravel. Father John fished his keys out of his jeans pocket, opened the front door, and reached in to turn on the lights. A lamp flicked on next to the worn, sagging sofa that, at one time, he suspected, had been blue and was now the color of the cottonwood fleece that floated across the mission grounds.

"Did you eat?" he said as the young man stepped into the small living room.

Mike nodded. "Mom brought me dinner in the barn."

"Make yourself at home," Father John said. "Try not to worry." He could tell by the slope of the young man's shoulders that would be impossible. He closed the door and walked back through the shadows and light, down the driveway and across Circle Drive to the residence. Walks-On was waiting in the front hall. He followed the dog into the kitchen and let him out into the backyard. He would smell the horse, he was thinking and, sure enough, Walks-On bolted down the steps and started barking. What new, strange thing had come to the mission?

20

ANGELA BOLTED UPRIGHT. She held herself still, hardly breathing. A noise of some kind outside, but now there was nothing but quiet, shades pulled partway down, shadows on the driveway, an occasional car floating down the street like a ghost. She hadn't meant to fall asleep. She squinted at the bleary red numbers on the clock—1:33—as if they were a trick someone had played on her. She had intended to stay awake all night, waiting for the call. Everything set in her mind, as real as if it had already happened. As if the man in the black ski mask had called, and she had known his voice immediately, a voice from hell.

But the call hadn't come. She felt drained and limp, hair damp and matted against her head, eyes caked with sleep. She checked the messages on her mobile. Five calls from St. Francis Mission. She didn't know the priest at the mission. He was nothing to her. Why was he calling? She had wanted to scream, *Stop calling!* What if *he* was trying to call?

She sank back against the sofa. The call would come tonight. It had taken a while for the intruder to figure out what she had. He would have found what he was looking for on the computers. He had to make sure there were no copies. No flash drives. He had gone back to the office and searched in the desk drawers, the file drawers. Now there was only one other possibility. He would call.

Today had been a disaster. Madden sniffing around like an old dog. How long before he stumbled upon the possibility of a flash drive? The idea gripped her like a sudden, sharp pain. He could get a warrant, search her place, and what was she supposed to do? She had no lawyer. No one.

Her heart was thumping, and she made herself draw in a long breath. It was just as well Vicky Holden had dropped her. Always probing, insisting she was hiding something. Well, she was hiding the flash drive, and if Vicky had hung around any longer, she probably would have figured it out.

A scratching noise came from outside, as muffled and faint as a pebble rolling inside a drum. She felt her muscles tense. She pushed herself off the sofa bed, legs wobbly and unsure. She went to the front window and pulled back the edge of the stiff, grayish curtain. The odor of dust came at her. Through the slit between the curtain and the window frame, she scoured the outside. A faint light from the rear windows in the house fell over the driveway. Weeds sprouted through the cracks; a patch of grass looked like dried plastic. She could see the bumper of her car, but there were no other cars in sight. She let the curtain fall back and breathed in another whiff of dust. She was imagining things. She was upset, nervous, that was all; worried about Skip. The terrible waiting, the uncertainty.

Skip had probably assumed she'd left the flash drive in the office. The secretary carrying around a flash drive with all the office business on it? He would have been furious. So he must have told the man in the black mask it was in the office. But she had wanted to be sure there would be no more loss of documents. She had kept the flash drive with her. Now she would use it to free him. He would be proud of her.

The noise again. More distinct and rhythmic, footsteps on dry grass. She checked the front door to make sure she had thrown the lock. There was no bolt, just the button on the knob. She went back to the window and looked again through the slit. Nothing had changed; shadows blotted the driveway. She made her way past the sofa bed to the little alcove that jutted off the side of the house and peered past the window curtain, breathing in the dust. She stared at the black hulk of the hatchback, expecting someone or something—she didn't know what; an animal, maybe—to disturb the darkness. Nothing.

Except the noise, and this time she realized it came from the back of the house. She slipped past the kitchen counter, threw herself against the door, and jammed her thumb on the knob. The noise was loud, and confident. Confident footsteps planting themselves through the strip of dried grass outside.

VICKY WAS WIDE awake, staring into the darkness, aware of the uneasy feeling that gripped her. Beside her, Adam had settled into the steady breathing of deep, unconcerned sleep. She envied him. He could go to the office, handle the business, do what had to be done, and let it go. He could sleep. She couldn't let it go. The interview with Madden kept looping through her mind. A faint light shone past the blinds at the window; slats of black shadows lay over the walls. She couldn't erase the image of Madden: big head and bulky shoulders, pockmarked face. Another image of Angela, small and closed in on whatever she was hiding.

Vicky pushed back the sheet and slid out of bed. She settled herself on the window seat, grasped her legs against the coolness, and set her chin on her knees. She had told Adam about excusing herself as Angela's attorney, and he had agreed to call a friend—Lakota—in Casper. Caveat. Always a caveat with Adam. Angela would have to call Adam's friend. He wasn't an ambulance chaser; he didn't call prospective clients.

The feeling of unease tightened like a cramp in her stomach. She tried to put what she did know about Angela into some logical order. Logical order, the way John O'Malley did. She kept her gaze on Adam and the slow movement of his chest and pushed away the thought of John O'Malley. It had been months since any case had brought them together. Life had gone on, settled into its natural rhythms. Enough distance had opened between them that when she thought of John O'Malley, it was with profound respect. A man who had given up everything, dedicated himself to helping others. Who stayed on the path he had chosen.

She forced her thoughts back. Where was the logic in anything Angela Running Bear had done? Falling in love with her boss, a man twice her age involved with a real-estate agent in Riverton. A secretary who didn't know anything about the clients, the cases? There wasn't anything Annie didn't know about the office. There were times when Vicky thought Annie knew more than she did. More details, more irrelevant information about clients that proved to be relevant and important.

Angela knew something, and she was in love with Skip Burrows. And that led to the logical conclusion—God, she should have seen it earlier. Whatever Angela was hiding, she was covering for Skip Burrows.

Vicky shivered. The cool night air penetrated the apartment

and drove off the stuffiness and heat of the day. She pulled her knees closer to her chest. What did Angela know? That Skip had withdrawn money from the bank on Friday before they left for Jackson? The girl had seen the briefcase. Where was it now? In the trunk of Skip's missing car? Is that why he was abducted? Someone had seen him withdraw the money, followed him, waited until he came into the office Monday morning, and abducted him?

Then what was Angela hiding, if it wasn't the money? What was she covering up for him? Some case he was involved in? Something he was doing? Something his abductors knew about?

Vicky pitched herself off the bench and began tracing out a little circle between the bed and the window. She tried to focus on the abduction. Computers gone, backup gone, drawers and files ransacked. Whoever had taken Skip had intended to take something else. Had returned and searched the office again. Which meant he hadn't found what he wanted.

She made another circle, widening it to the dresser, the foot of the bed, the window. Adam was starting to stir, reaching across the bed, pawing at the empty space on her side. Then he flopped over. "Come back to bed," he said, before sinking back into sleep.

She kept circling. He hadn't gotten it all! Despite the computers and the backups, the intruder hadn't gotten it all. That was it: Angela had another backup she was hiding. Keeping for Skip. Probably a flash drive of some sort.

My God, the girl was playing a high-stakes game. She must have figured out she had what the abductor wanted, and thought she could trade it for Skip. But Skip Burrows could be dead. And whoever had taken him would come for Angela next.

*   *   *

THE MAN IN the black ski mask crashed through the door, which splintered and fell apart. Angela backed against the refrigerator, barely aware of the hard metal handle against her ribs. Someone was screaming, and she realized it was her voice. Screaming, crying, and shaking against the refrigerator as the man in the black ski mask moved along the counter like a snake. He stopped and looked down at her key ring—keys to the house, the car. The flash drive. He scooped them up and dropped them into the pocket of his black shirt.

There were a couple of feet between them, and Angela darted into the space, the screams surrounding her, and threw herself at the front door, but he was behind her, gripping her around the waist, arms like anvils, fists digging into her stomach, pulling her backward. A big, fleshy hand clamped over her mouth and nose and bent her head back until she thought it would snap off her neck. Arrows of pain shot through her. The screaming had stopped, leaving only the sounds of her own feet scraping the carpet as he dragged her backward. She scratched at the mask, at the white neck in the black shirt, the gloved hands tightening around her neck, blocking the air. A part of her draining away, water flowing over rocks. She couldn't breathe. Darkness had started to close around her. She was vaguely aware of the taste of blood and acid, the tightness in her nostrils, and the thick, heavy pain that exploded in her chest.

THE RINGING PHONE burst through the quiet. Vicky threw off the sheet and blanket and sat up, groping for the phone on the nightstand, a knot of dread tightening inside her. The numbers on the clock radio registered 2:40. Her fingers grasped the cold plastic receiver and lifted it to her ear. The ringing stopped.

"Madden here." The detective sounded wide awake, gruff, and to-the-point. "There's been some trouble."

"Who's calling at this hour?" Adam's voice was sleep-filled and groggy, muffled in the pillow.

"Angela?"

"We're at her place now."

We? Madden and who else?

"Your client, Angela Running Bear, has been murdered."

She closed her eyes and pictured a whole phalanx of police officers—plainclothes, uniforms, coroner's deputies. Cars stacked in the driveway; blue, red, and yellow roof lights twirling into the darkness.

"What is it?" Adam was sitting next to her, his arm like a cushion laid across her back.

"Murdered," she repeated. "When?"

"Who's been murdered?"

"About an hour ago. The landlady heard screaming and called 911. An officer responded within ten minutes, but there was no one on the premises. The back door had been broken in. Angela was on the floor."

"Oh my God." Vicky leaned into Adam's shoulder. "Angela," she whispered.

"Who do you think did it?"

"The man in the black mask, Madden. He came looking for . . ." She hesitated. She had no proof. Angela had never admitted to holding on to a backup of any kind, and yet Vicky was sure it was true. "Flash drive. Did you find a flash drive in the house?"

"We're not done looking yet."

"You won't find it."

"We need to contact family on the rez. Can you help us out?"

"I'm on my way."

She was in the bathroom now, unsure of how she had gotten there. The receiver lay on the counter next to the sink. She could hear the dull buzzing noise as she splashed cold water in her face. Adam stood in the doorway. She could sense his presence looming behind her.

"Why are you going over there? You don't have to go. You told me you weren't representing her."

"She was murdered." Vicky splashed cold water inside her mouth, as if she could wash away the word. She swung toward Adam. "Murdered, Adam! She was helpless and alone, and a man in a black mask murdered her."

"Let the police handle it."

"Someone has to tell her family."

"You told me you don't even know them."

"I know who they are." She brushed past him, slipped out of her nightgown, and started pulling on jeans and a tee shirt from the pile on the floor.

"For godssakes, Vicky. You don't have to go."

She stuffed her feet into sandals and hurried past him down the hallway, grabbing her bag off the kitchen counter as she went. She slammed the door and ran for the elevator, pushing the call button again and again until the cage cranked and rattled upward and the doors parted. She leaned against the cold metal panel inside the cage, watching the doors close and feeling the steady pull of gravity. "It's who I am." She mopped at the moisture on her cheeks. "It's who I am."

21

THE HOUSE LOOKED like a stage prop: lights shining in the windows, blue and yellow police lights revolving over the exterior, stagehands in dark uniforms, everything suffused in unreality. Vicky slid to a stop alongside an SUV with Fremont County Coroner in black letters across the doors. Her headlights splayed over the front of the house. The door opened, a blur of dark figures moving about inside, and Detective Madden outside talking to a tall man in a cowboy hat. It always came as a surprise, the way John O'Malley knew what was going on with her people before she did.

She got out of the car and walked through the kaleidoscope of shadows and light, conscious of the way the two men stopped talking and turned partway toward her. "What happened to her?" she said.

"Coroner says the marks on the body indicate she was strangled. The killer burst through the back door."

The body! Vicky looked away. The dark uniforms coming and going, boots scratching gravel. Somewhere inside the house was the lifeless body of a girl, Angela Running Bear. Vicky could see the hard set of her jaw and eyes as she'd gotten out of the Ford only a few hours ago, the rigid line of her back as she'd hurried into the little house. Scared and obstinate, determined to find her own way, to be someone, to live.

"I'm sorry, Vicky." A calm depth of understanding shone in John O'Malley's eyes. How much she had missed him these past months. Missed the understanding that passed between them without the need for explanations.

Madden cleared his throat, his forehead furrowed with thought. This afternoon, Vicky was thinking, he had been interviewing Angela across a table. An ordinary interview, the kind that took place every day. People didn't walk away and die. "We won't know for certain what happened until we get the autopsy results. The landlady . . ." He shot a glance across the top of a police car to an older-looking woman with gray hair straggling from the bun at the back of her head. She stood with arms folded across her middle and neck craned toward the house. The colored lights revolved over her face, and Vicky saw the look of betrayal, as if Angela, in her murder, had defiled the property.

Madden was going on about how the landlady had called 911 at 1:45 and reported screaming in the rental house. "Wasn't the first call."

"Tonight?"

"She had called around eleven thirty. Reported a window peeper. Not unusual for her. She had a habit of calling 911, complaining about suspicious persons nosing around, loud music in the rental. Nuisance calls. Everything bothered her. We showed up when we had the time. A patrol car swung by tonight after the first call, didn't see anyone about. But the next call . . ." He let the words trail off and focused on the officers gathering in the doorway. "Dispatcher thought something was different. She claimed there was a disturbance in the rental house. She was sure the man she'd seen peering into the windows must have broken in. Says she had gotten a good look at his face in the light of the windows. A car was here in five minutes. It was too late. The perpetrator was gone. We've made casts of boot prints. He was in and out of here in a hurry. Doesn't look like he left anything behind."

"You're sure it was a man?"

"Or a very strong woman. The girl put up a fight. She was dragged about ten feet from the front door."

"Did you find any computer flash drives?"

The detective was shaking his head. "I wouldn't say a definite no. It will take a while to go through the house. We found her cell." He swung toward John O'Malley. "Looks like you had been trying to reach her. Must be three or four messages about her nephew."

"I thought she'd like to know where he was staying."

"Somebody else was real anxious to talk to her. Left six messages. Last one said he was going to come and get her. Colin Morningside. Made himself real scarce today. On his way to the Sioux, I suspect. Looks like he changed his mind and came back."

Vicky caught the flicker of surprise on John O'Malley's face. So Madden knew Colin Morningside had left the rez, which meant the police were talking to Colin and Mike Longshot and the other warriors in the parade.

Someone had opened the rear doors on the coroner's SUV, and the shadowy figures in the doorway started rolling out a gurney. The lumps of a small body poked through the body bag. Madden threw up a hand, stepped over, and said something to the attendants. Then he motioned to John O'Malley.

Vicky followed Father John over to the gurney. So many murders and wrongful, stupid deaths, so many times she had found herself at a crime scene with John O'Malley. She could predict what would come next. She could have closed her eyes and watched what he would do. An attendant had zipped the bag back enough to expose Angela's face. She might have been sleeping but for the dark smudges about her neck, as if someone had dabbed mascara on the wrong places.

John O'Malley lifted his hand over Angela's face and made the sign of the cross. "May the Great Spirit have mercy on your soul," he said. "May all His angels and spirits lead you into the next world, and may you find peace and joy in the everlasting love that He promised through his son, Jesus."

A soft chorus of *amens* came through the shadows, followed by the ripping sound of the zipper and the crackling of the body bag as the attendants lifted Angela into the SUV. A uniformed officer, like a guard, waited until the attendants had stepped back, then slammed the doors.

"Any family, besides the nephew?" Madden said.

"She has a sister on the rez," Father John said. "I'm not sure she's around, but I can check."

Madden nodded. "I'd appreciate it."

John O'Malley gave Vicky a slow, comprehending look, as if he knew what she would say and was merely waiting to hear the words.

"I'll go with you."

*   *   *

"WHAT DO YOU know about Angela's sister?" Vicky sat in the passenger seat of the Toyota pickup that rattled and shook around her. She had offered to drive, but she hadn't pushed the matter. A deep tiredness dragged at her arms and legs. She represented Garrett's widow. She had been so intent on distancing herself from Angela Running Bear after she'd realized there could be a connection between Burrows's disappearance and Garrett's murder. The conflict of interest had weighed on her like a heavy coat. She hadn't bothered to get to know the girl. Who had she been close to? Who cared about her? Everyone on the rez knew the Running Bear family, stalked by tragedy. Mother murdered, grandparents dead. A sister who may or may not be around. Pieces of information floating like debris in the wind.

"I've met Claire a few times," John said. "Her son, Ollie, plays for the Eagles. Nice kid. The kind who has a sense of what he wants."

"And he wants off the rez?" They had crossed the border, following the headlight beams through the darkness on Blue Sky Highway.

"His mother left him alone."

"Drinking?"

"Ollie's learned how to get along. His mother wasn't around today."

"So he's staying with somebody else."

"The Makepeace family."

Arranged by you, Vicky was thinking. A white man so close to her people, his life so intertwined with theirs that she wondered how either would manage when he left. They followed the curve of the headlights right onto Seventeen-Mile Road, driving east. Then left toward a cluster of small houses. John slowed the pickup

and turned through the borrow ditch into a dirt yard. The headlights swept past the hulk of an old pickup, what looked like a
washing machine turned on its side, and a carton with bottles poking out of the top. The house looked dark and closed up. Another
pickup stood near the front door. Little points of red lights flitted
above the pickup bed.

"Wait here," John said, swinging out. He left the motor running, headlights cutting across the back of the pickup.

Vicky opened her door and got out. The faint noise of giggling
and the slurred sound of voices drifted in the air. "Hello!" John
called.

The red dot of a cigarette rose out of the pickup bed, and behind it, the head and wide shoulders of a man caught in the headlights. "Who's there?" The voice strained with the effort to sound
sober. The second red light also floated upward with a woman's
voice, bleary and full of alcohol. "You cops? We haven't done anything wrong." A bottle clinked against the pickup bed.

"Claire? It's Father John and Vicky Holden."

The woman seemed to snap to attention, as if the alcohol had
drained from her body and left her sober. "What do you want?
Ollie's all right. Nothing's happened to my boy. He's sleeping in the
house."

"Ollie's staying with Lester Makepeace."

"What? He's sleeping inside. I checked on him. You think I
don't care about my kid? I love that boy more than anything."

Except alcohol, Vicky thought.

"You never checked on the kid yet." The man took a long draw
from the cigarette and the red light flared against his face. A cloud
of smoke rose around his head. "You was gonna check on him
soon's we finished the bottle."

"That's a big, fat lie!"

"We're here about Angela," Vicky said.

"My know-it-all, higher-than-God sister? Too good for us. Got off the rez like a bat outta hell, said she was never coming back. Like white people were gonna treat her good. Like they give a hoot about Indians. What's she gone and gotten herself mixed up in?"

John O'Malley moved closer to the side of the pickup, as if he wanted to be ready to reach for the woman, steady her. "I'm sorry, Claire. Your sister was killed tonight."

The woman sank against the rear window of the cab. Her eyes rolled back until she was staring out of white sockets. John took hold of her hand as the man beside her slipped an arm around her shoulders and pulled her into his chest.

"You better know what you're talking about, coming out here and scaring her to death."

"The police found Angela's body at her place a while ago."

The woman made a rhythmic, muffled noise into the man's shirt.

"I'm sorry," Father John said again.

"Who done it?"

"The police don't know."

"They're never gonna find out. Arapaho girl killed? Who cares?" Claire lifted her head and made an effort to turn sideways. Eyes black and wild looking now. "What'd he do to her?"

"The coroner believes she was strangled."

"Who do you think might have done it?" Vicky said.

"Take your pick. Any white man in town. I told her, stay away. Nothing good's gonna happen to you across the border. Keep with your own people."

"Is there anything we can do for you?" John O'Malley said.

The Indian man gave him a long, appraising look. "I'm gonna take care of her just fine. We don't need your help." He cocked his head toward Vicky. "Yours, either. Go back to your white friends."

JOHN BACKED THE pickup out of the yard and onto the road, then shifted into drive and drove north, deeper into the rez. "Colin will want to know. He left this morning, but Lou will know how to reach him." He gave her a sideways glance. "Colin's a person of interest in Garret's murder. Copspeak," he said. "I knew he'd gotten scared after Madden wanted to interview him a second time. Mike Longshot is also scared. They were the only Arapahos who went to the theater to hear Garrett speak. He went on and on about Custer's exploits. I can't blame either Colin or Mike for being upset."

"Upset enough to kill the man?"

John O'Malley shook his head. "Upset enough to want to be absolutely sure they wanted to teach him a lesson, remind him of what happened at the Little Bighorn." A faint pink light had begun to glow in the eastern sky, and the headlights searched the pink haze. Vicky felt his eyes on her again. "They both need a lawyer," he said. "Mike's staying at the guesthouse. I told him I'd bring him to your office tomorrow."

Vicky was quiet a long moment. How to explain? The words fell away. "I can't help him. I can't help either of them." She could sense the disappointment and questions in the silence between them. "I'm representing Garrett's widow," she heard herself say. Representing a white woman, when her own people needed her. How had it come to this? Maybe Claire and her boyfriend were right. She had become like a white person. "It would be a conflict of interest," she managed. "There are other lawyers."

"Adam?"

"He's too close to me."

John flinched, she thought, but then she told herself she had imagined it.

22

THE SKY FELL all around in long streaks of red, magenta, pink, and orange. Sunrise always brought a sense of renewal, Vicky thought. A new day, new opportunities, new things coming, but not this morning. This morning she kept her eyes straight ahead. An occasional house passed, bathed in pink. John had flipped the switch on the CD player on the seat and the music of some opera—*Cosi fan tutte*, he had told her—drifted over the hum of the tires. She was grateful not to have to keep up a conversation. It had always been like that with John O'Malley. Often there was no need to talk.

The hard knot of failure tightened inside her. She could see Angela's face, still and final. No more experiences, no more joys or sorrows, no more laughter. The girl had kept something back—Vicky had felt it; she hadn't challenged her. Later, she had realized what it was. So obvious, she thought now. Skip Burrows's office ransacked, computers taken. The man in the mask had returned, looking for what Angela had hidden.

Angela, trying to be brave, when she had been scared.

"You couldn't have prevented it." John's voice floated through an aria, as if he had read her mind. "Try not to blame yourself."

"I could have taken her someplace else. A motel the killer wouldn't have known about." The pickup started to slow down, making rattling, coughing noises as they turned onto a dirt road. The sky had faded into a palette of pastels, and the prairie had turned to gold. "I think she had a flash drive with office files on it," she said. "It was what the killer wanted."

John was quiet a moment. "She must have known he would come after it. Maybe she thought she could trade it for Skip's life."

"Bargain with a killer? What chance did she have? I should have found a way to help her." Vicky took a moment, trying to bring into focus the thoughts jammed in her mind. "Skip Burrows could be dead," she said. "He had a briefcase of money that he'd withdrawn Friday. There was something on the office computers the killer wanted. People were always in and out of Skip's office. Anyone might have seen Angela insert the flash drive. The killer couldn't risk leaving it in Angela's possession."

They were rolling east, a few houses outside, gold and pink under the sky. John made another turn, and the pickup bounced down a dirt road toward a ranch house. Left onto a graveled drive-way. He stopped behind a green truck. Vicky managed to let her-self out, legs heavy, dragging her forward, the sense of failure weighing her down. She followed John O'Malley around the truck to the small, white house that glowed in the first rays of the sun. He had just lifted his hand to knock when a man's voice inside said, "Come in."

He pushed the door open. "Lou?"

"Yeah, I'm here."

Vicky stepped into a narrow living room. John O'Malley close beside her, brushing her shoulder. Shadows fell over the sofa and easy chair, the small tables scattered about. The window blinds were closed, and the house had the feeling of early morning, the smell of freshly brewed coffee in the air. Everything about the living room was neat and orderly—the stack of newspapers on the table, the balanced look of the lampshades, the pictures that might have been hung with a level. Across the room was an alcove that extended from the kitchen. Seated at one end of the table, hands curled around a mug of coffee, eyes half-closed, was Lou Morningside.

"Priest and lawyer." The Arapaho shook his head. "Sit down. I need a minute before I get the bad news."

Vicky took the chair next to Lou. She was quiet. It was John, seated at the end of the table, who said, "We're here to get a message to Colin, Grandfather," he said, using the term of respect for an elder.

"Colin?" Lou's eyes snapped upward. He straightened his shoulders toward John O'Malley. "You mean, he's not dead? He's okay? You aren't telling me they found his body in a ditch somewhere? I been worrying myself sick about that boy. Up all night waiting for him to get home, straining my ears so hard they're about to fall off. I been debating with myself about going into Lander to look for him, but where would I go? Some old Indian wandering around town in the middle of the night, waiting for a cop to pull me over. *What business you got here?* I didn't see how that would help Colin."

"I thought he left for Pine Ridge," John said.

"Drove halfway there, then turned around. Blew in last night. Ate himself some supper and took a snooze on the sofa, then woke up and said he'd be back later. That's all he said, but I know the boy. I told him he should've gone to his Crazy Horse relatives and not come back until they solved that Custer murder. The police are going to put it on him. Him and his Crazy Horse regalia. No call for him and Mike to go into town and listen to the lies about the Old Time, but they went anyway. Now the cops can't take their eyes off them. He came back 'cause of that girl. Got to worrying about her, thought he had to come home and save her from herself. Loved her since they were kids. Soon as he tore out of here, I knew something bad would happen. I could feel it in my bones."

He stopped. Jaw hanging slack; eyes switching between her and John. "That's why you come here. You're gonna tell me what happened. What'd Colin do? Take her away, like Crazy Horse did his woman?"

Vicky leaned toward the old man. "We came to tell Colin about Angela." She tried for a soft tone, the kind she would have wanted if someone told her something horrific had happened to one of her own kids.

"What about her?"

"Angela was murdered."

"Murdered!" The Arapaho kept repeating the word. "Murdered. Murdered." He tilted his head back and stared at the ceiling. The kitchen nook had gotten lighter, sunshine filtering past the flimsy curtains at the window. "Colin didn't do it," he said, looking again between her and John. He shifted toward Vicky. "You gotta help him. You gotta make those white detectives know there's no way he would've harmed that girl. She meant everything to him. Just about killed him when she left the rez. Little ranch we got here wasn't good enough. All the ceremonies and celebrations, powwows and picnics, having her own pony to ride over the prairie—none of that was good enough. She wanted a white life on the other side of the border."

"What time did Colin leave here?" John said.

Vicky caught his eye, and in that instant she knew what he was thinking. Angela's landlady had seen a man around the rental house. She could have seen Colin. The sense of failure turned into a deep feeling of dread.

"Must've been about eleven. I was getting ready for bed. I begged him. 'Colin, don't get involved in that girl's business. Stay out of it. You got enough worries.'"

"What do you think she was involved in?" Vicky said. She was thinking that Angela could have told Colin about the flash drive. He had realized the danger she was in and gone to help her. Bring her back to the rez. Hide her where the killer couldn't have found her.

"All I know is the white lawyer she worked for disappeared. I heard there was a fight and the office got trashed. Angela was his secretary. So I asked myself, What did she know? What was she up to? I told Colin, 'It's white man's business. Stay out of it,' I said. 'If that girl got mixed up in what don't concern her, that's her problem.'"

He scraped the chair backward and, laying the palms of his hands on the table, pushed to his feet. "Not minding my manners, I been worried about the boy. Should've offered you coffee," he said, stepping along the counter. "Just made a new pot." Lou poured the coffee into a pair of mugs and set them on the table.

"Thank you," Vicky said. She could use a cup of coffee, a jolt of caffeine, anything that might help her get a grip on the unfolding day.

"Don't get me wrong," he said. "It's awful what happened to

the girl. She was a pretty thing. Colin couldn't ever get her out of his mind. But she was headstrong as a mule. Nobody could tell her anything. She would've been safe here with Colin. Nobody would've hurt her."

Vicky sipped at the coffee. The warmth radiated through her and settled into her stomach. She began to feel as if she were coming back to herself. "Where do you think Colin is now?"

"I wish I knew." Lou lowered his gaze to the table and the half-full mug. He twisted it between his hands. "I'm praying he's driving back to Pine Ridge. He seen she was okay, and he took off to save himself." He looked up at John O'Malley a moment, then turned sideways toward her. "All the boys are scared. Hiding out, trying to stay away from the police, but that Lander detective won't let up. Keeps coming on the rez. Either got the fed with him or one of the BIA cops, keeps it legal. Otherwise he don't have any business on the rez. One after the other, he finds the warriors that rode in the parade Sunday. All it took was one snitch wanting to stay out of the clutches of that detective to give up a name. That got Madden started. One name, then another. There's all kinds of clubs he can hold over their heads. Outstanding DUI, traffic ticket, probation. He rides them hard, threatens trouble if they don't cooperate. So they cooperate. Well, don't blame them. They tell the truth. All the warriors wanted to do was remind the Custer guy who was boss. He might brag all he wanted about the great things Custer did killing our people, but at the Little Bighorn, the tables got turned. The warriors sent a message at the parade."

"But the idea was Colin's," John said.

Lou nodded. "Madden's taking a hard look at him and Mike Longshot. Mike's the one that trained the warriors how to race the horses in a tight circle. Something else about him . . ."

"I understand," John said.

"Some of these modern warriors forget the Creator makes us the way he wants us. In the Old Time, Mike would've been holy. Nobody would've dared hurt him." Lou leveled his gaze again at Vicky. His eyes were like black pools, shiny and sad. She clutched her hands into fists and waited for the words. "Those boys need a good lawyer. You always take care of our people."

"It's different this time, Grandfather," Vicky said. "I have a conflict of interest." Her own words sounded tight and far away. God. Two young Arapahos who could stand trial and be convicted of murder on nothing but flimsy circumstantial evidence. They were in the proximity, they were Indians, they hated Custer. And now this: Angela, Colin's ex-girlfriend, murdered, and every chance that Colin had gone to her house tonight. Colin could be in even more trouble than Lou imagined. She heard herself stumbling: Other lawyers in the area; someone would represent them. Lou had already turned away. She could see the beads of sweat on the profile of his forehead and nose.

THEY THREADED THEIR way across the reservation and over the border through Hudson, the sky a perfect blue and the prairies, arroyos, and sand hills clear in the morning light. "I can't recommend any lawyers. I can't be involved." Explaining, explaining to the white man behind the steering wheel, when he hadn't asked for any explanation. He understood. Explaining for herself, she thought. All the years getting a law degree, training in a Denver firm, preparing to help her people, to change the way matters had always been. She would use the white man's law for her people, instead of against them. A one-woman crusader. She turned and laughed into the passenger window.

"I know a couple of lawyers." John glanced over. She could feel the warmth of his eyes on her. "I'll see if they'll take on Colin and Mike."

She didn't say anything. The reality was like a boulder that had dropped between them. The Indian lawyer was representing a white woman.

23

SUNLIGHT SPLASHED THE pews and the few old faithfuls scattered about. Father John lifted his hand and made the sign of the cross over the little congregation. "Go in peace," he said, the last words of the Mass. He walked down the aisle and out into a morning that promised a hot day, his mind full of Angela Running Bear, a girl he couldn't remember meeting. Perhaps years ago, with her sister, Claire. Two little girls squirming next to their grandmother at Sunday Mass. After their grandmother died, they had never come back.

He had offered Mass for the girl. He had asked the congregation to pray for the repose of the soul of Angela Running Bear, who had died tragically last night. Wrinkled brown faces had looked up at him with uncomprehending eyes. Only a few heads nodded, as if the news hadn't surprised them. A girl who had left her own people, gone off to be somebody else.

News about Angela's murder hadn't reached the moccasin tele-graph yet, or there would have been more people at Mass. There was always a crowd after a tragedy, as if it took a tragedy to re-mind people of their own mortality. But the news was probably filtering across the border by now. People discussing it over coffee and doughnuts at the senior center. Over the tanks at the gas sta-tions as they filled up their pickups. In the convenience store where Mike worked. There would be a big crowd at Mass tomorrow.

One by one the parishioners walked out and he took their hands, the roughened palms warm against his own. "What hap-pened to her?" they wanted to know. "She was murdered," he said again and again, the words scratching at his throat. "The police are investigating." One of the grandfathers shook his head. "So many murders. Cops will be looking at the rez, wanting to blame an Indian. More trouble," he said.

After the last pickup had driven around Circle Drive and into the cottonwoods, Father John walked back through the church. The sound of his boots on the carpet broke through the heavy still-ness that always permeated the church after the congregation had filed out, as if some of the energy, the breath, of the people who had knelt in the pews were still present.

He knelt on the altar step and prayed again for the soul of An-gela Running Bear, and for the people who had loved her. Claire and Colin Morningside. Ten minutes later he had hung his alb and chasuble in the sacristy, placed the Mass books in the cabinet, and retraced his steps down the center aisle. He crossed the mission grounds to the residence. Sporadic gusts of wind whipped at the wild grasses, and birds chirped in the cottonwoods. Walks-On rose off the stoop and came loping to meet him, gripping a Frisbee in his teeth. Father John managed to coax the Frisbee free, then threw it across the field enclosed by Circle Drive. The dog went after it, brought it back and, this time, dropped it at Father John's feet. The game went on for several minutes, until he threw the Frisbee in the direction of the residence and ran after the dog. "More later," he said, letting himself through the front door. The dog stood on the stoop shaking the Frisbee, disappointment flashing in his brown eyes.

The bishop had already eaten breakfast and was sipping at what was probably a third mug of coffee when Father John walked into the kitchen. "You didn't get much sleep," the bishop said.

He hadn't gotten any sleep, Father John was thinking. He had stayed up late working on the budget that never wanted to balance itself; it lived in the perpetual state of hovering over a cliff. Then he had taken a book to bed—*Custer in the Civil War*—and had been about to drop off when the phone rang. Detective Madden. A young Arapaho woman murdered. The detective thought he might like to know.

Elena stood at the stove ladling oatmeal into a bowl. He wondered if she had heard the news, but the moment she turned around and set the bowl on the table, he knew that she had. "My nephew called first thing this morning. Told me about Angela Running Bear."

"I'm afraid it's true."

"God have mercy on her." The bishop set the mug onto the table.

Father John pulled out a chair with his boot and sat down in front of the oatmeal. He was aware of the hollow space in his stomach, but he didn't feel hungry. He reached for the mug of coffee Elena handed him and took a couple of long sips. The kitchen went quiet. He could feel the unasked questions floating over the table. After a moment, he told them what he knew about the murder. He was thinking that he didn't know much.

"What did that girl get herself mixed up in?" Elena said. "Boss kidnapped, place ransacked. You ask me, the poor man is dead. Now Angela murdered. What did they have going on?"

Father John took a drink of coffee and stared at the woman. She had seen enough to cut a straight line through the conjectures and theories and possibilities to what was most obvious: whatever Skip Burrows had been involved in, he had also involved his secretary. Father John poured milk over the oatmeal and took a spoonful. It was like swallowing a lump of coal. He couldn't shake the feeling that Madden would look first to the rez, to Angela's Arapaho connections. Family. Ex-boyfriend.

"Sometime in the middle of the night," the bishop said, "I thought I heard a pickup on Circle Drive."

Father John stopped eating and waited for the old man to go on. "We usually don't get visitors that late. Took me a while to get out of bed, but when I got to the window, everything looked quiet. No sign of any vehicle."

Father John pushed his chair back and headed down the hallway. He slammed out the door and took off running, down the sidewalk, across Circle Drive, and through the field, across Circle Drive again and down the driveway bathed in the shadows of the church and the administration building. He was aware of Mike's horse stomping and whinnying in the makeshift pasture behind the church. He ran on. A pickup stood next to the side of the guesthouse, almost lost in the shadows. When he got close, he saw the bumper sticker: Crazy Horse Lives.

He knocked on the door of the guesthouse. He was breathing hard. Before he could knock again, the door swung open. Mike stood in the doorway, disheveled and sleepy-eyed. He moved backward and Father John stepped inside. In the narrow kitchen off the living room was Colin Morningside.

"Texted me last night and said he needed a place to stay," Mike said.

Colin turned away from the counter and the cereal bowl with the spoon sticking up above the edge and walked to the doorway. He leaned a shoulder against the frame. Wide-awake, tense, and wired, as if he might burst across the room and out the door. Blue jeans and checkered shirt looked worn and wrinkled. One knee poked through a wide tear in his jeans.

They hadn't heard about Angela, Father John was thinking. The moccasin telegraph would be buzzing by now, but they must not have checked their phones or text messages. "I have bad news," he said. "We'd better sit down."

"Sit down?" Mike dropped onto the armrest of the sofa. He looked as if a gust of wind had blown him over.

"You're going to tell us Madden's looking for us," Colin said, straightening himself in the doorway. "He's had us in his sights since Garrett got shot." He was shaking his head. "He's been harassing warriors all over the rez. Doesn't surprise me if one of them said, 'Yeah, Colin could've done it. Crazy Horse hated Custer. Surrounded the cavalry so he could kill that white man.'"

"Listen to me Colin. The news is about Angela."

The young man regarded him for a long moment, sizing him up, wondering what the priest at St. Francis Mission knew about Angela Running Bear that he didn't know. "She's okay." He shook his head, as if to brush off whatever initial concerns he might have felt. "I saw her last night, and she's fine. She's still living in that rental house in Lander."

"She was murdered last night," Father John said. "I'm sorry, Colin."

The Arapaho's face went perfectly still, as if his breath had stopped in his throat. His eyes narrowed into hard, black slits. For a moment, Father John thought the man would fall facedown onto the floor. A strangled gasp came from the sofa, and he was aware of Mike struggling to his feet, leaning over the armrest, holding on. Then Colin stepped back and swung a fist, like a sledgehammer, onto the counter. The cereal bowl skittered to the edge and crashed on the floor, splashing Cheerios and milk over the linoleum. The spoon spun like a top into the living room.

"Who?" The word gurgled out of his throat. He was still leaning forward, pounding the counter, but now the pounding was a metronome of helplessness.

"The police don't know yet."

"She was fine when I saw her."

"Did you talk to her?"

After a moment, the pounding stopped and Colin turned around. "She didn't want to talk to me. I must have left five or six messages. Told her I was coming for her. I wanted to get her out of there. She didn't even call me back. I wanted to bust down the door and take her, so she'd be safe. All I did was look in the window. Saw her sitting there like she knew what she was doing. What business did I have to pull her away? What did I know about her new life in Lander? Nothing. That's when I knew it was over between us. She made it clear when she came to the ranch Monday afternoon that she didn't want me in her life."

"You shouldn't have come back," Mike said.

Colin stared into space, swaying on his feet. "I couldn't stop loving her. Worrying about her. Couldn't sleep. I'd close my eyes, and there she was. I could see the shadows around her, like dark spirits at her heels. She was in danger. I felt it in every part of me. I decided to give it one more chance. Crazy Horse went and got his woman. I had the notion I could do the same. I should've saved her." The words came like a long wail of grief. "I should have taken her away. What did he do to her?"

"It looks like she was strangled."

"Strangled! Oh God, why did I leave her there?"

Father John gave him a moment before he said, "What time were you there?"

Colin sank against the edge of the counter and rubbed at his eyes. "Around eleven thirty. I wasn't thinking about the time."

"The landlady might have seen you." Father John could hear the tight worry in his voice. "She claims she saw a man in looking in Angela's windows."

Colin nodded. "I walked around the house, trying to decide what to do."

Father John could hear Madden's voice: *The killer burst through the back door.*

"So Madden's got another reason to arrest me. He figures I shot Garrett and had nothing to lose by killing Angela. He'll say I killed her 'cause she broke up with me."

"He'll need solid evidence." Dear Lord. Madden would build two murder cases against Colin. "You both need to talk to a lawyer." He glanced from Colin to the man straddling the armrest. "I'll make a couple of phone calls."

"You said Vicky Holden can help," Mike said.

Father John shook his head and told them that Vicky was already representing Garrett's widow. The helplessness he had sensed in her was as strong as if she were standing beside him. "It would be a conflict of interest." Echoing her words. "There are other good lawyers in the area."

"I'm out of here." Colin pushed off the counter and flung himself through the doorway and across the living room. He yanked open the door. "You got any sense, you'll come with me," he shouted over one shoulder. Mike jumped off the armrest and followed him out the door.

Father John stepped onto the stoop and watched the pickup skid backwards, then shoot down the driveway. He could hear the motor screaming through the cottonwoods and out on Seventeen-Mile Road. He might have tried to stop them, he thought. It would have been the logical thing to do. Running to Pine Ridge would make them look guilty, add ammunition to whatever theory Madden was entertaining. They should get a lawyer, take their chances. A couple of Arapahos? What did he know? They would be safer at Pine Ridge.

He walked back to the residence. When he got into the office, he intended to call Mike's mother and find out what she wanted to do about the horse. He wouldn't tell her where Mike had gone. The less she knew when the cops came around, the better it would be.

24

"I'VE BEEN WORRIED." Adam stood in the center of the kitchen, freshly showered, crisp white shirt and blue jeans, hair still damp. Gripping a coffee mug in one hand. Coffee smells filled the apartment. From outside came the muffled sounds of the morning traffic and Lander coughing to life.

Vicky shut the door behind her. She should have called him, let him know where she was going. A simple phone call. It was wrong and distracted of her not to think about him. *Woman Alone.* She shook her head at the name the grandmothers had given her. She had been Woman Alone for so long, she had forgotten how to be anything else.

She started to apologize when Adam lifted his other hand, palm outward in the Plains Indian sign of peace. "I understand. You went to the rez to notify relatives. Tough job." He shook his head.

"I keep wondering what I could have done." Vicky walked over to the counter that divided the kitchen from the small dining area, took a stool, and let her bag fall on the floor. She dropped her face into her hands. She couldn't shake the image of Angela Running Bear, back straight, shoulders squared, rushing toward the front door, as if she knew where she was going. She was aware that Adam had set a mug of coffee in front of her. The aroma floated like clouds around the image.

"You're not psychic. She told you what she wanted to tell you."

Vicky sipped at the coffee, grateful for the warmth and the faint feeling of normality. "The last thing I told her was that I couldn't help her."

"You didn't have a choice."

Vicky stayed with the coffee. It was true. Her client was Belinda Clark, and the minute Madden had let on that he was looking at a connection between the murder of Belinda's husband and the abduction of Angela's boss, she knew she had a conflict of interest.

"Angela wasn't the only one I couldn't help," she said. "Lou Morningside, Colin's grandfather, is pretty sure Colin went to her place last night. The landlady may have seen him. Angela had broken up with him when she started working for Skip. Now Madden will think Colin murdered Angela. He's already convinced that Colin and Mike Longshot conspired to murder Garrett. It fits his scenario. Crazy Horse leading the charge against Custer. Both Colin and Mike need legal representation, and I can't help them."

"There are other lawyers. The court will appoint lawyers . . ."

Vicky waved away the rest of it. She knew how it worked. Court-appointed attorneys, straight out of law school, their only experience with Indians was passing them on the street, and somewhere, deep in their hearts, believing Indians were different. Who knew what Indians might do?

"You practice law in a white town. A white woman walked in needing a lawyer and you agreed to represent her. Were you supposed to turn her away at the door? Tell her to get a white lawyer and wait for Arapahos to come in? I don't remember anything in the oath we took specifying the type of people we should help."

"You don't understand." Vicky got up and stepped around the counter, brushing Adam's back. She rinsed her mug in the sink.

"I'm trying."

She turned and faced him. "I crossed the border, like Angela. Became part of another world the way she did. Caught up in other ways, other problems. My own people need me, but I'm too busy with *them*."

"Come on, Vicky." She heard the familiar, rising note of anger in Adam's voice. "We both practice close to the courts, close to the jail. What sense would it make to practice on the rez and spend time driving back and forth to Lander? So you're on the other side of the border. So what?"

Vicky watched him while he was speaking, the way his mouth moved around the words, as if he were translating from Lakota to English, the way his black eyes bore straight into her. A formidable opponent in the courtroom or the conference room, Adam Lone Eagle. He had a great ability to convince anybody that he was right. Except for her.

"I know it makes sense . . ."

He cut her off before she could say the rest of it—"to you." "We both have work to do." He swung around the counter, picked up the briefcase on the dining room table, and started for the door. Holding the door opened, he looked back. "Tonight?"

She didn't say anything, which he seemed to take for a yes because he nodded, stepped into the corridor, and closed the door behind him. She listened to the tread of his footsteps retreating down the corridor, the elevator rattling into life.

VICKY GOT TO the office before Annie or Roger had arrived. No smells of freshly brewed coffee, no phones ringing, no sense of bustling about. Just the residual stillness of the night. She opened the windows that overlooked the backyard, dropped into the swivel chair, and turned on the computer. The morning breeze ruffled the blank pages of the legal pad on her desk as the computer whirred into life and icons settled onto the screen. She thought about Colin. Worrying about Angela, feeling guilty about leaving her alone in Lander, as if she were stranded in another country with no way to get home.

Colin, going to Angela's place last night. God. If Madden couldn't find enough evidence to charge Colin with the murder of Edward Garrett, he wouldn't have any trouble finding evidence to connect him to Angela's murder. Boot prints outside the house. Fingerprints who knew where? The landlady peering out the window, certain she could identify the man she saw. A white woman who probably thought all Indians looked alike. And Colin, returning for his woman, like Crazy Horse.

Vicky typed "wife of Crazy Horse" in the search engine and watched the black lines of text come up. Pages of Web sites, but only one or two looked interesting. She clicked on "Crazy Horse and Black Buffalo Woman" and glanced through the text.

From the time they were children, Crazy Horse had loved the solemn-faced, black-eyed girl, but when they were grown, she married another Sioux warrior, No Water. The marriage didn't stop Crazy Horse from loving her, and one day, he went to her camp and took her away. No Water bided his time, but eventually he came after her and shot Crazy Horse in the face. His father begged him to let the matter drop, not to take revenge. Keep peace within the tribe, and Crazy Horse listened. He carried the scar from No Water's bullet the rest of his life.

A whoosh of air lifted the top page of the legal pad as the front door opened and closed. On the other side of the beveled glass doors, Annie and Roger moved about, a blurred dance step. There was the low murmur of voices. The phone rang twice, then stopped. Vicky looked back at the text. She hated the doubt nipping at her. God, she was thinking like a defense attorney, trying to convince herself her client was innocent so that she could convince a jury. Not asking her client if he was guilty, not wanting to know the truth. Truth? Some clients were guilty.

"Morning, Vicky." The beveled doors opened and Annie stepped inside, Roger close behind, the same worried, tired, up-most-the-night look on their faces. "Can we talk?"

Vicky closed the Web site and motioned them to the chairs on the other side of the desk. The first whiff of brewing coffee trailed after them. "You've heard?"

They nodded in unison and sat down, holding hands across the space between the chairs, Annie's brown hand lost in the white, pawlike hand of the attorney Vicky and Adam had hired to handle the little cases. Cases like those of Angela Running Bear and Colin Morningside and Mike Longshot.

"Friend in the Lander PD called after he got to the house and saw the murder victim was Indian." Roger sat tall in the chair, long legs folded in front of him. He used his free hand to push at the brown hair that kept falling onto his forehead. A mixture of worry and sadness dulled his eyes as he threw a sideways glance at Annie. "Figured the victim was from the rez and Annie might know her."

Vicky didn't say anything. She was thinking that the moccasin telegraph worked on both sides of the border. "I'm sorry," she said.

"She didn't deserve to die." Annie's voice swelled and cracked with tears. "She was trying to find her own way. You could have helped her."

Vicky flinched at the stab of pain, as if Annie had shot her with an invisible arrow. "No, I couldn't."

Annie's black eyes were locked in a stare of incomprehension, and Vicky realized she hadn't yet told either Annie or Roger about Madden investigating a possible connection between murder and abduction. "There could be a conflict of interest." The words hollow and meaningless in her own ears. Then she told them about the investigation. "I told Angela she would have to find another attorney, someone not connected to this firm." She paused. "Or to me."

Annie looked away, which sent another pang of regret shooting through Vicky. "Do you know Colin Morningside?" she managed.

"Crazy Horse?" Annie turned back and shrugged. "Nickname. Everybody knows it. No surprise Detective Madden thinks he wanted to kill that man playing Custer. But the cops can't think . . ." The glance she gave Roger was filled with the panic of sudden realization. "Colin could never have killed Angela. He was crazy for her."

"You never know what cops are thinking," Roger said.

"You ask me, they should be looking at what happened to her boss. Angela might've known something . . ."

"Could she have taken a flash drive from the office? Could that be possible?"

Annie hesitated. Then she said, "She was really happy with her job and"—she shot a glance at Roger—"she was in love with her boss. She wouldn't have done anything to ruin things."

She had been so certain, Vicky was thinking. She had needed to find a connection, some reason for the man in the black mask to come after Angela. She'd been grasping at thin air. Angela wouldn't have done anything to jeopardize her job or her relationship with Skip.

"Angela did have some trouble . . ." Annie had pulled her hand free from Roger's and was shifting about in the chair. "The school district she worked for . . ." She took a couple of seconds. "Well, she told me she'd hit some wrong keys on the computer and erased a lot of important documents, so they let her go. Told her she was incompetent."

"They weren't able to get the documents back?"

"Oh yeah. They called in the IT people and found the lost documents, but they still said she was incompetent."

"Are you saying she might have started making her own backups?"

Annie was quiet a moment. "You think that's what the killer was looking for?"

"Yes." Vicky could feel the certitude settling over her.

Annie nodded, then got to her feet. Roger stood up beside her, and they started toward the beveled doors. "I almost forgot," Annie said, looking back. "Wyoming Central Bank called. They have the records you subpoenaed."

Vicky nodded. Another reminder of the white world, the white client. "Will you get Madden on the phone for me?" she said as Annie let herself out the door.

She turned back to the computer, a part of her wanting to know more about Crazy Horse going after his woman, but she'd had enough. When Madden learned about the episode—and he would learn; some enterprising young intern in the police department would Google the Indian chief that Colin had portrayed in the parade—it would add to his case that Colin Morningside had patterned his life after the man he idolized.

The phone rang, and Vicky stared at it, trying to recollect why she had wanted to speak to Madden. Then she remembered. She lifted the receiver. "Detective Madden?"

"What's up?"

"Did you find the flash drive at Angela's house?" she asked again.

"No flash drive. What's this all about?"

"I have reason to believe that Angela Running Bear had in her possession a flash drive with documents from Skip Burrows's office."

"That's your theory?"

"I'm trying to help your investigation. The man who abducted Burrows went back to the office looking for something. He didn't find it. So he went looking at Angela's. You didn't find the flash drive because he took it."

"You have evidence? Angela tell you something?"

"It's what she didn't tell me."

25

A STERILE QUALITY to banks. Waxed, shiny floors, teller's compartments in geometric shapes, glass-enclosed cubicles on the opposite wall. Vicky stopped at the front desk and waited for a blond-haired woman with quick, blue eyes to finish a phone conversation. She wore a white shirt with a long, pointed collar, like the shirts worn by the tellers and the bank employees moving about the cubicles—the bank uniform. Neat black letters on the plastic tag below the collar spelled Monica Pugh.

Vicky pushed a business card across the desk the instant the phone call ended. "I'm here to see Mr. Mason."

"Oh yes." Recognition sounded in Monica Pugh's voice. "Please come with me." She swung around and started along the cubicles. Vicky stayed close behind. Hushed conversations floated through the openings, a series of heads nodded over papers spread across desks. Computer screens were black, but that was because they were meant to be seen only by the bankers in front of them.

"Ah, Ms. Holden." The thin man with a concave chest inside a point-collared white shirt rose from the desk in the last cubicle and came toward her, extending a white-freckled hand. His palm felt moist and warm. She stepped inside the cubicle as Monica Pugh disappeared on the other side of the glass wall.

"Curtis Mason." He might have been in his forties, brown hair receding above a wide forehead and sun creases at the corners of his blue eyes. He swept a hand in the direction of two chairs and dropped back into a swivel chair. Extracting a thin file of papers from a brown envelope that materialized from a desk drawer, he said, "Sorry about Mr. Garrett. I was standing a block away with my wife and kids. Couldn't believe what happened. I did hear the shot, though. Thought it was a truck backfiring."

"Belinda Clark, Garrett's wife, is entitled to know what became of his assets. She was surprised to learn he had withdrawn the money from his account here."

"I helped him with that withdrawal four months ago." Mason shook his head, as if everything about Garrett was a matter of deep regret. "He came into the bank to close the account. Wrote a check for every last penny. Five hundred thousand dollars. I explained he might want to leave enough in the account for unexpected expenses. He refused. You understand, it was his money. He could do whatever he wanted with it."

"It also belonged to his wife."

"Edward Garrett was the only name on the account. It is our policy to talk to a client intent on withdrawing large sums. We don't assume he is dissatisfied with our bank and simply wishes to move to another, which is his choice. But we try to ascertain if that is the case. Naturally we would want to know why a client is dissatisfied and try to rectify the matter. There is always the possibility the client has been targeted in some get-rich-quick scheme which may or may not be legal."

He was nodding over the papers, and Vicky asked if he believed Garrett had been targeted in such a scheme.

"I regret to say that my interview with him left me with a very uneasy feeling. He insisted he knew what he was doing. Oh, I can still hear him saying, 'May I remind you, Mr. Mason, I am an adult male in full control of my capacities. I am no man's fool.' He had a funny way of speaking, like somebody from another time. When he told me he portrayed General Custer, it made sense. Later, after he was killed, I did some research on Custer. Garrett even looked like him! I read that Custer was stubborn, always sure of himself. Well, that was Garrett, seated right where you're seated now, basically telling me to mind my own business because he knew what was best."

"What became of the money?"

Mason thumbed through the records. "He told me he had the chance of a lifetime to make a good investment. Expected a thirty percent return in a few months. I tried to press him. Thirty percent? It raised my hackles. I cautioned him to be wary. Legitimate investments don't pay out like that in a matter of months." He lifted his shoulders and spread both hands over the papers. "There are always exceptions. Garrett believed he had come upon one."

He began laying the records in front of Vicky, one at a time. "You can see the major deposit he made six months ago. Five hundred thousand. He told me he had just closed on his ranch near Laramie. Before that, as you can see . . ."—he slipped another record to the top—"he kept a few thousand dollars in the account, wrote occasional checks, and made new deposits when the balance began to slip. He had banked here for a year. He said his daughter had moved to Lander, and he hoped to spend more time here. He had been coming to the area for a number of years on the way to rodeos and parades."

"Did he say where he intended to invest the money?"

Mason had pulled out a stack of checks. He peeled off one and handed it across the desk. Vicky studied the loopy, sprawling handwriting: "Granite Group. Five Hundred Thousand." The signature line was almost indistinct: a large E followed by a wavy line, then a G and another wavy line. She turned the check over. A stamped endorsement said Granite Group, with the faint outline of a mountain peak in the background.

"Where was this deposited?"

"Bank of the West." He glanced over one shoulder. "Down the street. We have the routing number."

"Any idea who the principals are in the Granite Group?"

"No. But I believe it is a legitimate company. We've had other clients write checks to them."

"For large sums?"

"I would say as large or larger than Mr. Garrett's."

She thanked him and got to her feet. She was going around in circles. Edward Garrett had the right to write a check for any amount on the account, and he had exercised his right. He had just forgotten to mention it to his wife. The money could still be invested, in which case Belinda would have a right to claim half of the assets. The other half would belong to Garrett's daughter.

First, Vicky had to get in touch with the Granite Group, whatever it was.

*　*　*

SHE RETRACED HER steps through the bank and down the sidewalk to the Ford parked at the curb. She started the engine, lowered the windows, and pulled her cell from her bag. In a moment, Annie's voice was on the phone: "Holden Law Offices."

"I want you to contact the secretary of state's office," Vicky said. "I need to know the officers and registered agent for an investment company called the Granite Group. That's right. Granite Group. They bank at the Bank of the West on Main Street."

BELINDA CLARK OPENED the front door of the trailer at the first knock, which took Vicky by surprise. Before she made a U-turn and started for the RV lot, she had tried calling her client and gotten a flat, routine message: "Leave your name and number. I'll get back to you." She drove up to the hard-packed, scrub-studded mesa and slowed down the dirt road between rows of RVs. Wind squealed between the metal vehicles like trapped animals. Vicky parked in front of the white RV at the end of the row and waited, but no one came out. Finally she took the three metal steps at the door and knocked.

"I saw you called," Belinda said. She looked older, as if she had aged in the last few days. Brown hair damp with perspiration. Sunbonnet tossed on the table that nearly bisected the vehicle. She wore the same old-fashioned dress, wilted and tired-looking, the same white lace-up boots. She seemed hesitant, lost in thought. Then she stepped backward and beckoned Vicky inside. "You haven't found the money."

"What makes you think that?" The vehicle was stuffy, filled with odors of grease, old coffee, and food cooked hours ago.

"I know my husband." Belinda plopped down on a red-plastic

bench behind the table and motioned Vicky to a chair. "He never asked advice. Didn't want it. Didn't need it. He always knew what was best."

"Did you talk about your investments?"

"Investments? After we were married, he put a paper in front of me and said, 'Sign it.' My permission for him to make investments on our behalf." She shrugged. "I had no choice. He never discussed investments with me. All the sure-to-succeed schemes to make him as rich as he deserved to be." She laughed deep inside her throat. "He did deserve to be rich. He deserved to have his genius recognized. Money could have done that. Money would have made him president."

Vicky stared at the woman a moment. She was Libbie Custer, waiting at Fort Lincoln for the return of her husband from an illustrious victory over the renegade Sioux and Cheyenne. Hardening herself for the bad news she had always known was coming.

"We're talking about your husband, Edward Garrett."

Belinda brushed the tabletop with her hands. "I know. I know. But it was the same. Always taking chances, betting on the long shot. He deserved to be recognized for the genius he was. No one could channel the great general like Edward."

"Are you familiar with the Granite Group?"

"Can't say I ever heard of it."

"Edward wrote a check for five hundred thousand to the Granite Group. He told the banker he expected a thirty percent return in a few months."

"Did he get it?" A look of hope flared in the woman's eyes.

"I have to locate the company and subpoena a copy of your husband's account."

"How ironic. Just when he would have had the money to provide the life and recognition he deserved, those Indians killed him. It's all part of her plot."

"Whose plot?"

"His daughter. He tried to forget she existed, but she kept at him. Calling all the time. Going through a rough divorce. Crying on her daddy's shoulder. She paid the Indians to kill him. You want to know who's behind the Granite Group? Ask her. She's probably already gotten the money."

26

A HAMMER POUNDED in the quiet. Vicky left the Ford in the dirt driveway that connected the road to a two-story log house with a wide front porch. She followed the noise around the corner. Halfway up a ladder perched against the house was a stout woman with thick, muscular legs, blue sneakers, and blond hair hanging below the brim of a straw hat.

"Dorothy Winslow?"

"Who wants to know?" The woman glanced down along one leg of the ladder, hammer inert in her hand.

"Vicky Holden. I represent your stepmother, Belinda Clark."

The woman's expression changed from annoyance to curiosity. She started down the ladder, one sneaker reaching for the lower step, then the other, hammer in hand. She wore khaki shorts that bunched around her thighs and a white tee shirt with Indian Country stamped on the back. She reached the ground, balanced the hammer on the lowest step, and squared herself toward Vicky. "You a funeral director?"

"An attorney."

Amusement moved into her expression. Her eyes were blue, flecked with light. "Well, that's ironic."

"I don't understand."

"You don't understand that my stepmother hates all Indians because they killed her beloved Autie? You don't see the irony in her hiring an Indian lawyer?" She waved Vicky after her. "You came all the way out here to talk, we'd better talk."

Dorothy Winslow took the two steps to the porch and dropped into a wooden chair that rocked and creaked beneath her. She waited until Vicky took the other chair. "My stepmother is a nutcase. You've probably got that much figured out."

"You mean the fact that she impersonates Libbie Custer?"

"Impersonates." The woman let out a snort of laughter. "One way to put it. How about, lives like her, talks like her, dresses like her, mourns for a man she never met, except in her dreams. I call that nuts."

"She worked with your father."

Dorothy Winslow looked as if a door had slammed in her face. She took a moment before she said, "So that makes them both nuts. My dad, the good old boy. Happened to like the past better than he liked the present and anybody in it. Custer and Libbie never had kids, and most the time, Dad forgot he had a daughter. You talk to the Indians . . ." She twisted around and stared at Vicky. "What am I saying? Naturally you talk to Indians. You know what the Cheyennes say? Custer had a daughter with a Cheyenne woman he took from the Washita. After he killed Chief Black Kettle. Nice guy my dad was enamored with."

She stopped talking and looked straight ahead. Sandstone out-croppings bunching against the golden brown hills, houses here and there, brown ribbons of roads and dry landscapes, the roofs of Lander in the distance. "Used to say there were real heroes back then. Not like today where the only heroes are in video games. Looked just like Custer. Maybe that dictated the historical charac-ter he should impersonate. He was sure to find somebody, rooting around in the past like he did. Looked even more like Custer when he dyed his hair blond." Her nails drummed out a fast rhythm on the wood armrest. "Wouldn't have been my choice of a hero, but Dad shouldn't have died for it. Go ahead. Lay it on me."

"Lay what on you?"

"My stepmother's theory that I had something to do with his getting shot. What did she tell you? Who did I hire to pull the trig-ger? Indians, am I right? I've heard the rumors. That's the story she's putting about."

Vicky didn't say anything. She kept her face a mask. Unread-able. Inscrutable. Isn't that what whites expected from Indians?

It was a moment before the woman went on: "An Indian who thinks he's Crazy Horse—now that's the kind of story my step-mother would love. The perfect reenactment."

"She's trying to track assets that have disappeared."

"You don't say?" Astonishment flashed in Dorothy Winslow's eyes. "You mean Dad actually hid his money from her? Maybe he wasn't as crazy as I thought. What's this about? Money from the ranch in Laramie?"

"He placed the money in an account with Wyoming Central Bank."

"On my advice."

"You advised him to put the money in a bank in Lander?"

"A bank she didn't know about so she couldn't withdraw every penny and blow it."

"You and your father were close?"

Dorothy looked away. "Closer in the last year, after he figured out his wife wasn't the sweet, obliging Libbie of his dreams. You ask me, Belinda played the role to perfection. Libbie Custer was hard as nails. Nobody crossed her, not even Ulysses S. Grant. Anybody who dared to suggest that Custer might have been responsible for what happened at the Little Bighorn faced the wrath of Libbie. For fifty years she wove a magical web around the battle and kept the truth from being told." She twisted around again. "The money should have been safe."

"He withdrew it."

"All of it?" Dorothy sank against the back of the chair. The legs skittered on the wood floor. "So it worked. He had hidden the money until he found a ranch near Dubois. Naturally she didn't want him to purchase another ranch. Tied her down too much. I mean, Autie never owned a ranch. He was free. Galloping over the plains, the horizon always ahead. She trekked along, basking in his glory." Dorothy unwound her fingers and leaned forward as if to confide an important secret. "Invitations to appear all over the country. Rodeos, county fairs in places you'd never guess: Florida. New England. California beach towns. Everybody wanted Custer. He brought along the Seventh Cavalry. Enough troopers to give folks the idea. Brought along Libbie, the adoring wife. No ranch for her, no sirree. She nagged my father until he sold out in Laramie, which broke his heart. He loved that place."

"Is that how they made their living? Playing Custer and Libbie?" Vicky had seen the deposits on the bank records, sporadic, small amounts. Then the big deposit after he sold the ranch.

"County fairs and a few head of cattle he'd sell every year."

Dorothy shook her head. "He wanted something more secure. He wasn't getting any younger. He'd already lived twenty years longer than Custer. Saw some buddies die in Desert Storm. I encouraged him to look at ranches in this area. I knew she'd hate it. 'Libbie's happiest when we're roaming the plains,' Dad said. You want to know the real reason I encouraged him? I was hoping she'd leave him. Find another Custer."

She let out a little laugh, tilting her head upward and staring at something inside her head. "I'll bet she found a way to break open his safe and get the bank records. Oh, what I would have given to see the look on her face when she saw the balance. He must have gotten his ranch after all."

Granite Group. It would explain the check, Vicky was thinking. The ranch was owned by the Granite Group. Except the broker at the real-estate company said the deal hadn't closed. If it hadn't closed, where was the money? She said, "The sale hadn't yet gone through."

"Hadn't gone through?" Dorothy drew in her lower lip and frowned. "He was worried."

"About what."

"Couldn't make the asking price. I told him, give them a down payment, take a mortgage. You have to understand. He was from another time in a lot of ways. Don't owe anybody. Don't take out mortgages. Pay your own way. He said he would buy the ranch outright. Own it lock, stock, and barrel. It would've been his, and his money would've been safe from her."

"Did he ever mention the Granite Group?"

She shook her head.

"He wrote a five-hundred-thousand-dollar check to the Granite Group."

"What?" The woman jumped to her feet and grabbed hold of

the porch railing, as if she wanted to yank it out of the floor. She swung back. "Dad was a sucker for get-rich schemes. Give me your money and I'll double it in two weeks? After he got back from Iraq, he took everything we had and plunked it down on a high-tech start-up. Going to make enough money to buy us a ranch. Killed my mother, all the worry. For a couple years, she didn't know where the money was going to come from to feed us. Dad never lost faith, and you know what? Doubled, tripled his money when the company went public. Got his ranch after all. By then Mom was so sick, she didn't care. Died a year after we moved in. Is that what he did? Another high flyer?"

"I was hoping you might know." The sound of Dorothy Winslow's rapid intakes of breath broke the silence that hung between them.

"Ask your client."

"She's asked me to help her."

"Always the smart move. Always a step ahead."

"If she knew what your father did with the money, why would she have hired me to help her find it?"

Dorothy pivoted and sank back into the chair. It rocked backward. "You're right. He wouldn't have told her. He wouldn't have taken any chances on her making trouble, keeping him from investing the money. He had his heart set on that ranch."

"You said he lived in another time." Edward Garrett, dressed like Custer, riding ahead of rows of cavalry down Main Street. A bugle blaring "Garry Owen." The clip-clop of horses' hooves on asphalt. Whinnying. Vicky could see the floats passing, she and Adam on the curb a half block away, clutching Styrofoam cups of coffee. "Who would a man who felt comfortable in the nineteenth century have trusted to invest his money? Did he ever mention anyone?"

Dorothy took so long to answer that Vicky began to wonder if the woman had heard her questions. Finally she exhaled a long breath. "Army buddies. He felt comfortable with old army buddies. Why do you think he played a man who was made general on the battlefield? Custer was his kind of man. Brave and independent. Fighting the undesirables. Killing. Dad was in the army when Desert Storm started. Colonel. Fought for seven months. It changed him. I was still a kid, but I remember that he was different when he came back. He retired but he couldn't break free. Oh, he wanted the ranch in Laramie all right, but the military life had taken him over. He saw himself as a soldier. Retired solder running a ranch. Then he found Custer, and he could do both. Run a ranch and pretend to be a soldier. Better than staying in the army. Going to Iraq. Afghanistan. He could relive the battle of the Bighorn, over and over and over, and nobody got killed. Until last Sunday."

"An army buddy like Skip Burrows?" Angela had said they were buddies, Edward and Skip.

Dorothy nodded. "At least Burrows got out of the army and went on with his life. There were others, like Dad. Never got free. The military in their blood. Planning battles, riding off to defeat the enemy. Lived for reenactments. Couldn't reenact Iraq, so they hit on the Civil War. Dad and his buddies specialized in Custer and the Seventh."

"What buddies? Who are you talking about?"

"All of them."

There was the faint sound of ringing. Vicky reached into her bag and pulled out her phone. A name she didn't recognize. "Sorry," she said to the woman next to her.

Dorothy gave a dismissive wave. "No matter. As far as I'm concerned, we're done here." She lifted herself out of the chair, yanked open the screened door. "Good luck in dealing with Libbie." She disappeared into the house.

Vicky pressed the phone to her ear as she made her way down the steps and across the yard. A woman's voice, faint. She had to stop and press the volume button. "You said to call if I seen Deborah."

"Deborah Boynton?" A picture was emerging—the skinny girl with white, gangly legs pushing the baby carriage outside the Realtor's house.

"Yeah. She come home this morning. Drove away again, most likely going to work. You can probably catch her there."

Vicky thanked the girl and started the Ford. Driving down the brown hills, around the curves, Lander rising to meet her, wondering what Deborah Boynton might know about Garrett's empty bank account.

27

"WHAT DO WE tell them?"

"The truth."

The bishop placed an open hand against the door frame and leaned into it, as if he were leaning against the wind.

"I meant, to give them peace of mind."

Father John sat back in his chair and studied the cottonwood branches swaying outside the window. They moved silently, and yet he knew the soft, whishing sound they made. The phone had been ringing all morning, and he and the bishop had taken turns fielding the calls. *Who could have strangled that poor girl? What did she do to deserve that? Who cares about her?*

He looked back at the old man in the doorway, the shadows of the corridor falling behind him. "We have to trust that the police will conduct a fair and impartial investigation."

"They're Arapahos."

"Yes." Father John took the point. How many times had the police come to Bishop Harry's mission in Patna looking for those without resources, the most vulnerable? Easy way to conclude an investigation. Records closed. Case solved. He wanted to say, *It's not like that here*. He remained quiet. Bishop Harry was no fool.

The rumbling noise came from far away, then grew closer, like the sound of horses stampeding. He got up and went over to the window as the black truck with the white horse trailer came around Circle Drive, the trailer shimmying, dried leaves and little clouds of dust in its wake. Darleen Longshot peered out through the windshield.

"Here to collect Brownie, I take it," the bishop said. "Rather nice to have him around. I enjoyed speaking with him on my walk this morning. Very intelligent animal."

The phone had started ringing again, and Father John realized how pleasant the last ten minutes of quiet had been.

"You'll probably want to say good-bye," the bishop said, starting along the corridor toward his office in the back.

"I'll tell him good-bye for you." By the time Father John reached the front door, the telephone had stopped ringing. The bishop's voice drifted behind him. "St. Francis Mission. Bishop Harry here."

Darleen had already opened the tailgate and was jiggling the chain at the fence when Father John came down the driveway. "Let me help you," he said, hurrying around the rig. He took hold of the chain, worked it loose, and swung open the gate. The sun burned down; there was no shade. The metal fence was like a hot iron. Brownie pawed at the thin grass in the enclosure, tossed his head, and snorted until Darleen stepped over and extended a hand. The horse nosed toward her and began licking the sugar cubes that glistened in her palm. "You miss him, don't you, boy?" she said, running her other hand over the horse's withers. He shivered beneath her touch, then settled down and nuzzled her palm.

A few motions, and the bridle was on Brownie's head, the lead rope clipped to a ring under his chin. Fluid. Smooth. "We're going home." She led him out the gate, her round face red in the sun. Clicking her teeth, urging the horse up the ramp into the trailer.

She shut the tailgate and turned to Father John, a deliberate motion, like the final step of a powwow dance. Little circles of sweat spread in the armpits of her pink blouse. "Where's Mikey?" Brownie blew a gust of air and tapped out another dance routine.

"He's not here."

"I know that. Otherwise he wouldn't have left Brownie. Where did he go?"

"Darleen," Father John said, grabbing a moment. "He didn't tell me."

"I get it. You didn't ask, so he didn't tell. That way neither of us knows. Right? Cops come around, and we can tell the truth." She let out a loud cough. "The Jesuit Way."

"Something like that." He could feel the sun burning across his shoulders and searing his head. He'd run out without his cowboy hat, and now he squinted at the woman standing guard behind the horse trailer, as if she could protect everything—her son, the horse.

"Alone?" She put up one hand. "Don't tell me. Something else we shouldn't know." She glanced away, eyes darting across the mission grounds, the expanse of wild grasses and stunted bushes that ran to the Little Wind River. From somewhere came the faint sound of sirens.

"Cops are all over the rez." She turned in the direction of the sounds. "They want Mike and Colin. How can they think they had anything to do with killing that girl? Colin loved her his whole life.

But the cops think they have it figured. Shot a white man, killed an Arapaho girl. Cops can solve two murders, they don't care how. Moccasin telegraph says the cops have witnesses. Witnesses! Some Arapaho that's scared his parole will be revoked, so he says what the cops want to hear? He saw Crazy Horse shoot Custer? Mike covering for Colin, riding in to shield him so nobody would see? Mike could do it. He could do anything with horses. But he didn't help kill anybody."

She stretched a hand between the slats of the trailer and ran it along the horse's flank. "Brownie here could tell them a thing or two. Mike talked to him all the time. Brownie talked back. Told each other secrets." She withdrew her hand, buckling, knees giving in, and Father John reached for her arm to steady her.

"We can't give up hope."

"It's not much, is it?"

"It's all we have."

The sirens had swelled to a screech that echoed through the hot, dry air. She pulled away and, hanging on to the side of the trailer, made her way to the driver's side of the truck. She flung open the door. "I have to get out of here."

Past the corner of the administration building, Father John saw the line of gray police cars, roof lights flashing through the cottonwoods. "It's too late," Father John said. "Wait here."

He jogged to the end of the driveway, turned into Circle Drive, and walked toward the vehicles swinging into the curb. *In an ambush, go to the enemy.* It was what Crazy Horse had done.

Detective Madden was lifting himself out of the passenger seat of the first car. He came along the drive, dark uniforms behind him, waving a white piece of paper, like a flag. "Where are they?" he called.

Father John waited until he had closed the space between them. White detective, alone on the rez, out of his own territory, BIA Police backup, dark, serious faces and intense black eyes watching, ridge of black hair below their caps. "Who are you looking for?" Playing for time again.

"I have warrants to arrest Colin Morningside and Mike Longshot for first degree murder and conspiracy to commit—"

"On what evidence?" Father John locked eyes with the man until he looked away, still waving the white sheet of paper.

"Enough evidence to convince the district court judge. No disrespect, Father, but this is out of your jurisdiction."

"You have the wrong men."

"Well, see, that's the problem. We don't have them yet. We will get them, however. They cannot hide on the rez forever."

"I'm telling you, they're not guilty of murdering anybody."

"You know that how?"

"I know them," Father John said. "They aren't capable of it."

"A priest telling me that? I wonder if you believe it. Maybe you haven't heard enough confessions. Let me tell you, I've heard more than I want to think about. Cleanest-cut, best-looking, best sons in the world, until they took a few too many shots of whiskey, got to brooding on all the wrongs done them, picked up a knife or a pistol or a baseball bat, and went looking for revenge." The detective moved in closer, head bent, staring up at Father John. "You think we can really ever know another person?"

"I'm telling you, you've got the wrong men."

"Where are they?"

"They're not here."

"We can search the entire mission."

"Help yourself."

Off his shoulder, Father John heard the familiar rumble and clank of the truck and trailer. Brakes squeaking followed by the ragged sound of gears shifting, engine revving. Father John glanced around as the rig drove straight for Detective Madden and the mass of blue uniforms. Darleen Longshot hunched over the wheel, hands on the top, white-knuckled, and the wildness of a grizzly in her eyes.

"Stop!" He leapt out in front, holding up both hands, the truck only a few feet away. Barely aware of the police officers stumbling and scattering, flinging themselves off the drive and into the grass. A hand, like iron, gripping his arm, yanking him backward, the bumper knocking against his leg.

"Are you crazy?" Madden's voice was a half octave higher, terror and shock racking the words.

Out of the corner of his eyes, Father John saw the officer crouched on the curve, in shooting position. God! The pistol pointed at the cab of the truck heading into the curve on Circle Drive.

"Don't shoot!" Father John yelled. "For godssakes, don't shoot."

Time stopped. The pistol poised in the air, moving slowly, tracking the trailer, the horse stamping. Then the trailer turning into the curve. Now, a clear view of the dark head in the rear window.

"Don't shoot her!" He shouted into the abyss of a battlefield, nothing but confusion, instinct, adrenaline pumping.

"Stop!" The detective's voice now, and the pistol slowly came down, and there was silence except for the receding rattle of the trailer heading through the cottonwoods.

"Damned Indian tried to kill us." The officer holstered the pistol and stood up. Father John could see his legs shaking, his hands trembling.

"We'll pick her up," Madden said. "She's not going far." He turned to Father John, eyes narrowed in barely controlled rage. "You see what we're dealing with."

"She's distraught."

"Where are they?" The detective sounded as if he were at the end of his rope. No more conversation. No more theories. Only the stark nearness of death.

"They left," Father John said. "They didn't say where they were going."

"But you know." He straightened his shoulders. "Both of them were here." Talking to himself now. "Darleen Longshot in the truck, crazy as her son. The whole lot of 'em crazy. Heading for the Sioux. Like we won't be able to get them there. It's a matter of time."

Madden gestured to the BIA Police who had accompanied him—a white man on the rez. Trying to arrest two Arapahos. It was dangerous.

One by one, the officers lowered themselves into the cars. A radio screeched. "Come in. Come in. Do you have an officer down?"

Madden yanked a mike off a hook and shouted. "No officer down. Stop a black pickup pulling a white horse trailer. Seventeen-Mile Road. Darleen Longshot driving. Approach with caution. Dangerous. Arrest her for attempted murder."

He replaced the mike and stared at Father John a moment. Then he started to pull the door shut, shouting, "Better have that leg looked at."

Father John watched the cars backing around, pulling out, roof lights dark. Driving out of the mission. It was then that he felt the sharp stabbing pain working its way through his left leg.

28

THE REAL-ESTATE office was quiet, window shades half-drawn against the sun, photos of houses fading to light bronze. Vicky had left the Ford at the curb and let herself through the glass door. The bell on a red rope was still jangling. On the left, an empty reception desk. No one around. She gave it a minute to allow the sound of the bell to register on someone in the back cubicles. Linda Lewin, the broker. Maybe even Deborah Boynton.

Linda Lewin came through the door wearing an expression that ran like water from hopeful to resigned. "You just missed her," she said.

"Deborah? Where can I find her?"

"As I said before, I don't keep tracking devices on the Realtors." A harmony of phones rang in the cubicles behind her.

"You can probably help me . . ."

"Oh yeah. A subpoena if I refuse. Well, maybe I'll just let you get one."

Vicky was quiet. Something had changed. "What are you afraid of?"

"Afraid of?" She pulled the door closed behind her and motioned to the plastic chairs lined up below a plate glass window. "Look," she said, patting her short dark skirt over her thighs. "I don't want any trouble, okay?"

"Why would you have any trouble?"

"I don't know what Deborah's up to. Next time she comes in, I intend to tell her I don't want her here anymore. Soon's a Realtor gets squirrelly . . ."

"Squirrelly?"

"Unreliable. Shows up when she wants. Voice mail full. Clients calling me, saying, 'Where's my Realtor?' Last time that happened with one of the Realtors, we had the real-estate board crawling all over us, investigating the company. Understand what I'm saying? I don't need that."

"You said she was just here."

"Blew in. Picked up a stack of mail and blew out."

"Look, Linda," Vicky began, "I'm trying to find out what happened to a large sum of money that my client's husband invested . . ."

"You mean, in real estate?"

"Possibly." Vicky stopped. The Granite Group could be right here, a real-estate investment fund handled in this office by Deborah Boynton. There could have been some delay in transferring the money from one fund to another so that Garrett could purchase the ranch. "What do you know about the Granite Group?" she said.

Linda Lewin seemed puzzled, at sea, blinking at the name. "Sounds familiar," she said. "Some time ago . . ." She got to her feet, sidled past the desk, and sat down. Typing. The computer screen lighting up. "Here we go. Eight months ago, the company purchased an apartment building in Casper. Two months later, seven houses in Cheyenne." She looked past the edge of the screen. "Deborah handled the transactions, if that's what you want to know."

"Who owns the company? Where is it located?"

The woman leaned back in the chair and clasped her hands on her waist. "Same questions I asked Deborah. A group of investors, she told me. I shouldn't worry. Everything legitimate. The transactions went smoothly. No problems."

"The company still has the properties?"

"If they've sold, they didn't list with us. Hold on." More typing, Linda hunching over the screen. "Here we go. County records in Casper show Granite Group as owner of the apartment building." Another moment passed, studying the screen. "Same ownership on the houses."

"Any names?"

Linda Lewin shook her head. Timing was everything, Vicky was thinking, and the timing wasn't right. Garrett hadn't transferred money to the Granite Group until four months ago. "What about the ranch near Dubois that Edward Garrett wanted to buy. Who owns it?"

The computer keys snapped like marbles rolling across the floor. It took a few moments before the woman said, "Stockton Ranch, located off the highway ten miles south of Dubois. Still for sale. Owners Jocelyn and Ernest Stockton, Richmond, Virginia."

Vicky stood up. She felt as if she had been running down dark corridors into solid walls, with no way out. Deborah Boynton knew the principals behind the Granite Group, but the woman wasn't here, and she wouldn't be at home. In and out, picking up mail and messages. "Did you ask Deborah to call me?"

"I gave her your card." The broker lifted herself over the computer and came back around the desk. "Don't expect a call. She was—how should I put it?—preoccupied."

Vicky left the woman standing in the reception area, stepped off the curb, and got into the Ford. She caught a view of the woman through the glass door. A silent, dark figure, as if she were staring at shredded papers, trying to piece them together.

She turned the ignition and rolled down the windows. Little clouds of dust swirled around the parking lot, nipped at the tires of cars parked farther along the curb, blew across the open windows. Her nostrils felt dry and scratchy. She concentrated on the cell cupped in one hand, calling the office.

A moment, then Annie's voice saying she had been about to call. "I just got off the phone with the secretary of state's office. You're not going to believe it, but the Granite Group doesn't exist. There is no company registered by that name."

Vicky stared straight ahead. The figure had disappeared from behind the glass door, leaving the real-estate office with a shutdown, end-of-the-day look. It surprised her that she wasn't surprised. The Granite Group didn't exist, except in the mind of whoever had set it up. Whoever had taken Edward Garrett's money.

She asked Annie to keep trying, sensing the pointlessness even as she issued the request. Legal documents filed with the county clerk that might reference the Granite Group. The Internet. Bulletin boards where investors might have posted something on the Granite Group. Like looking for a needle in a haystack. She backed into the lot and drove forward. Onto Federal, then south to Highway 789. Past the road to St. Francis Mission. Past the Wind River

Casino and Hotel perched on the hill, and on until she had crossed the border and was slowing through Hudson, scrub brushes dancing in the wind outside.

She followed the Popo Agie River around the curve and on into Lander. The town had settled into the heat and quiet of the afternoon. She turned into the asphalt lot along the side of the square, tan-brick building, and slid into one of the slots behind the sign that said Bank Customers Only. Inside, cool air streamed across an open area with shiny floors that resembled Wyoming Central Bank down the street. Glass-enclosed cubicles on one side, and on the other, a row of tellers behind a long counter. It struck her that all banks had a similar feeling—solidity, dependability, trustworthiness.

"How can I help you?" A young man with a scrubbed, eager look and short-cropped blond hair, who looked like the frat boy he had probably been not long ago, rose from a desk that faced the front door. He wore a light blue shirt with a dark blue tie that bisected the front of his shirt. A ballpoint pen was clipped in the pocket.

"Vicky Holden," Vicky said, handing a business card across the desk. "I'm here on behalf of a client. I'd like to speak with an officer."

The man frowned at the card a moment. "I'll call Mr. Welton," he said, backing away from the desk, still studying the card.

Vicky watched the charade play out in the third cubicle along the wall. The young man standing, nodding, tilting his head toward the front door; an older man with broad shoulders sitting behind the desk, studying her business card, poised, tense. He rose, came around the desk, and led the young man across the lobby, footsteps making a soft scuffing noise on the carpet.

"Ms. Holden," he said. He wore a short-sleeved, light blue shirt and dark tie identical to the young man's. "Clark Welton," he extended his hand. His grip was firm and confident. "We've been expecting you. Follow me, please."

Vicky followed the man through the lobby, past the cubicles and a small table topped with a metal coffeepot and stacks of Styrofoam cups. He halted for a half second at the table. "Coffee?"

"No, thank you," she said. Then they were through a walnut door that fit so closely into the walnut wall at the rear of the bank, she hadn't realized it was a door. They walked down a short hallway, and he ushered her into a conference room with a long, polished walnut table surrounded by chairs upholstered in dark blue tweed. A computer sat on a small table against the wall, and that is where he headed. Waving her to an upholstered chair close by, he sat down at the computer and swiveled toward her.

"I understand you represent Edward Garrett's widow. We were informed by Wyoming Central Bank that you are trying to trace a large sum of money Garrett paid into one of our accounts. You understand the privacy issues here, I trust. Certain matters must remain confidential."

Vicky pulled the file folder out of her bag and opened it on the table. "Belinda Clark has given me her power of attorney in this matter. We have also opened a probate action in district court. The money her husband transferred to the Granite Group was communal property. She is entitled to know if the money is still in the account."

He steered the chair around to the computer and started typing. From where she sat, the screen looked black, but Welton kept alternating between watching the keyboard and looking up at the screen. "Difficult to say." He seemed to be talking to himself. "Ongoing deposits and withdrawals. Garrett's check for five hundred thousand cleared, but there was activity after that. This was a very active account."

"Was?"

Welton turned from the computer and eyed her steadily for a moment. "The Granite Group account was closed. The full balance, four hundred thousand dollars, withdrawn. This removes our bank from the matter. We have no responsibility—or, indeed, knowledge—of what became of Mr. Garrett's money."

"When was the account closed?"

The man did a half turn and tapped at the keyboard with one finger. He leaned in closer to the screen. "Recently. Last Friday at two thirty-nine p.m."

"Where was the money transferred?"

"Transferred?" He swung back. "It was received in cash. One-hundred-dollar bills."

"By whom? I need to know the principals behind the Granite Group."

"And I'm afraid that is information that must remain confidential." He put up a hand before Vicky could say anything. "Naturally we would honor a subpoena."

Vicky laid a fist on the table. "We both know who is behind the Granite Group," she said. "His name is on that screen."

Welton jerked his head sideways, a panicky movement, as if she had read the black screen.

"Skip Burrows."

"You did not hear that from me. I have not divulged his identity."

"You just did," she said. "You'll have the subpoena as fast as I can issue it."

*   *   *

OUTSIDE, THE ENGINE hummed and a hot breeze blew through the Ford. Vicky pressed the mobile against her ear and counted the rings—one, two, three—until Annie's voice came on. "Everything okay?"

"Listen, Annie," Vicky said, ignoring the question. "We need a subpoena to force Bank of the West to provide information due Belinda Clark."

"Got it."

"Let me talk to Roger."

It was a moment before Roger Hurst picked up. "Sorry, Vicky. I was on the other line. What's going on?"

"I need some names. You know Skip Burrows . . ."

"Knew him, yeah. Shook his hand a couple dozen times. We threw back a couple beers together. You know, another lawyer in town. We commiserated with each other."

"You joined the search after he disappeared."

"Along with about seventy others."

"What do you know about him?"

"Excuse me?" Roger hesitated as if he were waiting for a clarification. "Not much," he said.

"Was he investing money for clients?"

Roger took a long moment before he said, "Skip is a funny guy. Friendly, outgoing. Left the impression he'd bail you out of jail, if that's what you needed. But"—another deliberative pause—"he kept a wall up. There was a way he had that let you know how far you could go, what questions you could ask."

"You never heard about any investments?"

"He had what you might call a club. I got the impression a few people were closer to him than others. And they were all the same. I mean, with the wall up."

"Anybody in particular?"

"If I wanted to find out about Skip, I guess I'd start with Hank Colton at the Wind Bar. He owns the place."

29

DANK LIGHT SHONE on the pine walls and tables inside the Wind Bar. The air was thick with odors of beer and hot grease. From the speakers fixed near the ceiling in opposite corners came the voice of Willie Nelson over a rumble of guitars. Except for the man leaning over a newspaper opened on the bar in back, the place was empty. Vicky threaded her way among the tables and barrel-shaped chairs. A silver stand with menus and salt and pepper shakers occupied the center of each table.

The man turned over a newspaper page and looked up. "What can I do for you?"

"Hank Colton?"

"So they say." Everybody's idea of a western movie star, handsome and rugged in a blue-striped shirt and jeans. Brown hair cut short, jaw squared, and wrinkles sun-etched at the corners of eyes that looked sky blue even in the dim light.

"Vicky Holden. I'm an attorney."

"I know you. Indian lawyer. Seen you around town with that other Indian lawyer. What brings you here?"

"I understand you are a friend of Skip Burrows."

He spread his arms in an arc as if he might lift the whole world. "Includes about everybody in town. Skip was a good guy. Took time to get to know people. Always wanted to know how the wife and kids were getting along."

Vicky slid onto a stool. "Was a good guy? You believe he's dead?"

"How long has it been, three days since he got dragged out of his office? Police don't have squat. Nobody's asked for a ransom, and believe me, if there had been any ransom calls, I would've been the first to hear. Nothing goes on in this town that doesn't come to this bar." He thumped a fist on top of the newspaper that shifted and crackled. "The confessional. All kinds come in here, talk about everything. Man, if this bar could write a book, it would be a bestseller exposé of the whole area. What's your piece of this?"

"I represent the widow of Edward Garrett, the man who was killed out there." She motioned with her head toward the front of the bar and Main Street beyond.

"I was there. I seen it. Those Indians pulled a fast one. Surrounded old Custer once again and shot him down."

"The investigation is still going on," Vicky said, making an effort to tamp down the hot shoots of anger rising inside her. It was so easy to blame the Indians, jump to conclusions. "The warriors sent a message. It didn't mean one of them shot Garrett."

"Yeah, right." Colton tilted his head back and stared at the ceiling. "You Indians stick together. You ask me, nobody else around here had any reason to kill Garrett. Nobody else was close enough to pull the trigger. How do you account for that?"

"I don't. It's Detective Madden's problem." Vicky waited a moment for the point to sink in. "I'm here about Skip."

"What's he got to do with the guy that got killed?"

"I understand he made investments for clients. I believe he invested for Garrett, and his widow is trying to trace the funds."

Hank Colton settled back on his heels and regarded her a long moment, as if he had to readjust his initial opinion. "What makes you think Skip was investing?"

"This isn't the only place where you can pick up on what's going on." She tapped a knuckle against the shiny wood. "What can you tell me about the Granite Group?"

Hank took his time folding the newspaper and pushing it aside. Then he pulled a cloth from beneath the bar and began running it over the space between them. "What Skip did, he did for his friends. He didn't broadcast all the good he did. The way he helped people grow their money, put them in a better place. It was private, nobody's business."

"You invested with him?" Vicky could sense the tension around them, like electricity crackling silently.

"If I did, I wouldn't have anything to say. It was between Skip and his closest friends. A real tight club. A lot of people wanted to get in, but Skip was particular." He twisted the cloth and snapped it at the corner of the bar. "You didn't just walk up to Skip and say, 'I got some money I'd like to invest.' He'd tell you to go see a broker."

"So who was in the club?"

Hank was looking off into the bar, something unfolding behind his eyes. "We were having a beer, just Skip and me. Middle of the afternoon, like now, nobody else around, and I said, 'Skip, old buddy. What's this I hear about you getting real good returns on investments?' I told him I'd heard rumors he was doubling people's money in a short time. Hell, I've been working this place for five years, barely squeezing out a living. Then my old man died and left me ten thousand. So I thought, here's my ticket. I had something to grow."

"What did he say?"

"Nothing, at first. Pretended he didn't know what I was talking about. I told you, the club was private. Big locked door that only a few got past. I told him I had a lot of money I wanted to invest, and I remember he took a long drink of beer before he said, 'How much?' 'Ten K,' I told him, and he . . ." Colton shook his head, then brought his eyes back to hers. "He said, 'Put it in the bank.'"

Vicky made a little fist and blew into it. After a moment she said, "How much did it take to join the club?" She was thinking that Edward Garrett had walked away from the sale of his ranch in Laramie with five hundred thousand dollars.

"I got the picture after that. Ten K was a pittance. Skip was interested in the high rollers. He knew what he was doing, all right. I mean, how much could he make off a measly ten K?"

"Where did he find investors?" Vicky was thinking that Garrett had found him, an old army buddy, a man he trusted.

"Jackson."

"Jackson." Vicky spun sideways and studied the mixture of shadows and sunlight creeping across the tables and the floor, the little motes of dust floating in the sunlight. Skip spent a lot of time in Jackson, Angela had said. He had friends there.

She spun back and faced the man across from her. "Then how did the rumors about the investments get here?"

"Lot of people from Jackson stop in. Probably came to see Skip, check up on their money, collect their interest." He shrugged. "The club was private, but folks like to brag, you know? Tell strangers how they belong to a real private club."

"Anybody you know?"

Colton shook his head.

"Anybody from this area in the club?"

"Maybe," he said. "Nobody ever came right out and said so, but they'd brag about making a fistful of money on a great investment." He snapped the cloth on the edge of the bar again, making a sharp whacking noise. "Try Reece Mishko, artist moved to town from Jackson last year. He liked to brag a lot about the great investments he had. Yeah, try that dude."

REECE MISHKO WAS easy to find, as if the artist had laid out a pathway for anybody with enough cash and art appreciation to connect with him. Vicky stopped into the art gallery halfway down the block from Wind Bar. A pair of oil paintings, one of the Wind River range and the other of the Tetons, stood on easels in the front window. Scrawled in the right corner was the name Reese Mishko.

"Beautiful, aren't they?" The woman's voice floated through the sound of the bell jangling over the door as Vicky stepped inside. "I saw you admiring the paintings." She was short and wide-shouldered, dressed in a black blouse and a long black skirt with a belt studded in turquoise, coral, and silver. Her light brown hair, cut straight and shoulder-length, mingled with her dangling turquoise earrings. "Reese does a wonderful job of capturing the colors and grandeur of our local mountains." She waved at other paintings on the wall. "Notice the shadows of the pines in the creek at the bottom of the Wind River scene."

Vicky moved toward the side wall and studied the arrangement of paintings. Buffalo, horses, a stunning portrait of a wolf with a glint of desperation in his eyes.

"He's great with wildlife." A pencil had materialized, and the woman thumped it against her palm.

"Are these the only paintings you have?"

A look of annoyance flickered in her eyes. "For the moment. Reece is very prolific. He has other pieces in the gallery at his house, which we also represent. If you don't find what you like here, I'm sure he'd be happy to show you more. Are you interested in making a purchase?"

Vicky gave the woman a slow, assuring smile. She was thinking of the framed posters on the wall in her office, and the one original painting that she had bought when she'd started her practice, a beautiful rendition of an Indian village in the vastness of the plains painted by an Indian artist she had met at a powwow. She always imagined it was the village of her great-grandparents. "If I found something that appealed to me."

"Something different from the pieces here?"

"Yes. I'm in the market for new art for my office, and I like Mishko's work very much." She extracted a business card from her bag and handed it to the woman.

"You're a lawyer?" The woman cleared her throat, as if she could clear away the sound of surprise. Then moved sideways to a large desk with a polished surface and an upholstered side chair pushed into the well. She picked up a mobile, pressed a key, and, throwing a watchful look Vicky's way, said, "Reece! Are you busy?" A moment passed. "I agree. That was a stupid question. I have a client here, a lawyer looking for paintings to display in her office. She likes what we have, but"—she drew in a long breath—"it's not quite what she wants." She nodded at Vicky, as if to confirm the truth of what she had said, then shifted her eyes sideways, her attention focused on whatever the man at the other end was saying.

"Fine, darling. I appreciate it. See you soon." Setting the mobile back on the desk, she said, "If you go right away, he will take a few moments to show you his gallery. You can make your selection, and we'll handle everything. We'll deliver the paintings to your office, even hang them for you."

She opened a drawer, pulled out a small white pad, and started scribbling. Then she tore off the top sheet and held it out to Vicky. "His house and studio are not far from here. In the hills west of town. Large ranch style with a big porch and black-tiled roof."

30

THE RANCH-STYLE house with white wicker sofa and chairs on the front porch sat isolated at the end of a road that corkscrewed uphill. The area was familiar. Dorothy Winslow's place was on the other side of the hill, not far away. Vicky got out of the Ford as the front door swung open. Wild grasses bumped against the sidewalk to the wooden front steps. The wind gusted around her. The porch was like an oasis, the air quiet and ten degrees cooler. A young woman—not much older than Angela, Vicky thought—blond and curly headed, wearing cutoff denim shorts and a too-tight tee shirt, stood in the doorway. Chin hoisted in the air, eyes narrowed in disapproval.

"Vicky Holden. I'm here to see Reece."

"Reece is very busy." The blond woman had a little girl's voice, a shaky edge to the confidence she was obviously trying to convey. "He doesn't like to be bothered in the middle of the day. Annette . . ."

"Annette?"

"At the gallery, should know better. He has hours when the public can visit his private gallery. Two to four on Saturdays. Annette should have told you that. Trouble is, all she can think about is collecting her stinking commission. I don't know why Reece . . ."

"Invite Ms. Holden in." The voice, low and raspy, came from somewhere inside the house.

"All I can say is, make it quick." She stepped to the side and nodded Vicky into an entry as large as her office, with a ceiling that soared above an expanse of wood floors and white walls covered with paintings that resembled those in the gallery—a collage of the Wind River and the Tetons. She glanced around the paintings. Any of them would be beautiful in her office.

"Reece has work to finish this afternoon," the woman was saying. "Annette's isn't the only gallery that represents him. He has galleries in Jackson and Aspen, you know."

"Vicky Holden, attorney-at-law." The man appeared in the arched doorway that led somewhere to the back of the house. Gray hair, thick and tangled, long, ropey muscles. He wore khaki shorts and a blue shirt with tails hanging loose, top buttons unfastened. He was in his sixties, which meant the girl could have been his granddaughter, except for the worshipful gaze she fastened on him. Enormous hands, like baseball gloves, dangled at his side. "See anything you like?"

"They're all beautiful."

"Well, Prissy here"—a glance at the girl standing first on one bare foot, then the other—"will be happy to show you through my private gallery on the second floor. Excuse me if I don't accompany you. Works calls. I'm sure you can understand. Prissy was good enough to open up the gallery."

"If you don't mind, Mr. Mishko . . ."

"Reece. We're not in New York."

"I'd like a few words with you."

"I told you, work . . ."

"About Skip Burrows."

Reece Mishko rocked back on the heels of his leather sandals, not taking his eyes from her. "You used subterfuge to get here."

"I do admire your work, and I could use more art in my office."

"Okay, okay." The man put up the palm of one hand. "We can talk in my studio."

"Reece . . ." The name had hardly emerged from the girl's mouth when his palm turned sideways and sliced the air in her direction. "Bring us some coffee."

She seemed to melt backward, past the large staircase and through a door on the other side of the entry. The door made a hissing noise as it opened and closed.

"This way." Reece swung around. Head high, gray hair brushing the collar of his shirt, calf muscles flexing, he headed through the archway. Vicky followed him into a large, light-filled room with black leather sofas and chairs and tiled tables arranged beneath a wall of windows that framed the foothills. The view resembled the view in one of the paintings in the entry. Large paintings covered the walls at either end of the room.

Vicky realized that Reece Mishko had already taken a turn to the right and disappeared through a door in the corner. She walked over and stepped into another room filled with a suffused light from the overhead skylight. In the center was a large easel with a painting that looked half finished. Another view of the Wind River range. All of Mishko's paintings seemed familiar, as if she could step inside and find her way.

Scattered around the studio were tables with jars of different colors of paint crowding the surfaces. Paint dribbled down the sides of the jars. There were wads of cloth and paper towels, buckets of brushes, a desk in one corner cluttered with papers, and shelves along the far wall filled with books that toppled against one another. A mixture of odors—alcohol, turpentine, paint—clogged the air. From outside came the soft whooshing noise of the wind in a cottonwood.

In front of the easel was a black metal stool that Reece Mishko spun around and straddled, leaning against the top bar of the back. "Sit anywhere." He motioned toward a pair of chairs near the desk.

Vicky went over and pulled one chair into the center of the room. She was about to sit down when she realized she would be looking up at the famous Reece Mishko, which, she also realized, was exactly what he had intended. "I'm more comfortable standing," she said.

"Whatever suits you." A smile creased the corners of his mouth. They were playing a game, and she wasn't sure of the rules.

"Any news on Skip?"

"I'm afraid not." Vicky began pacing. Back and forth in front of the man with the bemused expression on his face. She forced herself to stand still and lock eyes with him. "My client is the widow of Edward Garrett."

"Do I know him?"

"He was murdered last Sunday on Main Street."

"The crazy Custer guy."

"He was a friend of Skip's. They were army buddies. He was a member of Skip's club."

Reece Mishko dipped his chin into his chest and examined the paint caked under his fingernails. "And this affects me how?"

"The money he invested with Skip is missing. I was hoping you could tell me about the Granite Group."

"You're assuming . . ."

"I know you were in the club." Vicky held her breath. All she knew was that a man who ran a bar had told her Reece Mishko liked to brag about his investments. "Look, all I want to know is whether Skip paid you back your principal."

Reece was shaking his head. "The club was for a few friends of Skip's who had money to invest and needed good returns. Once in a while, Skip made an offering to club members of securities in oil and gas start-ups. Skip said the securities were exempted from registration under the federal securities laws, since all of us are seasoned investors. He was a darn good lawyer. He knew what he was doing. The offerings were private. I suppose the widow told you about this. All I can say is I was privileged to know Skip. Privileged that he allowed me to invest with him." He spread his hands as if he might take in the whole studio, the house, the grassy, wind-blown hills. "Things look good to you, right? I mean, I have a big house. Paintings on sale in galleries. Problem is, the economy tanked and even rich folks stopped buying paintings. Why art that feeds the soul should be considered nonessential is something I will never understand. Is food nonessential?" He shrugged. "So I tightened up, started watching my money. Moved here from Jackson to cut down on expenses. Then I got lucky. An uncle died and left me a nice sum of money. Of course, I knew Skip. Who didn't? Spent a lot of time socializing in Jackson. Great skier. I'd heard rumors about Skip and his investment club from some well-heeled clients in Jackson, so I made a few phone calls. Skip had never mentioned anything about the club. It wasn't his way."

"What was his way?"

"You'd hear about it. Rumors, innuendos. You'd get Skip in a corner of a bar and ask about joining. If you were lucky, you got in. Very few got in. Usually he'd deny there was any club." He pulled himself upright, straightened his shoulders, then went back to leaning on the chair. "Half a mil was the entrance fee. I made it in the club two years ago. Been collecting thirty percent every quarter since. Keeps this place and my business running. Why would I want my principal back?"

"What kind of investments did he make?"

"Real estate. Oil. Gas. Look, I've got the paperwork. Records for each investment, amount paid out. All in black and white."

Vicky started pacing again. She thought better when she was moving, not stuck to the ground like a fence post. Her people had always been moving, she knew. Moving, thinking, planning, deciding, all at the same time. The words *black and white* rang in her ears. Records composed on Angela's computer, spit out of Angela's printer, and saved on Angela's flash drive. "Skip's still missing," she said.

"He's dead."

Vicky stopped and turned toward the man. "What makes you so sure?"

"Indians killed him." He tossed his head and shrugged, as if that were the end of the matter. "Killed that Custer maniac, then they killed Skip."

"Why would they do that?" Here it was again, the spokes of white-hot anger turning inside her.

"Why does anybody do stupid things? For the money. You heard about Skip's club. Other Indians heard about it, too. Probably from that Indian girl that worked for him. I figure she put them up to it, promised they'd get their hands on the money Skip had coming in. Let's face it, she was in a position to transfer interest payments to her friends. My guess is the interest on Garrett's account started going to Indians. Must have seemed like Custer owed them. I figure Garrett caught on, so they killed him. Skip also caught on, so he disappeared."

"You're not worried about your money?" The principal was gone, Vicky was thinking. Gone the way Garrett's money was gone.

Reece Mishko was smiling now, shaking his head and smiling. "They didn't break into my account. Checks arrive like clockwork. I figure it doesn't matter what hole they dropped Skip into, the Granite Group is still solid. Somebody will take it over and manage it, maybe a bank or a club member that knows finances."

The door opened and the girl sidled into the studio, balancing a tray, coffee cups rattling, a creamer and sugar bowl sliding toward the edge. "Coffee?"

"You're a dear, Prissy. Set it over there." Reece nodded toward a table. The girl slid the tray against an array of paint cans, then drew herself upright. A satisfied expression printed itself on her face.

"Leave us."

The young woman blinked, the look of satisfaction fading into one of confusion. She moved sideways, retracing her steps across the room and through the door.

"Fresh coffee?" Reece wrinkled his nose.

Coffee smells wrapped in the smells of paint and turpentine, Vicky thought, like the darkness wrapped inside the light-filled room and the big house with the soaring ceiling. "I've taken enough of your time." She fought the urge to pivot about and run from the studio. From the house and the area, from the disaster about to take place. Half a million dollars gone, and Reece Mishko had no idea.

Vicky opened the door, then turned back. "You should talk to Detective Madden," she said. "Tell him what you've told me." She waited, trying to gauge the man's reaction. Was there a hint of discomfort in the way he clasped his hands and rolled his shoulders, as if she had seen something he had been ignoring, like a botched tree in a finished painting? "For your own good," she said.

VICKY SAT IN the car several minutes, engine humming, the air hot and dry in her throat. The picture clear now, as clear as a photograph with none of the smeared edges of oil paints on canvas. As clear as if she were in Skip Burrows's office, a witness to what was happening. Edward Garrett demanding his principal so that he could buy the ranch near Dubois. Skip trying to put him off. Cajoling. Reasoning. Why would he want the principal withdrawn from the Granite Group when he was making thirty percent? Where could he get that kind of money? They had a great thing going.

Garrett insisted. They had argued, Angela said, and Garrett had stormed off. But what had he said before he stormed off? What had he threatened? To go to the police? To blow the whistle on Skip Burrows's Ponzi scheme?

Because that was what he was running. Collecting money—a half mil was the minimum—from new investors to make interest payments to old investors. It worked, as long as new investors came in, and Skip had made sure that happened. Visiting Jackson, but not living there! Not staying too close, where people could ask too many questions. All working, until Edward Garrett demanded to withddraw his money.

She shifted into reverse and twisted around to watch the driveway unfurl behind her. Then, in drive, she started down the winding road and struggled to contain the fear that welled inside her. Skip had cashed out on Friday afternoon. He had decided to take off with what he had. A briefcase full of money. Then, a moment of what? Panic? Remorse? Fright? He had called her office. Another lawyer. Maybe he'd had second thoughts. Maybe he wanted to stop the whole thing, the running, the waiting—there had to be the waiting—for the moment when everything crashed down around him.

She hadn't been in the office. And he hadn't run. He'd gone to Jackson with Angela. On Monday morning he was back in his own office. Had he intended to call her again?

But Angela had seen the briefcase of money. What if she had told Colin?

Vicky turned into the outskirts of Lander and slowed for the stoplight ahead. She swallowed hard against the taste of acid erupting in her throat. Maybe everybody was right. Madden, the bartender, Reece Mishko. Colin had killed Garrett. Then, Monday morning, he had abducted Skip and his briefcase of money. My God. She hadn't wanted to believe it could be true. She had been blindfolded.

At the red light, she drew out her mobile and punched the key for St. Francis Mission. John O'Malley would test her theory, tell her where she had taken a wrong turn, set her back on the right trail. She had to speak with him! The need running through her was like a dull ache she had tried for a long time to ignore.

"St. Francis Mission." The voice was only slightly familiar.

"Is Father John in?"

"It's you, Vicky?" the Bishop said. "He's at Riverton Memorial. Colin Morningside was shot this afternoon."

31

THE WAITING ROOM was empty except for Lou Morningside crouched on a plastic chair in a far corner, eyes fixed on the metal swinging doors in the opposite wall. Father John walked over, laid his hand on the old man's shoulder, then sat down beside him. He didn't say anything. It was enough that Lou knew he was there.

A long moment passed. Then Lou made a gurgling noise, as though he had to swallow the whole terrible reality before he could speak of it. "They tried to kill my grandson."

"What do the doctors say?"

"Nothing. Just worked on him, peered down at him, punched needles in his arm, hooked him up to plastic bags." His shrug was filled with hopelessness. "They're going to take him into surgery. Told me to wait out here."

Father John felt the faintest prick of hope. Colin was alive! "We can pray for him."

The old man nodded. "All I been doing. Praying and praying. I'm begging the Creator not to take him. Not yet. He still has a lot to do, so much good to do."

Father John patted the old man's shoulder again, then clasped his hands between his knees and bowed his head. "Dear Lord." He was whispering, but the words seemed to fill up the empty space. "Have mercy on your child, Colin. Remember him and hold him close to you. Have mercy on the doctors and guide their hands. We place our trust in you."

He waited. Whatever had happened to Colin, Lou wasn't ready to talk about it yet. They might have been in a vacuum, the muffled sounds of traffic far away, the click of footsteps and traces of conversation wrapped in hospital quiet.

Several minutes passed before Lou cleared his throat again. "No need to shoot the boy. All they had to do was tell him what they wanted, where they were gonna take him. I been thinking on what happened since I got the call from the tribal police saying Colin was shot and I should get over to the hospital. He was so close to being free. Thirty miles from South Dakota, then over the border into Pine Ridge. Mike and him could've stayed there until this business got cleared up and the cops stopped blaming them for killing Custer. Stopped blaming Colin for murdering the girl he loved all his life, and started looking for the real killers. Instead they went after Colin and Mike. Got word to all the cops in Wyoming and South Dakota to be on the lookout for them. Well, they found them. State patrol pulled them over, handcuffed Mike, started to handcuff Colin . . ."

"He took off." It was like a movie running in Father John's head. Colin, trapped like an animal, smelling the hopelessness. How would he ever prove himself innocent? Dear Lord, Madden had enough circumstantial evidence to file charges of murder against both Colin and Mike.

"Where was he gonna go? Nothing but the plains going on forever. Arroyos and hills and no water. Shot him in the lower back, crazy bastards. Didn't want him making it across the border."

"Why did they bring him here?" Father John knew the answer even before he had finished the question. He tried to push down the thought that they had brought him close to home to die.

"It's good he's here," Lou said. "He needs people around that love him."

Father John glanced about the empty space. Odd it wasn't crowded with Arapahos, cousins and relatives so far removed that nobody was sure how they were related, friends and the grandmothers who always showed up to sit with the grieving. "Can I call someone?"

Lou nodded. "Lorene Morningside, my brother's granddaughter. I left the rez so fast, didn't call anybody."

Father John slipped the cell out of his shirt pocket. It took a moment to find the woman's number, then he keyed it in and listened to the ringing noise that sounded close enough to be in the waiting room. Finally, a woman's voice, an anxious note in the way she said hello, as if she had been expecting bad news.

He told her Colin had been shot and was about to be taken into surgery at Riverton Memorial. He was in the waiting room with Lou.

"Oh my God." He could hear the heavy, sporadic breathing, as if the woman had run up a hill. "I'm on the way." What she didn't say was obvious: She would put out the word on the moccasin telegraph. She would make two or three calls, and the news would flash across the reservation. The waiting room would fill up.

Father John put the cell back into his pocket. Now there was only the waiting. Waiting and praying. He'd lost track of the number of times he had sat in this waiting room with parents and grandparents half-crazed with worry and grief, jumping off the seats the instant the steel doors swung open and a doctor from the labyrinth beyond appeared. You could always tell by the look on the doctor's face when the news was bad.

After a moment, he said, "What happened to Mike?"

"Took him to jail. Gonna charge him with conspiracy to murder, being an accomplice." He shook his head. "Nothing makes sense. They're even looking for his mother. Say she tried to run down that Lander detective, so they're going to get her for attempted assault."

Father John glanced out the glass doors at the thin steam of traffic crawling past the far side of the parking lot. He could picture Darleen Longshot driving a pickup attached to a horse trailer, a target as big as a house, down Seventeen-Mile Road. The cops would have pulled her over before she'd gotten home. Or they would have been waiting for her there. But he knew Darleen wouldn't have turned left onto Seventeen-Mile Road when she left the mission. She would have turned right and headed across the border into Riverton. The pickup and trailer would be parked in a shed in a trailer park where some of her relatives lived. Brownie grazing in the pasture. He felt the smile pull at his mouth. The woman had outsmarted a whole fleet of cops.

But they would find her. It was only a question of time. Mike and Colin would both face charges, and so would Darleen. He tried to ignore the spasm in his chest muscles. He couldn't shake the feeling that Colin and Mike were innocent. No matter the circumstantial evidence—it was still circumstantial. And yet he had watched other Arapahos sentenced to prison on circumstantial evidence not as strong as what Madden had against Colin: an eyewitness who could place him at the house where Angela Running Bear was murdered; a motive, since Angela had left him for Skip Burrows. By now an Arapaho warrior who had taken part in the dare run was probably willing to testify he had seen Colin pull out a pistol and shoot Garrett, willing to say Mike had covered for him, willing to say anything to stop the interviews, the suspicions, the chance of having his own parole rescinded.

The steel doors opened and a thin, wiry man in his forties, light-colored hair thinning away from his forehead, walked over. Father John stood up. Dr. Peter Mason was printed in black on the tag pinned to the man's white coat.

"Mr. Morningside." He bent over the old man, who was staring up with black, rheumy, frightened eyes. "Would you like to see your grandson before we wheel him into surgery to . . ." He stopped, compassion and hope in the words, the tone of his voice, and the fact that he hadn't said, "tell him good-bye."

Lou struggled forward in the chair, and Father John took hold of his elbow and helped him to his feet. He could feel the strength in the man, the sinewy muscles carved from years of hard, outdoor work, the work of a cowboy. Lou took a moment to steady himself, then started after Dr. Mason, who was holding open one of the steel doors.

Father John stayed with the old man down the green-lined corridor, smells of antiseptic floating in the air, hushed voices and clacking computer keys behind the closed doors. Around a corner and down another corridor. He could see the gurney ahead, the plastic bags hanging from steel poles, the yellowish hose running downward to the figure beneath the white sheet.

Dr. Mason lifted a hand, and three men in green scrubs stopped wheeling the gurney toward another bank of steel doors. He motioned Lou forward. The others made room.

Lou stood close to the side of the gurney, eyes fixed on the blood-drained face of his grandson. Colin's eyes were closed. Words formed in the old man's throat like a tentative rumbling of thunder. "My boy," he said. "My boy, my boy." Thin streams of tears started out of his eyes and gathered in the wrinkles of his cheeks. He touched the sheet over Colin's chest, then he gave Father John a pleading, beckoning look, as if he thought Father John might be a miracle worker, able to raise the dead.

Father John moved in closer, aware of the muscles in his chest, so tight that he had to gulp for air. He looked for some sign of life in Colin, a twitching finger, the flicker of an eyelid. Some will to live. Leaning over the gurney, he said, "Colin, it's Father John." There was no response. He could hear his own heart hammering. He had been present at the deaths of so many people. It was never easy. He had the sense he was talking to a corpse. "Listen to me," he said. "You are Colin Morningside. You are not Crazy Horse. You do not have to die. You must live. Your grandfather is here. He loves you and needs you. People are coming to the hospital, your relatives. They love you and need you. You must live for them, Colin."

There was an instant before the gurney started rolling toward the steel doors, the attendants and Dr. Mason alongside, the figure under the white sheet silent and still, that Father John wondered if he had detected the faintest movement behind the closed eyelids, or had only imagined it.

He steered the old man by the elbow back along the corridors. Even before they'd reached the waiting room, he could detect the change in the atmosphere, the sense of fullness, the undertone of conversation. He pushed through the steel doors and watched as the crowd of Arapahos surged toward Lou, enclosing him and leading him into the center of the room. Black heads bobbing about, brown arms reaching for the old man, patting the stooped back. A dozen voices, all asking the same questions: "How is he?" "Is he going to be all right?" "Where'd they shoot him?" "What's the doctor say?"

Loreen Morningside turned to Father John. As short and thin as a girl, narrow face frozen in worry. He knew her from St. Francis, where she volunteered to teach preschoolers in Sunday school. Gone was the cheerful and laughing and positive woman he saw on Sunday mornings. "It will kill him to lose Colin," she said.

Father John was quiet. There were no words, no platitudes that would allay the woman's worry, nothing but prayer and hope and the skill of doctors in the operating room.

"He didn't kill anybody," she said. "He doesn't have it in him. Cops got up a theory, and started turning the rez upside down looking for the warriors in the parade."

"What have you heard?"

"One of them said he saw Colin shoot that Custer guy, and Mike was right beside him."

Father John felt his jaw clench. It was what he and Lou had feared. Somebody desperate.

"The warrior just got out of Rawlins," Loreen was saying. "He's twenty-three years old, scared to death the cops will find some way to get his parole revoked. Says no way he can go back."

Father John looked over at the new group of Arapahos pushing past the glass door. A full-bore investigation on the rez, showing up at all hours, pulling people in for interviews, and finally, finally making a connection. A part of him felt sorry for the young man willing to lie to stay out of prison himself.

Outdoors, beyond the relatives sweeping into the waiting room, he watched a woman dart across the parking lot and thread her way around the parked cars. Before she lifted her head, he had known it was Vicky.

Loreen was leading Lou over to a chair, and Father John managed to catch the woman's attention and motion that he was going outside. Vicky was coming through the ambulance bay when he stepped past the glass doors.

32

"TELL ME." VICKY stood still with the wind whistling across the asphalt, whipping at her hair, wrapping her skirt against her legs.

"He's alive. They're operating now."

"Well, that's something," she said. Her shoulders relaxed a little. The faintest look of hope flared in her eyes. And yet there was something else. He knew her so well. It was as if he had memorized her, all the different shades of emotion and worry.

"What is it?"

"I have to talk to you."

A car door slammed behind them, and another group of relatives flowed toward the glass doors. He took her arm and guided her along the sidewalk to an iron bench in the shade of a cottonwood. Cigarette butts had been stamped out in the sand in the top of a small receptacle. The odor of tobacco smoke circled the bench.

He waited until Vicky had sat down, then sat down beside her. "What is it?"

She drew in a breath and gave him a long look. "I've been to two banks and talked to people who knew Skip Burrows."

"Burrows?" He felt a little pinch of surprise. Burrows was the last person he'd expected her to be investigating.

"You don't understand," she said, and he realized she had read his mind the way he often read hers.

"They're connected," she was saying. "Burrows, Garrett. Even Angela. What it comes down to is, Burrows was running a Ponzi scheme. The Granite Group. He and Garrett were army buddies from twenty years ago, and when Garrett sold his ranch in Laramie, he invested with Skip."

He was aware of her eyes searching his, waiting. "Let me guess," he said. "Garrett found another ranch he wanted to buy and asked for his money back."

"There was no money. At least not the full amount. I think Garrett threatened to go to the cops and blow the whole scheme out of the water. Angela told me they'd had a big argument in Skip's office and Garrett had stomped off. Friday afternoon, Skip withdrew all the money, then he called me. But I had already left the office. He didn't leave a message. I think he may have been panicking, looking for a way out."

Father John took a moment, turning over the pieces of information, examining each piece and its relationship to the others. "You think Skip decided to plan his own disappearance?"

Vicky nodded, then looked away, gaze roaming the parking lot, another car of Arapahos pulling in. "He had to make sure Garrett didn't report him before he could leave the country." She turned back. "Angela said he was building a house in Mexico. I suspect that's where he went. He took a briefcase of money, about four hundred thousand. I won't know the exact amount until I get access to records from the Granite Group. But there's more money, I'm sure of it, stashed away in the Cayman Islands or somewhere. He had investors in Jackson who liked belonging to a secret investment club that returned thirty percent. Of course, he had to keep finding new investors so he could pay off the old. The whole scheme was bound to collapse sooner or later. Garrett would have brought it down now."

"Skip had him killed."

Vicky lifted her hand and began rubbing her forehead, as if she could make the thoughts inside her head vanish. He understood. He didn't want to believe it either, he didn't want it to be true. "You believe he hired Colin to kill Garrett," he said finally.

"I don't see how it could be anything else." In her voice, he heard the same reluctance and sense of defeat that was moving inside him. "I've been turning it over and over," she went on. "I think Colin must have told Angela he and the warriors were planning a dare run at the parade. Angela told Skip, and Skip saw his chance. He got in contact with Colin. It wouldn't have been hard. Angela probably arranged a meeting. He knew Colin thought of himself as Crazy Horse. He appealed to Colin's sense of reliving the past, getting justice once again for the tribes, defeating the Seventh Cavalry."

She stood up and started pacing out a little circle. "Garrett didn't help matters by going on stage at the theater and bragging about Custer's massacres, like the Washita. It awoke so many memories, so many of the old stories. Children run down and shot. Women put into brothels for the army. Warriors killed trying to protect their families. All those memories still here, just below the surface."

Father John had to look away. He tried to take in the whole

scenario from her point of view. The old sorrows, the historical events pushed away, but never completely forgotten. Logical. Except he didn't believe it was true. He knew Colin Morningside. He had talked with him in the guesthouse. He had seen the fear in the man that he would be arrested and charged with crimes he hadn't committed.

"Nobody knows who actually killed Custer," Father John said.

"Crazy Horse led the warriors that swarmed up Last Stand Hill where Custer died," Vicky said, her tone quiet, matter-of-fact, as if she were relating a story she had known all her life. "Colin could have been tempted, not only by the money, but by doing what Crazy Horse had done."

Father John stood up and walked a few paces, trying to organize his thoughts. He turned back. Vicky looked small and determined, holding her breath against whatever else he might say. "Colin may have looked up to Crazy Horse. Maybe he wanted to be like him, a leader others could depend upon. Crazy Horse was defending his village when Custer was killed. There was no village for Colin to defend. What Colin had wanted to do was make a statement, remind people that Indians had defeated the U.S. Army. He organized the dare run, but that's all there was to it. A dare run."

Vicky dropped back onto the bench, and he sat down beside her. "Colin isn't guilty, Vicky. I know him. I've talked with him. There has to be some other explanation."

"What if he needed the money?"

Father John was aware of the contrapuntal sounds of their breathing. She was stubborn. Fierce when she had made up her mind. They were alike, he was thinking. Is that why he couldn't accept that Colin might be guilty? Because of his own stubbornness? "Let's say Skip Burrows planned his own disappearance." He tried to find the logical path. "It doesn't mean he paid Colin to kill Garrett."

"He had to get rid of the man, John. He didn't have much time." She shifted toward him. "Colin was the perfect man for the job. Funny thing about Colin and Angela: She had left Colin for Skip, but she hadn't completely broken away. She would get lonely for the rez and call Colin. She went to the rez to see him. Skip worked with a Realtor in Riverton, Deborah Boynton, his ex-girlfriend. She helped him locate apartment buildings and houses to invest in a couple of years ago. I suspect that's when Skip started the Granite Group. He and Boynton might have broken up, but they stayed in touch. Couples like that tell things to one another. Colin must have told Angela about the dare run. Angela told Skip. That could have given Skip the idea for a way to stop Garrett. Permanently."

"So Skip took Angela to Jackson for the weekend to make sure he wouldn't be connected to Garrett's murder." Logic had a force of its own, Father John was thinking. A series of facts that rushed to an inevitable conclusion. It didn't mean it was true.

Vicky went on: "He wanted to assure his investors in Jackson that everything was going well, the investments were secure. He didn't want them running to the police when he disappeared. Angela said he met with clients while they were in Jackson. He staged his disappearance so Angela would find the office trashed when she came in Monday morning."

Father John stood up again and walked a couple of yards down the sidewalk. He turned back. "Skip must have staged the disappearance Sunday night after he and Angela returned from Jackson."

A little smile played at the corners of Vicky's mouth, as if she believed she had won him over. "Madden would have put out an alert Monday morning to every police and sheriff's department in Wyoming, as well as to the state patrol. Skip wouldn't have gotten very far. I agree, he left sometime Sunday night. He was in Colorado by the time Angela found him missing. His car is probably parked in a lot at the Denver airport. He's in Mexico."

Still . . . logic didn't square with the facts, Father John was thinking. "At some point Skip realized he hadn't taken all the records. There was Angela's flash drive."

"He must have called Colin. Offered him more money to go to the office, search it, and get the flash drive."

"But that was Monday night," Father John said. Here it was, the break in the sequence of facts. "It wasn't Colin Angela confronted in the office. Angela had gone to the rez to see him Monday afternoon. Lou told me Colin was upset by her visit. He didn't think they could ever put their relationship back on track. He said Colin didn't leave the house Monday evening. He was home all night and most of Tuesday. He didn't leave until Lou suggested he go to Pine Ridge and lay low until Garrett's killer was found."

He waited a moment, reading the expression on Vicky's face, the way the facts rearranged themselves behind her eyes. "Colin loved Angela," he said finally. "He would never have hurt her."

"I wish that were true. I wish I hadn't picked up too many newspapers and read about some woman murdered by the man who loved her." Vicky slid her eyes from his, then looked back. "Think about it, John. Angela knew about the investments. She prepared the reports. She had the evidence against Skip."

"It was Skip," Father John said, and he could see in the way Vicky lifted her hand and rubbed at her forehead that she was coming to the same conclusion. The force of logic. "He didn't leave the area right away. It was Skip searching the office when Angela confronted him."

"He wore a dark ski mask." Vicky's voice was quiet. She stood up and began carving out another small, thoughtful circle. Around the sidewalk, across the edge of the grass. "He could have taken the flash drive," she said. "Angela would have given it to him. Skip was her ticket off the rez. Across the border forever." She stopped on the lawn, the wind moving the branches behind her. "Even if he wore the ski mask when he came to her house, she could have recognized him and . . ." Vicky left the rest of the words unspoken in the empty space between them, and he knew that, had she gone on, she would have started weeping.

She turned away, and he went over and placed an arm around her shoulders. "I'm sorry," he said.

After a moment, she nodded and looked up at him. "I spoke with one of Skip's investors. He's convinced Skip invested his money in oil and gas investments that will continue to pay large interest rates despite Skip's disappearance. The other investors probably believe the same. Skip was a persuasive man. Everybody's best friend. People trusted him. Angela trusted him." Her voice faltered a little. "When the quarterly checks stop arriving, the investors will get worried and go to the police. Skip will be settled in Mexico by then."

"But he's not there now. He's probably hiding out someplace in the area. He could be anyplace with a garage to hide his car." Father John led Vicky back to the bench. "We'd better call Madden."

She pulled away. "And tell him we have a great theory that proves Colin didn't murder either Garrett or Angela when he's already marking the case closed. He has the perpetrator and his accomplice. Colin, who might be dying on the operating table." Another falter. She looked away. "Mike Longshot locked up at the Fremont County Detention Center. Madden will charge them with Skip's abduction. He'll claim Angela told Colin about the money Skip had in his briefcase. He'll find phone records that show the calls Angela made to Colin. He'll say Angela and Colin planned the abduction and theft of the money together. They got into a disagreement. Angela started to panic. Madden had interviewed her twice. Colin couldn't trust her not to break down and confess. He went to her apartment and . . ." She stopped and hid her face in her hands a moment. After several seconds, she looked up. "I may know where Skip's hiding," she said. "It's a long shot, but if I can spot the car and get a photo, we'll have the evidence to take to Madden."

"I'll drive." He was already guiding her toward the parking lot.

33

VICKY LAID OUT her theory as they drove out of the parking lot: Deborah Boynton, the Realtor that Skip might not have completely broken up with, had made herself scarce. Left town, except for coming into the office to check messages once or twice. Hadn't returned Vicky's messages. She had been handling the sale of the ranch near Dubois that Garrett planned to buy, until he couldn't get his money from Skip. "The owners live in Virginia," she said. Then she added: "It's just a hunch." Starting to second-guess herself, he knew.

"It's all we've got," he said. In the back of his mind was the white-sheeted figure of Colin Morningside on the gurney wheeling toward the steel doors. And Mike Longshot, scared out of his wits in a jail cell, waiting for the worst of it to come.

They took Highway 26, skirting through the northwestern part of Riverton and out across the wide, windy spaces that wrapped around occasional ranch houses and barns popping out of the brown earth. There were long periods where Vicky didn't say anything, and neither did he. It was impolite to interrupt someone else's thoughts and demand they turn their thoughts to you. He had turned the volume low on the CD player that sat between them.

Finally, Vicky said: "Skip and Deborah could both have left already. They would have taken her car. None of the police are looking for it."

"Then Skip's car is in the garage or barn. If we can get photos, Madden will have to consider the possibility that Colin and Mike are innocent."

They turned north. Rising ahead on the right were the red-rock formations that rose out of the plains and glowed in the afternoon sun. Everything in this land was a surprise, even the woman seated next to him. Holding back her hair in the wind, staring out the windshield.

He squinted against the brightness, looking for the milepost that marked the turnoff into the mountains. He had been to ranches in the area. Off dirt roads that threaded around the mountainsides and overlooked clear-blue lakes: Ring Lake, Torrey Lake. A beautiful, sequestered area ten miles from Dubois, miles and miles from everywhere else. The milepost flashed ahead. He slowed down, waited for an oncoming truck to pass, and turned onto a two-track that switched back and forth until it started up the mountain. A narrow and rutted road with only a couple of feet of shoulder ran along the mountainside on the right. On the left, a drop-off into a grassy valley crossed by a thin stream. The drop-off got steeper as they climbed.

Vicky pulled a sheet of paper out of her bag. She held the sheet against the dashboard and set a finger in the middle of a paragraph. "'To reach the Stockton Ranch, stay on the mountain road for twelve miles,'" she said. "'Turn left, cross a wooden bridge. A small brown framed building will be on the left. Continue on the dirt road that climbs past a small lake into the meadow where the ranch house, barns, and outbuildings are located. Ranch house has 2,450 square feet . . .'" She set the paper on her lap. "We should be getting close."

Father John spotted the bridge as he came around a wide curve. He slowed again and moved as far to the right as he could to allow an oncoming pickup to pass. A rancher with a cowboy hat and a thick hand that waved in their direction. Father John swung left through the cloud of dust clinging to the hood and the windshield and drove toward the bridge. He had to turn on the wipers to clear a space to see through. He could see the small brown framed building. "How far to the ranch house?"

Vicky leaned over the sheet of paper. "Half a mile."

"They'll hear us if they're here." Father John pulled off the road and slid to a stop behind the building. "Wait here. I'll hike up and see if I can spot the car."

Before he had gotten out, Vicky was out on her side. She didn't say anything, and he knew that no matter what he said, she was coming with him. They started up the dirt road, staying close to the right edge. It was quiet, nothing but the sound of the wind. Puffs of dust rose around their footsteps. The air smelled of dust and sage.

Beyond the rounded hill ahead, Father John spotted a peaked, green roof. "We'll go as far as the bend," he said. "We should be able to see the house and cars from there." An uneasiness had started over him, like brambles pricking at his skin. There was no telling what they could be walking into. They could come face-to-face with a killer. Even if Skip were gone, Deborah Boynton could be here, and she had been protecting him. What would she do to keep him safe?

Vicky had left her bag in the pickup, but she clutched a cell phone in one hand. She walked fast, and he stretched his legs to keep up. "We'll have to be careful." He wondered if she had heard him, she was so lost in her own thoughts.

"What a scam Skip had going," she said after a moment. "People clamoring to get into his private club, to be his special friend. It took a minimum of five hundred thousand to invest. He told a bartender in Lander to put his ten thousand in a bank. He wasn't rich enough for the club." She glanced at him over her shoulder. "People with a lot of money, greedy for more. Eager to join an exclusive club so they could tell themselves they were the elite, better than everybody else."

"They'll lose their investments."

"The money's already gone," Vicky said. "Skip used new investments to pay on the old. I suspect he helped himself to what was left. A new house in Mexico. Condo in Jackson. Expensive car. No doubt there's more in hidden bank accounts. Investors will be lucky to get pennies back on the dollar. You know what's funny?" She took a deep breath. "Everybody loved him."

They were approaching the bend. Scam artist, murderer. Skip Burrows would be a dangerous man to surprise, if he was at the ranch. Father John took Vicky's arm. "Let's slow down."

She pushed ahead, pulling away from him, and he hurried to pass her before they came around the bend. He heard the faint, rhythmic thuds of metal against earth before he saw the woman. Tall, reddish hair, in blue jeans and yellow tee shirt, tapping a shovel against the dirt piled around a fence post. Behind her was a stretch of field that wrapped around a log house with a wide front porch and a couple of chairs and a rocker that moved in the wind. Beyond the house was a wood-planked barn. The double doors were closed. There was no sign of Skip Burrows's silver BMW.

She looked up. She was pretty in a fierce, uncompromising way. Perspiration glistened on her forehead. "Who are you? What do you want?"

"Deborah Boynton? I'm Vicky Holden." Vicky had stepped out ahead again and was walking toward the woman, hand out-stretched, as if they had met at the shopping mall.

The woman jammed the point of the shovel into the dirt. She made no effort to take Vicky's hand. "The Indian lawyer and the priest from the mission. I've seen your photos in the newspaper. Crusaders for law and justice."

"I've been trying to reach you. I've left several messages on your phone and with your broker."

"I never responded. Didn't that tell you anything? I'm not look-ing for new clients, and I'm certainly not giving interviews. I sug-gest you turn around and hike out of here."

"I believe you can help us."

"I don't see how."

"My client is the widow of Edward Garrett. She wants to locate the money he had invested in the Granite Group."

Deborah Boynton shook her head and leaned on the shovel handle, as if to steady herself. Father John kept his eyes on her. The woman was as tense and coiled as a rattlesnake. He had counseled people like that. Backs against the wall. Ready to strike. She was shaking her head. "Why would that concern me?"

"You represented Garrett. He intended to purchase this ranch.

He couldn't get his money from the Granite Group, so the deal fell through. You must have been very disappointed."

"It is none of your business. Buyers come and go in real estate. Things don't always work out. There'll be another buyer. The place is an excellent investment. I've been spending time here tidying up a little. The living area is freshly painted." She had slipped into a robotic patter she had probably given hundreds of times. Her hand looked welded to the shovel handle. "Notice the new barn doors. I've made sure the furnace and water heater are in tip-top condition." She gave a quick glance toward the dirt road that ran past the barn and up the mountainside into a stand of stunted pines and sagebrush. "Unless you would like to make an offer, you had better leave."

"You also represented Skip Burrows, the man behind the Granite Group. He purchased residential property some time ago."

"You've done a lot of snooping. My broker told me you kept coming around. Let's cut to the chase. What do you want?"

Vicky took a moment before she said, "Skip Burrows."

Deborah shifted her gaze between them, deciding. Father John could almost see the thoughts colliding behind her eyes. "Skip is a lawyer and a legitimate businessman. He was abducted from his office. I wouldn't know where he is."

"You've been hiding him here." Vicky bore in, Father John thought. A lawyer questioning a reluctant witness in court. "Burrows has money that belongs to my client and other investors that he has bilked."

The woman curled around herself, face shadowed and eyes pinpricks of black lights. Father John moved in closer, between her and Vicky. "Burrows staged his own disappearance," he said.

"You have no proof."

"It's only a matter of time before Detective Madden shows up here." He wished that were true. He wished they had let someone know where he and Vicky were going.

The woman was still gripping the handle, hanging on hard, as if the shovel might evaporate and she would topple over. "So Skip got into a little financial trouble. He needed time to straighten things out. He's very smart. He makes good investments for his clients, but they've been slow paying off. The economy is cyclical. It falls. It rises." She lifted the shovel slowly, as if it weighed a couple hundred pounds and dropped it into the loose dirt, still gripping the handle.

Little clouds of dust rose over the pines on the mountainside. The quiet rumble of an engine mingled with the whoosh of the wind. The rumble grew louder, and a pickup the color of dirt sped out of the trees, disappeared behind the barn then came bouncing along the two-track toward them. A black Stetson bobbed over the steering wheel. Father John grabbed Vicky's arm and pulled her sideways just as the pickup swung off the road toward the barbed wire fence, tires churning the dirt and crunching sagebrush. The pickup stopped.

The driver got out. Face dark and indistinct beneath the low-tipped brim of the black Stetson. He turned toward the frame that held a rifle against the rear windshield, rammed a key into a lock, and removed the gun. Then he came around the back of the pickup. Chin thrust high, a band of sunshine across the center of his face. Father John could have identified Skip Burrows from the swagger in his walk, the confident, take-charge attitude in the way he gripped the rifle pointed at them.

34

SLIP BURROWS LOOKED different, Vicky thought. Shorter, leaner, altogether a smaller man than the lawyer she had occasionally run into on Main Street, in a coffee shop, at a meeting of the local bar association. Skip Burrows had always seemed taller than his five feet ten inches, bigger than the narrow shoulders hunched around the rifle. Everything about him louder, consuming space. One hand gripping yours, the other gripping your arm or shoulder. A smile as wide and open as the plains. *How are your kids, your practice, your life? How are you and Adam Long Eagle getting along? Any plans to form a firm together again?* He knew about you, and he cared. Who wouldn't want to be Skip Burrows's best friend, a member of his private club?

"You shouldn't have come here," he said.

"We came to talk to you." Vicky marveled at the calmness in John O'Malley's voice, the way he seemed to look past the barrel of the rifle, the black bore that went on forever. "No need for a weapon."

"I'll decide that."

"I've told them the truth," Deborah said.

"The truth?" Skip seemed to acknowledged the woman with the strands of red hair wafting in the wind, yet he gazed straight ahead. Staring at *them*. "You should keep your mouth shut."

"I told them it's a mistake. You need time to straighten things out, that's all. They understand. You do understand, don't you?" Deborah Boynton threw a pleading look at Vicky, then John O'Malley.

"I'm surprised you're still here," Vicky said. "I thought you would be in Mexico by now."

"I'll be there tonight. Unfortunately you're both here now. It's a problem I have to deal with."

"You didn't tell me we were leaving today." A whine had come into Deborah's voice.

"*We* aren't leaving."

"But you said you would take me with you. I've made plans. I've canceled meetings with clients, told them to find another Realtor." For a moment, Vicky thought the woman might burst into tears. "I'm going with you. You know you need me."

Deborah shifted toward Vicky. The top of the shovel handle rested against her chest. She looked scared, shriveled like a stalk of dried tumbleweed. "You're a lawyer. You know this will blow over. As soon as Skip recoups the money and starts getting the interest he expects, he'll pay off the investors. They know Skip. They know he'll do the right thing."

"Your boyfriend had Edward Garrett killed," Vicky said.

"That's a lie!" Deborah swung a half step toward Skip. "Tell them that's a lie. Everyone knows the Indians killed Garrett. What fool comes to a place where Indians live and brags about killing Indians? What did he think would happen? That Arapaho who thinks he's Crazy Horse is as big a fool as Garrett. Tell them! You didn't have anything to do with Garrett getting shot."

"For the last time, Deborah, shut up!"

"You need me, Skip. I can help you. I can make them understand."

"Garrett threatened to go to the police," Vicky said. "He wanted his money back But you didn't have his money. You had spent it, right? Houses? Expensive car? Accounts in the Cayman Islands? You were setting yourself up for life. Garrett had to be stopped."

The thick mountain quiet spread around them, the quiet of the sky interrupted by the sporadic hum of the wind through the brush. "It was not Colin Morningside you hired to kill Garrett." Father John's tone was low and as steady and certain as steel. Vicky caught his eye for an instant and understood what he was about to say, could feel it in her bones. "Indians weren't the only ones who hated Custer," he went on. "Benteen and Reno for starters. Custer refused to rescue Joel Elliott and his men at Washita. They all died. Elliott was their friend."

Skip Burrows gave a shout of laughter. "You think anybody but the Indians cares about what happened a hundred and forty years ago? Benteen and Reno are dead."

"What happened in Desert Storm?" Father John said. "Why would Osborne and Veraggi hate your commander so much that they were willing to kill him?"

Skip Burrows looked stunned, a little unsteady, the rifle weaving back and forth as if he and the rifle were caught in a windstorm. "You are going to die." His teeth were clamped together, jaw rigid.

"No, Skip! They're taking a wild guess. Tell them it's not

true. You couldn't have hired anyone to kill Garrett. The Indians did it, like you told me."

"Garrett deserved to die." Skip's voice sounded distant and disengaged, Vicky thought, as if Garrett had nothing to do with him. "Bastard led the men through sand dunes into an ambush. He didn't know anything about deserts, and he wouldn't listen to guys who had been out there. The arrogant sonofabitch did things his way, and damn the men under him. You know what it's like to live with the same guys twenty-four-seven? Listen to them cry out in their sleep with nightmares you were having? Watch the shadow of stubble grow on their chins? Smell their boots? We were the same. We were a single body. You know what it's like to watch yourself die? Feel the pain of the bullet that blew off the head of your buddy crouched beside you? Wipe the sand and sweat out of your eyes and look at your buddy's brains exploded all over you? Eight men died! Good men! But they weren't the only fatalities. We all died there. Only some of us stumbled back after the army helicopters arrived and started strafing the Iraqis. The helicopters got us out of that hellhole. The walking dead."

"You hated Garrett," John said. "Why keep up the old armybuddy routine? Why would Osborne and Veraggi be reenactors in the Seventh Cavalry with Garrett the commander, like Custer?"

"Revenge takes time." Burrows made a loud sucking noise. The rifle was still moving back and forth, and Father John could see the tremor in the man's hand. "Taking that bastard's money was the most pleasure I've had in a long time. Invested it in a ten-thousand-square-foot house in Mexico. You're right about the Cayman Islands. Stashed some down there. Osborne and Veraggi? They wanted a different kind of revenge. They wanted him dead. Bided their time, waiting for the right moment for an accident to occur. That's what kept them going. Custer must die! I handed them the opportunity. Sooner or later they would have found it on their own."

"My God, Skip. What are you saying?" Deborah was shouting, as if Skip were on the other side of the road, halfway up the mountain. "You hired them to kill Garrett? Why? Why would you do such a thing? You lied to me! You told me you needed more time, and everything would turn around. Interest money would start flowing. My God! I believed you!"

"I'm sick of you, Deborah." Skip spoke out of the side of his mouth, keeping his eyes from her, as if she weren't beside him, hunched over the shovel handle as if she might throw up. "Sick of your whining and nagging and your superior, know-it-all attitude. Sick of you understanding me. You don't understand anything. Garrett set a deadline. Either he got his money on Monday morning, or he went to the cops. The colonel giving the order, just like before. The arrogant sonofabitch. Forward! Over the sand dunes to destruction. Well, he was no longer in charge. He was no longer leading anybody. He had destroyed enough."

"What about Angela?" Vicky struggled to keep her own voice steady. "What had she destroyed?"

"Angela! That Arapaho girl you were involved with? My God! You had her killed, too!"

"Shut up! I won't tell you again."

"Angela loved you," Vicky said. "She would have given you the flash drive. All you had to do was ask. You didn't have to kill her."

"What? You did it yourself?"

"There was no way out for me. I thought there might be. I even tried to call you." He gave a little nod toward Vicky. "The fact is, Angela knew too much." Skip drew his lips into a thin, tight line.

The same look of disengagement, as if he were somewhere else, crossed his face like a shadow.

"She didn't know anything," Vicky said. "She prepared the phony statements you told her to prepare. She thought they were legitimate reports that your clients needed. Why wouldn't they be? She thought you were a god, a white god come to save her, take her away to Mexico and a dream life."

"You killed that girl? You bastard!"

"Let me tell you what you're going to do, Deborah," Skip said. "You are going to walk to the pickup and get the rope on the floor in back. You're going to bring it to me. Do it! As for you"—he pressed the butt of the rifle against his chest and looked from Father John to Vicky—"you are going to drop. Now. On your hands and knees, on your stomach, faces in the dirt. You won't be tied up long. Only as long as it takes us to dig your graves. Get the rope," he shouted as if he were now aware that Deborah hadn't moved.

"You're going to kill them?"

"Get it!"

"Murderer!" The woman grabbed the shovel handle and swung it backward over her shoulder, a swift, smooth motion. Just as Skip turned sideways, the shovel crashed into his temple. He staggered forward, the rifle loose and bouncing in his hands. Stunned, glassy-eyed. Blood was running down his cheek.

"No!" Vicky heard Father John shout as Deborah swung the shovel into the back of Skip's head. There was the sharp sound of metal splitting bone. Skip dropped onto the dirt, collapsing like a tree uprooted in the wind, the rifle sliding against the fence post. Again Deborah lifted the shovel, but John O'Malley had grabbed hold of her shoulders and pulled her away from the man sprawled at her feet, spasms running through his body, the back of his skull bashed in.

Vicky stooped over, picked up the rifle, and carried it to the borrow ditch alongside the dirt road. She set it down below the edge, where it couldn't be seen, aware of John O'Malley leading the woman backward. Holding on to her with one hand, as if she might bolt toward the fallen man and slam the shovel into his head again, he pried the shovel from her. Vicky saw him toss it hard into a clump of sagebrush. Deborah had started shaking, as if she were coming apart, as if she had returned to sanity from wherever she had gone, and reality—the terrible reality—was buffeting her. He led her up the porch steps to the chair rocking in the wind and guided her into the seat. "Stay here," he said. Then he came down the steps toward Skip.

He had stopped shivering. Stopped breathing, Vicky realized. She caught John O'Malley's eye as he went down on one knee beside the man.

Vicky crouched beside him. He kept one finger pressed against the side of Skip's neck. "I can't get a pulse," he said. "He's gone. God have mercy on his soul."

"Do you think there is mercy?" she heard herself say. An inanity. What difference did it make? Skip Burrows was dead. As dead as Edward Garrett and Angela Running Bear.

"There is always the hope," John said.

Vicky got to her feet, conscious of the weight of his hand on her arm, guiding her upright. Then he was pulling his cell out of his shirt pocket. She felt dazed, almost weightless, half expecting the shivering to start inside her, the shovel and the rifle looming presences in her mind. They were the ones who could have been dead. Tied up, shot in the head, and dumped into whatever shallow graves Skip and Deborah managed to dig in the hard ground. And Deborah. She would also have been dead.

"Send an ambulance," John was saying. Then came the

directions: Stockton Ranch, ten miles from Dubois, the dirt road on the west, twelve miles up the mountainside. Man struck in the head. No vital signs. Woman in shock.

"Ask them to get Madden on the line," Vicky said.

He repeated the request. "Vicky Holden wants to speak to Detective Madden. This concerns two murders he has been investigating." He handed her the cell.

Silence on the other end, and for a moment Vicky wondered if the connection had been lost. "Vicky? What's going on?" Madden sounded loud and impatient.

"We found Skip Burrows. We found the murderer."

Behind her, she heard the coughing noise of a motor turning over, the ratcheting of gears. She swung around as the pickup charged like a bull down the dirt road, rocking back and forth, Deborah Boynton hunched over the steering wheel. And John O'Malley running toward the pickup, waving both hands, shouting. "Stop! Stop!"

She heard the thud and watched him flying, flying, lifting into the air with the wind, and the terrible, scudding noise as his body dropped onto the ground and slid forward. Barely aware of the pickup speeding past her, the whooshing sound as the rush of air grabbed at her skirt. The pickup raced down the dirt road, the smell of exhaust filling her nostrils.

She dropped the phone and ran to John O'Malley.

35

SOME THINGS HE couldn't remember.

He couldn't remember what he had been doing in the moment before the darkness.

He couldn't remember the medics, sheriff's deputies, and state patrol officers swarming the ranch, although he learned later that had been the case.

He couldn't remember the ambulance trip to Riverton Memorial.

He decided they weren't important. He remembered Vicky's face, blurred and wavy, swimming toward him out of the darkness, finally solidifying, becoming real. "How do you feel?" she had asked, and he had tried to assure her he was okay. What he knew was that he was alive.

That was three days ago. He had spent the night in the hospital. For observation, the doctors told him. He'd taken quite a blow from the bumper of the speeding pickup. Slight concussion. Chipped rib and a bruise that ran from his shoulder to his hip and had already started to fade at the edges from black to shades of purple and yellow. His muscles felt as hard and stiff as rocks. The next morning Vicky had appeared at the hospital and driven him to the mission. She told him Skip Burrows was dead. The state patrol had picked up Deborah Boynton before she reached the outskirts of Riverton, and she had spent a night in jail. No charges would be brought against her. She had acted in the defense of others. She had saved their lives.

Vicky had brought the bishop, who rescued the old Toyota pickup from the hospital parking lot and drove it home. A cavalcade, he had thought, as they rolled through town and out onto the highway. Everything had looked vivid and alive in the hot June morning. The wild grasses in the open fields, bending in the sun, the cottonwood leaves swaying against the glass-clear blue sky.

They had driven in silence except for a few perfunctory remarks. Was he sure he was okay? He was fine. He should take it easy. So the doctor said. But he wouldn't, would he? No, he probably wouldn't. He could have been killed. She had thought he was dead. And she told him she didn't know what she would have done if that had been the case, how she would *be*.

He had turned away from the anguish in her voice and stared at the scrub brush passing outside, grateful they were both alive.

In the residence, he had managed to get up the stairs to his bedroom, the bishop trailing behind as if he might catch him should Father John tumble backwards, and that would have been a sight—the frail, white-haired man trying to hold him up with nothing but an indomitable spirit and determination. Bishop Harry had insisted upon saying the early Mass the last two mornings, visiting parishioners, counseling people who wandered into the administration building. Father John should rest. An old man recovering from heart surgery was taking charge. It was as if the bishop and he had exchanged places.

He had gotten to the office early this morning. There was only so much resting he could stand, and there were always things that needed attention. He had spent a couple hours working on the budget for the summer. *Cosi fan tutte* played on the CD. Tourists meant the Sunday collections might be larger than usual, but he could never count on that. Better to try to adjust the expenditures to the average amount of money that came in. As if the budget at St. Francis Mission could ever be balanced. He tried to stop the laugh that rumbled through him and knocked about the sore places. Then he pushed himself to his feet and walked down the corridor.

Bishop Harry was curled over a book opened flat on the desk. The ceiling light glowed in the pink bald spot on top of his head. He glanced up, and Father John told him he was going out for a while. He gave what he thought was a friendly wave and headed back down the corridor before the bishop could voice the objections that flashed in his blue eyes.

Ten minutes later, Father John was back at Riverton Memorial, turning into the parking lot, and driving for the empty spot marked by the sign that said Clergy. Lou had called yesterday and said that Colin had regained consciousness. He was going to be okay. The mixture of relief and gladness in the old man's voice had been like the bass undercurrent in an aria. The boy would like to see him, Lou had said.

He made his way across the asphalt lot and let himself through the double glass doors, trying to ignore the stiffness and the bullets of pain that shot through him as he walked. A gray-haired woman with glasses that hung against her chest from a string of beads directed him to Colin Morningside's room. Third floor. Elevators straight ahead. He knew that. He thanked her and headed down the corridor.

Colin lay under a white blanket, blanched looking, thin, like a shadow of himself, eyes closed, eyelids trembling as if he were dreaming. A hose ran from beneath the blankets into a blue bag attached to the edge of the bed frame. Father John waited, not wanting to disturb whatever dream Colin was having. He felt a sense of the relief and gladness he had heard in Lou's voice. Colin was alive!

"Hey, Father." The lids shot up, and Colin Morningside was looking at him out of eyes as black and opaque as river stones. "Thanks for coming."

Father John set a hand on the young man's shoulder. "How are you feeling?"

"Okay." Father John could hear the same bravado in Colin's voice that he knew had leached into his own. "I been thinking about that dog of yours."

"Walks-On?"

"Keeps going on three legs. I'm gonna have to figure out how to keep going with only one kidney." Colin gave a little shrug. "Doc says it's all I need. Guess I shouldn't have taken off when the cops pulled me and Mike over. All I could think was how close we were to the border. We could've run into South Dakota and kept running to Pine Ridge. I seen an arroyo the other side of the highway, and I thought, If I can get there . . . Almost made it."

Colin drew in a long breath that lifted the blanket over his chest. "When I seen them coming at me with handcuffs, I guess I went crazy."

"It doesn't matter. You're alive and you're going to be okay."

"Crazy Horse didn't get so lucky." Colin turned his head and stared up at him a moment. "I knew Skip Burrows was no good. I tried to tell Angela. He was cheating on her with that Realtor in Riverton, but I couldn't get Angela to believe it. She was crazy about him. He was like meth or something that she couldn't get enough of. Couldn't get off it." Colin blinked against the moisture filling his black eyes. "I loved that girl. That's what made me crazy, the cops thinking I murdered her. I felt"—he hesitated—"hopeless."

Colin took a moment before he went on. "At least Mike's out of jail. He must've been crazy locked up behind bars. Kid never did anything to deserve that. County attorney dropped all charges against me and Mike. Even that busybody landlady at Angela's place decided she couldn't identify the man looking into Angela's windows. It was me, but when I left, Angela was alive. She looked good, sitting on that little sofa, like she had some peace, like she knew what was best for her." He stopped and dabbed a finger at the corners of his eyes. "A lot of people must be surprised that it wasn't Indians who killed Garrett and . . ." He paused. Finally he said, "Angela. You could've been the one that got killed going after that bastard. Mike and I owe you and Vicky."

"You don't owe us anything. Just go on with your lives."

"I'm always going to miss her."

Father John patted the young man's arm. "I understand," he said. "If you ever want to talk, you know where to find me."

HIS MUSCLES FELT rigid, locking themselves down, Father John thought, as he drove back to the mission. He hated the waves of weakness that came over him. Rest. Rest. Rest. He could hear Bishop Harry echoing what the doctor had said. He didn't want to rest.

He made a left turn in front of the billboard that loomed over Seventeen-Mile Road with St. Francis Mission in white letters against a blue background of sky and mountains, and drove through the cottonwoods. The branches scraped the top of the pickup. As he swung onto Circle Drive, he saw Vicky's Ford, black hair above the steering wheel, hand pressing a cell against her ear, shoulders rounded into whatever conversation she was having. She glanced over as he pulled in beside her. It took him a moment to convince his muscles to lift him out of the pickup. She was already at his door, reaching out a hand to help him. Dear Lord, he was an invalid.

"I thought you were supposed to stay home," she said.

"I went to see Colin."

Vicky nodded. She knew him, he was thinking. He walked alongside her across the gravel, up the stairs, and through the heavy wooden door that, he realized, she was holding for him. He told her that Colin was going to be okay. He'd probably be in the hospital for a while.

She didn't say anything, and he figured she'd already had the news. The moccasin telegraph had been in overdrive the last three days. He motioned her to one of the side chairs and dropped down beside her. "Coffee?" he said. "I can make some."

She laughed. "I doubt you could get up. I'll make it."

Father John watched her go over to the little table behind the door, spoon coffee grounds into the container, and carry the glass pot into the corridor. Her heels made a tap tap sound on the old wood floor. The sound of running water filtered through the walls, then she was back. Setting the pot in place, pushing a button. By the time she sat down, a thin smell of brewing coffee had worked around them.

"The Montana state patrol arrested Osborne and Veraggi yesterday," she said. "They were in the RV, on the way to the site of the Battle of the Little Bighorn. Planning to take part in the reenactment, as if they hadn't killed a man. The police found the murder weapon in the RV. A twenty-two Ruger LCR. I understand Veraggi was drunk. After he sobered up he claimed Osborne had pulled the trigger and killed Garrett. He had tried to ride close in to give him cover. Funny, Osborne says Veraggi pulled the trigger. They'll both face charges of homicide and conspiracy to commit homicide. They'll be brought back to Wyoming today. How did you know they were the killers?"

Father John told her what had happened at the Washita, how part of Custer's command, led by Joel Elliott, had been surrounded and killed by hostile Indians, and how Custer, even though he knew about the attack, had refused to go to their aid. Benteen and Reno had been friends with Elliott. They hated Custer for what he had failed to do. "When I talked to Garrett's widow, she was dressed like Libbie Custer. She told me how Osborne and Veraggi hated her husband. She said they were jealous of him and blamed him for things that had happened. I thought she was talking about Benteen and Reno. It wasn't until Skip showed up at the ranch that I realized she had been talking about Osborne and Veraggi and about something that happened in Kuwait. How is she doing?"

"She's in Montana getting ready for the reenactment. Calls three times a day about the money. She isn't the only one trying to be repaid from the Granite Group. It will take the probate judge months to figure out where Skip stashed the money, liquidate what's left, and pay the investors. I suspect they will get pennies on the dollar."

Vicky jumped to her feet, poured two mugs of coffee, and

handed him one. "I do have some good news," she said, dropping onto the chair again. The coffee was hot and strong, the way he liked it, but she knew that.

"Darleen Longshot called me after the Riverton police found her rig in the trailer park across the highway. They arrested her and turned her over to the tribal police. She's been charged with attempted assault on an officer. Fortunately, the incident occurred on the rez. More than likely, the tribal judge will consider the extenuating circumstances, the fact she was distraught over the possibility of her son being charged with murders he didn't commit. I suspect the judge will give her a suspended sentence, require some community service, and warn her to stay out of trouble. Won't be hard. Darleen has never been in trouble."

"How's Mike?"

"Traumatized, but he'll be okay. He's finding his way. He's the best horseman on the rez, and now everybody knows." Vicky lifted her mug and took a long drink. "The dare ride shouldn't have ended in murder, but what the warriors did was something, and Mike was the one who taught them how to do it." She drained her mug, stood up, and set the mug on the table. Then moved toward the door, streams of sunlight floating through the corridor behind her.

He had a sinking feeling, another wave of weakness coming on. He tried to look away, but he couldn't take his eyes from her. He would not see her like this again for a long while, just the two of them. Maybe he would spot her on the other side of the powwow grounds, a group of Arapahos watching the dancers, Vicky in the center of the group. Walking down Main Street in Lander, Adam Lone Eagle walking on the curbside. He would hear how she had convinced the tribal judge to show mercy on Darleen Longshot, or managed to get the charges reduced for some Arapaho who had gotten drunk and wrecked a pickup, or handled the final adoption decree for grandparents caring for grandkids whose parents had left. A hundred different cases. She would never stop.

He realized she had paused at the door and was slowly turning back. "I can't help thinking about Angela," Vicky said. "How she wanted to get away from the rez, and yet she couldn't. Not really. She kept being drawn back. She was trying to find her way between two worlds." He knew she was speaking of herself. "Moving across borders, trying to find her own place." She lifted both hands. "Longing to be home and, at the same time, longing to be away."

"Maybe that is in all of us."

"Not in you," she said. "I don't think it is in you." She smiled, and he was reminded of the way her black eyes lit up when she smiled. "I should get back to the office."

"I'll walk you out," he said as she started to move into the corridor.

She glanced back. "Please don't. I want to think of you here."